CARETAKERS

OF

ETERNITY

EDWARD GORDON

BLACK

SPIRIT

Black Spirit Publishing
P.O. Box 2428, PMB# 8443
Pensacola, FL 32513

http://edwardgordonbooks.com

ISBN 978-0-9838971-4-9

For rights information, contact Black Spirit Publishing by mail or e-mail:

information@blackspiritpublishing.com

Second Edition

10 9 8 7 6 5 4 3 2 1

For

Michelle

PROLOGUE

———•———

Kerrie cried. It started as a whimper but changed to a hopeless, inconsolable lamenting. She huddled close to Whitney in their shared bed listening to the footfalls of their father's boots taking each step of the stairs. As he walked the hall toward their room, Kerrie screamed through a whisper: "He's going to get us!" She looked to Whitney, eyes wild and bulging.

"No, he won't." Whitney, said, and pulled her sister in close. "I won't let him."

But Kerrie moaned as the sound of the pounding steps grew louder. Whitney wanted to turn on a light, but their room wasn't wired for electricity. Only the downstairs rooms had electric light. Their nightlight was nothing more than the blue-white moon that shone on Eternity Vineyards and through the open drapes.

For all her consolations, Whitney knew Kerrie was right: he was coming for them—and there was nothing she could do to stop him. Not wanting her little sister to see her in tears, she held her tightly to her chest. It was important to be strong for her, but she knew this was the moment of their death. It had to be. He hadn't found another child in months.

Whitney wished her mother were there to protect them. The hurt of her absence stung worse than the fear of what she knew was about to come. But her mother had left them vulnerable to him, and he couldn't control himself.

He'd even told her he couldn't control himself blatantly and without any shame the night of their mother's funeral. "I have to do those things," he explained, as if somehow his calm confession could bring about her acceptance. Or maybe, she thought, he actually believed it could germinate in her some kind of an apprenticeship with him, but it never did, and now she knew he hated her for what he was and what she would never be. So, she had to pay.

His boots stopped outside their room. Whitney stared at the firelight reflecting on the polished hardwood beneath the door. When the doorknob clicked, Kerrie no longer contained her terror; she screamed, and her screaming made Whitney pull away.

Whitney's own panic took hold of her, and she screamed with Kerrie but no longer heard her sister. She only fathomed a primal self-interest. She fell from the bed taking their quilted blanket to the floor along with her. Kerrie remained on the mattress, exposed in the moonlight, covered only by a thin, pink nightgown she got for her eighth birthday. She clung to the oak headboard for safety even as her wailing continued and her eyes widened in terror. Then the door opened, and a human form moved in.

William Maddock was large. He wore a denim jacket she and Kerrie helped their mother make him two years back when he was still *Daddy* and it was Father's Day. But he wasn't their father anymore; now he was a man-monster Whitney couldn't comprehend. He held a blazing hurricane lantern out in front of him. The orange flame glowed on his angry expression, and as he entered their room, he illuminated the terror within it.

Whitney crawled backward on the floor dragging the quilt with her to a corner of the room. It was unimaginable; he was unimaginable. Her screams inflamed her throat, and she felt the pain, but she screamed in reflex because she couldn't help it.

Maddock walked past the bed where the eight-year-old howled and moved with single-minded purpose toward his twelve-year-old daughter. As he came for her, Whitney swung her thin arms at the air desperately hoping to form a barrier between her body and his, but Maddock easily grabbed an arm in his free fist and dragged her out of the corner.

She felt herself transform into her fear. Her thoughts vanished leaving only directionless panic. On her knees before him, she begged for her life: "No, Daddy, please, please, not me!" Her eyes darted to the bed. "Take Kerrie, Daddy! Take Kerrie. Take her." Then she softened from screaming into selling: "I can do things for you. You know I can. I'll do anything you want. We can sleep together, if you want. We can sleep together tonight!"

Maddock paused but still held on to her wrist. Looking down into the scared blue eyes beneath him, he seemed to calculate the benefits of preserving the more sexually developed of the two. He glanced over to Kerrie, his eyes dilating to black from the excitement. Whitney felt a fleeting twinge of hope, but Kerrie did not.

The child perceived her father's shift in attention and screamed with greater force. She continued on like a tortured animal, one scream after another echoing in the room as she devolved from the ability to communicate in any other way.

Maddock released Whitney's arm, letting her recoil back to her protective corner. She sobbed behind her hands and tried to believe it wasn't true, that the present reality wasn't happening.

He moved to the bed, reached across and took hold of his younger daughter's nightgown. He yanked it hard, but she clutched the headboard, unwilling to give up her only security. With the very next pull, the nightgown ripped away.

"Shit!" Maddock growled, and grabbed Kerrie's long, brown hair. He pulled it, tilting her neck back and changing her screams into morbidly distorted tones. He pulled harder, but she wouldn't release. He punched at her left flank, and his fist sank deep into her side. She grunted then and let go.

He yanked her off the bed by her hair. The flesh of her naked body slapped against the wooden floor, and for a moment, with her wind knocked out, she stopped screaming, and Whitney heard only the sound of her own whimpering. She watched him drag her to the bedroom door. Along the way, Kerrie finally found the air to scream what would be her final words: "Whitney, help me!"

But Whitney didn't move. Assistance was suicide. Her body wouldn't let her move, and besides, she had a deal with him, and she would survive the night. *Just don't move*, she told herself. *That's all you have to do.*

At the door, Kerrie latched on to the doorframe, the same as she had the headboard, but two of her fingernails gave way under the force of Maddock's wrenching. She let go with a shriek, and from then on her screams changed to infantile wails, no longer an eight-year-old girl, but a fetus pulled freshly from her mother's womb.

Through her fingers, the last Whitney ever saw of her sister was that of a flailing naked girl with a bloody hand being dragged by her hair through the bedroom doorway. Dark streaks marked the floor as she went. Then her father reached back and slammed the door shut. The bedroom, with Whitney in it, returned to the dark.

She tried to listen. Kerrie's squalling and the beating of her heels and palms on the floor faded as Maddock dragged her away. She heard thumping as he mercilessly pulled her down the stairs toward the basement door. But even that grew quieter as their distance from the bedroom increased. She strained to hear, as if counting the time between lightning and thunder; she wanted the sound to fade. It had to fade eventually. Her mind fought to turn away from it, but the sound of her sister dying kept interfering with her denial of it.

Whitney remained in the corner with her hands over her face and knees pulled up to her chest. She knew when he finished with Kerrie, he'd want to make good on her promise to him, but that didn't matter now. She wasn't in the cellar. She pulled the blanket over her shivering body and listened to the diffuse screams from the basement that filled the house. They seemed to come from nowhere and everywhere at the same time, but then suddenly she heard nothing. A silence came at last that could mean only one thing: Kerrie was gone. The house had fallen into the silence of her death.

Outside, there was no wind, nor was there any light in the room, save for the pale lunar light shining through the window. Whitney settled into the corner. "I want my, mom," she whispered to herself, as if wishing it could make it happen.

* * *

Hours later, the sky gave its first hint of morning. The sun hadn't risen, but the dark surrendered to the gray. Whitney had not slept; she'd only stared at the bedroom door expecting her father's return for the execution of his dirty deeds. *What if he gives me a baby?* she thought. *What if he kills me anyway?* But after the quiet that followed the end of her sister's life, the house persisted in grim silence.

He must still be in the basement, she thought. *He must still be making the wine.* The wine always took precedence over anything else he might want to do. The process possessed him, and he had to consume its final product, but something in her mind had broken. She wasn't afraid of him anymore. Through the last moments of the night, she'd found a solution.

It came to her as the guilt of betraying her sister began to outweigh the fear of her father. When she was calmer, when she could think, it settled in solid and took over the pounding revulsion she felt for what she'd done to Kerrie.

Suddenly it was clear. She'd betrayed her sister, and now her sister was dead. Even worse than doing nothing at all, she was the instrument of that death. She'd sold her sister to her father to escape what was meant for her. It amazed her that she hadn't thought of the solution before—especially when it was always there, always waiting for her to simply pick it up.

She rose and let the blanket fall to the floor. It was cold in the room, and she trembled, but she didn't care. Sitting down at the writing desk, where so many nights were spent doing schoolwork, she opened the top drawer and removed a Big Chief tablet. She opened her fountain pen and wrote on it: *I gave her to him.* Then she signed and dated it, *Whitney, 1957.*

She got up from the desk and moved to the bedroom door. She half-expected her father to be standing there when she opened it. She expected him to reach in and grab her, but it didn't matter to her now. The connection to her body had ceased. It had become a block of ice, and she was in the center of that ice looking out. Her body wasn't for her anymore. She'd offered it to her father the night before, just as she'd offered Kerrie's life to him.

She opened the door and nothing was there, so she walked down the hallway to the stairs. She ignored the bloody streaks she came across along the way. *I have a solution*, she kept telling herself. She thought it like a mantra, and it kept the revulsion at bay.

She descended the stairs to the first floor of the mission-styled winery. The ancient house was empty, and she knew her father was still working in the cellar, working feverishly on his latest batch of wine and drinking it nearly as fast. She walked cautiously across the stone floor, her bare feet silent on its surface as she moved. To the left of the foyer, she entered her father's study, his private library he forbade them to enter. But she'd entered it many times before.

Secretly, the elegant study was as much hers and Kerrie's as it was their father's. They played in it on the long days and nights when he buried himself in the cellar making wine. She and Kerrie were often left to themselves for two, even three days during those stretches, so they played a game in the office.

They took turns sitting behind the large redwood desk in the high back leather chair, and pretended to be *The Boss*, and the boss could command the other to do all sorts of menial tasks, the object being to enjoy the servitude of the other, at least until your turn was up.

On one of those days, after ordering Kerrie to make them both peanut butter-and-jelly sandwiches, Whitney opened the top drawer that her father had inadvertently left a key in. On a stack of old letters and papers lay the real object of authority for any boss. It scared her then, so she quickly closed the drawer and locked it, but this morning she would retrieve it.

She pulled the knob of the desk drawer, but it was locked, and the key was missing. She didn't try twice. She went to the

cold, black fireplace across the room and retrieved an iron pok-
er from its stand. Sticking the pointed end into the gap between
the desktop and the drawer, she pried until the wood snapped,
taking the lock and drawer's front panel along with it. She slid
out the drawer. It was still there just as it had been before. She
reached inside and removed her father's nickel-plated revolver.

It was heavier than it looked, and she could see the rims of
the brass cartridges in the cylinder, but this time she wasn't
afraid of it. Now it was a beautiful liberator that she put close to
her face and studied the distorted reflection in the bends of its
shape. *It's a true reflection*, she thought, and it represented a
final solution to the problem of William Maddock.

Of course, he'd used the gun in front of them before. She
recalled very clearly him shooting at cans and bottles in the
vineyard. He just pulled the hammer back, pointed it, and
pulled the trigger. He even shot a stray dog once.

She aimed the gun at the door of the study, strengthening
her abilities, pretending to aim it, rehearsing her next move.

She thought back to the day she and Kerrie found the dog
wandering in the vineyard. It was shortly after their mother's
death that the dog had come to them. It was panting and confused, but when they called to it, it approached them with a
wagging tail.

The dog was dumped on their property; she knew it. There
were no other houses in any direction around Eternity Vineyards, not for three miles at least; someone had to have abandoned it.

Kerrie gave it water and a hotdog from the icebox and
brought the shepherd-mix to their father, who looked at it with
a mixture of disgust and fear. When she and Kerrie asked to
keep it, he promptly retrieved the revolver from his desk and
fired two shots into the dog without explanation, one in the
chest that dropped it, one in the head that killed it.

Afterward, he made them him burry it with him. He seemed not want to be alone with it. He worked fast and didn't speak while they shoveled out the dirt of the grave and filled it back in, leaving a hump in the ground just about the size of the dog itself.

That was a day of crying for Whitney and Kerrie, and Whitney noticed the irony of it now: when she needed to the most, she knew how to kill a living thing.

She took the gun and walked out of the study across the lower floor of the Spanish estate. She went to the basement door and put her ear to it. She could hear bottles being jostled, and she knew he would never stop. Her sister was only one of many more children that would join him in Eternity's cellar. She was only one of many that had already been there before.

She turned from the cellar and went to the high double doors that hung as massive oak and ironclad guardians to the interior of Eternity. She squeezed the latch and pulled one of them open. There was resistance only from the weight of it. Once started, it swung open nearly on its own without even a squeak.

She felt the winter air of the early morning in Southern Arizona. Her thin, blue nightgown left her exposed to the low temperature. Her teeth chattered uncontrollably, but it felt good to her. The future was going to be better. Finally, there would be a measure of hope and happiness.

She walked down the gravel drive that led to the northern vineyard fields. The rocks hurt her feet, but she didn't guard her steps. She continued with only the thought of her mother and little sister dominating her mind. The torment of their images spread throughout her entire being. It pushed out the cold and the stabbing stones.

She walked between the rows of the vines, trying with diligence to avoid contact with the plump, black Mourvèdre grapes hanging in clusters that shouldn't exist. They should be impossible to grow in December; her mother had told her so, but the rituals her father performed at the winery changed their nature. He harvested grapes all year long. He made wine in a never-ending supply. Once made, he and the wine consumed one another, and it changed him, and no one was near enough to notice.

She walked into the middle of the vineyard and cocked the hammer of the revolver. She put the gun into her mouth, just as she had seen her mother do two years before. Her last physical sensation was the cold, hard steel of the barrel on her tongue and against the roof of her mouth, and without a second thought or wince, she pulled the trigger. A red spray from the back of her head expressed itself in the new sunlight peeking over the foothills on the horizon. In that instant, her body died and crumpled to the dirt—but her consciousness remained.

ONE

Jennifer Dickerman sat intolerant behind the wheel of her Durango at a lowered railroad gate watching the long, slow train that separated her from the eastbound I-10. She needed to get sixty miles farther south to find Eternity Vineyards before five if she was going to get to the old geezer before his nurse arrived to feed him, clean him, and generally get in her way.

She needed to talk to Robert Maddock; she needed to close the deal. It was a make-or-break deal. It meant the difference between working for herself now, at forty-three, or continuing to work for McWilliam's Real Estate until they wore her out at sixty-five.

Her cell phone rang. She tapped the button on her headset and turned on her always-friendly-always-happy-always-glad-you-called tone of voice: "Call-It-Home Realty, this is Jen." No matter whom she talked to, she considered the sale. All conversations were an opportunity to close, and closing started with becoming the friend—whether the client wanted one or not.

Familiarity established high ground and control of the conversation. Therefore, to the customers, she had to be Jen—never Jennifer, and never, ever *Ms. Dickerman.*

"Hey Jennifer, how's the drive?" said a swish voice from the other end.

It was Mike, and so she relaxed. Mike Wilson was her partner and co-former employee of McWilliam's Real Estate. Now he wore many hats at Call-It-Home Realty including general contractor, office manager, property inspector, and anything else she didn't have a license for or couldn't do from her car.

"I'm fucking late," Jennifer said. "I had to get off the freeway to get gas, and now I'm stuck at a railroad crossing in Tucson—wait, I think I see the end of it." Jennifer leaned forward over the steering wheel and tried to look down the track.

"Tammy called," Mike said.

"Damn."

"She says she wants to come home on the fifteenth. She wants you to call her."

"Damn it. I can't call her right now; I have to concentrate on this thing. This is the one. This is going to be the deal of all deals if we can get it."

"You haven't told her about your change in circumstance, have you?" Mike asked. He was an annoyingly good friend, the kind who was irritatingly good for her.

"No, I haven't told her, but I will. I'll call her tomorrow. If she calls back, Mike, tell her I'll talk to her tomorrow, okay?"

"What are we going to do about you?"

"Make me rich," Jennifer said.

"Hey," Mike said, "don't forget to look at the basement when you get out there. I got a feeling there's going to be problems given the price. Don't forget, Jennifer, the basement matters: any sign of water or cracks in the walls; look at the floor beams for rot, that sort of thing—the basics."

"I know," Jennifer said, "I won't forget. If I get out of there early, I'll give you a call. If not, I'll see you in the morning."

"Sounds like a winner."

Jennifer disconnected and felt a sense of relief as the last of the railcars passed the intersection. The gate rose, and she entered the interstate headed out of Tucson. Traffic was heavy from the Prince Road exit to I-19, but lightened up significantly thereafter. She might make it to the vineyard on time after all, if luck was smiling.

Heading east, she thought about the phone call from Robert Maddock shortly after leaving McWilliam's. He wanted to sell his place, and he wanted to sell it to her. He represented their first client, and Maddock's deal, if it was the real thing, if the house was anything other than a complete wreck, was too good to pass up. This deal, if she closed it, was more important than any other marketing efforts they could make at the time. She knew damn well no matter how hard she tried to prepare for success, this kind of luck was essential to the startup of Call-It-Home Realty.

The sun crept toward the tips of the Santa Rita Mountains to the west as Jennifer turned south on Highway 83. That's when the terrain began to change from strictly desert into grassland. It surprised her. She hadn't thought of Arizona as a grassland state or an area where cattle grazed on the open range. She figured it was all red deserts leading into Mexico. But she never made it down this way. For the last twenty years, Arizona was home, but she'd never gone south of the I-10, or south of Tucson for that matter. She placed all her bets in Phoenix and would have easily wagered there were no wine vineyards in Southern Arizona. But after Robert Maddock called, she Googled his place and discovered there were a dozen wineries in his area, but no listings or images for Eternity Vineyards. She made a left at Sonoita and followed Highway 82 east.

At four-thirty she arrived at the dirt road that supposedly connected Maddock's property to Highway 82. She followed it per Maddock's instructions, and there was, as he told her, a large black mailbox on a fencepost marked 113 at the entrance to the road. The road wasn't well maintained, but it was easy enough to traverse in her SUV. Still, she regretted yesterday's $25.50 at the car wash.

A mile of dirt later, Jennifer began to question her own directions. What if she misunderstood him? What if Maddock, who admitted to her on the phone that he hadn't left the premises in over two years, forgot the directions to his own house?

She couldn't keep going down an unknown road. She stopped the car to re-consult her atlas. It had to be the right road. As it was, she could still turn the Dodge around and head back; the road was still wide enough, but it was getting slimmer, and it was only an hour until dark. After that, she'd be hopelessly lost. Give it one more mile, she thought, call him again in a mile. He already told her he couldn't see her after his nurse arrived, but maybe there'd be some leeway in that.

Putting the Durango back into drive, she headed up the incline in front of her, loose gravel shot from under her tires as she went, but at the top of it, to her utter relief, the house came into view. "Oh my God," she said at the sight of it, "that's got to be nine thousand square feet—and in the middle of nowhere."

The house sat off on a hill that overlooked what she had come to learn were thirty acres of actual grapevines and another eighty acres of undeveloped grassland. A hundred yards in front, the northern vineyard began, and the dirt road cut through rows of barren vines on the way up to the house. She ignored them, her attention remained fully on the stone, two-story, mission-style structure. Its roof was covered with red clay tiling, and along the lower half of the house another clay-tiled roof was supported by a series of stone archways. Together they formed a walkway that seemed to run the entire perimeter of the mansion.

Nowhere or not, Robert Maddock couldn't be serious about the kind of cash he was looking for. She felt a grand waste of her time unfolding in front of her—just an old coot out of his mind; she should have known. A self-kicking was in order. Still, as she drove closer to the property, a predatory excitement took over. This could easily be the deal of a lifetime. The closer she got, the more beautiful the house became, and the more easily she knew she could flip it. If Maddock was even close to serious, they were going to get this place, and they were going to get rich.

Eventually, she made it up to the house where it sat on a half-acre lot of medium-sized white gravel. There was no loose dirt, and with that observation, she calculated no mud when the monsoons came in July.

Monsoon rain, she soon learned after moving to Arizona, was the moisture that came up from the Sea of Cortez giving the state a third of its annual rainfall, and with it the most spectacular lightning shows in the country. The monsoons were a major selling point of country estates back in her McWilliam's days. If they didn't know any better, she always stressed the beauty of the monsoon season to her customers who came to Arizona to retire. But she'd only mention it if she could guarantee no mud on the property. If monsoons meant mud, she'd say nothing about them at all. Now, Jennifer imagined the beauty of the monsoons in the seclusion of this place. She was already falling in love with it, and with the profit to be made when they sold it.

TWO

• •

She parked the Durango near two other cars next to the house, and after shutting off the ignition, she looked in the visor mirror to check the three essentials: hair neat, no food on her teeth, and evenly applied lipstick. Then off came the cell phone headset along with a quick straightening of the bangs of her shoulder-length brown hair. It was cut in the bowl-style of a politician, and she didn't prefer the look. She preferred the longhair days of her bygone youth, but the style was practically required of a woman in the real estate game. It was part of the uniform business look. Just like a high-and-tight in the Army, it was essential to the profession.

She exited the car and slung her bag over her shoulder. Then she reached back in to grab her leather briefcase, but as she moved to lock the car door, she scanned the environment that in Phoenix never failed to be hostile. There were literally no other dwellings in sight, just soft, purple-brown mountains on the horizon. No crime here, she thought, no way, so she dropped her bag back on the seat.

The other two cars were a concern. One was an oxidized green Range Rover with a rusty back bumper and a broken driver's side mirror. She deduced that one was Robert Maddock's. The other was late model Honda. "Shit," she muttered to herself, realizing his nurse had already arrived. But surely there would be some wiggle room.

So she passed through an arch and trekked the cobblestone walkway to the front door. It was oak and stood a good eight feet high, and when she reached out her hand and ran it along the iron straps and nails that held it together, she surmised it was the original door. It had to be more than a hundred years old, she thought. What character! What a selling point!

There was no doorbell, only a large iron ring that she lifted and let fall—it was absolutely perfect. But of course a doorbell and modern alarm system would have to be installed after Maddock sold it to her. Clients from the city would expect it. The perfect knockers as it were would become a mere ornament, but who cared? She used the knocker again and rapped twice and waited.

A full minute passed, and she reached for the knocker to rap yet again, but the mechanical clack of the door latch sounded, and she watched the door open silently inward. The massive structure seemed to move effortlessly on its own, and Jennifer's attention was drawn upward along the height of it as it moved. Then a rude "May I help you?" drew her attention back down to a short Hispanic woman, at least fifty-plus, wearing wine-colored scrubs. The woman held the door as if she might shut it at any moment during Jennifer's answer.

Jennifer smiled broadly and went instinctively into damage control. "Hello, how are you? I'm Jen. I'm here to meet with Robert." Her false humility was a masterpiece in dramatic study.

There was a dichotomy in real estate, a paradox Jennifer learned early on: You have to look better than the client. Wear a good suit or dress, drive an expensive car, and speak like you went to school. It makes the client feel inferior to and of lower class than you. Then you bring the client up until they feel equal with you, and at that point they'll do anything you say in order to maintain the good feelings of their newfound artificial self-esteem—self-esteem created by identification with a high-class friend. Jennifer wanted to be this woman's high-class friend, at least for the next sixty seconds.

"Well, Mr. Maddock isn't seeing anyone right now," the nurse began, oblivious to her chance at high-class identification. "He—"

"Who the hell is it?" a shout sounded from the dark bowels of the Spanish winery.

"Someone named, Jen!" the nurse shouted back over her shoulder as if her answer couldn't possibly mean anything to the voice from within, and as if she couldn't risk leaving the open door unattended by moving away from it. Jennifer continued to beam her smile at the aid. Five years ago she got her braces off and a set of veneers installed. She could hold a smile for twenty minutes if she had to. No one can resist a persistent smile. She'd learned that at a sales conference in Seattle one year.

"I told her I couldn't see her after four." The harsh voice yelled. "Tell her I told her I can't see her after four. I have to get my bath!"

Jennifer's mind screamed to her, He told me four-thirty, and it's fifteen after! Her smile still beamed, but to it she added slight "oooh, gosh" of feigned disappointment. "I am soooo sorry I'm late," Jennifer said. "I got held up on the 10, and I made a wrong turn on the 83—"

The aid began yelling over her shoulder in translation: "She says she got stuck on the freeway and made a wrong turn!"

"Well, I'm taking my bath!

"You want me to tell her to come back?"

There was silence. Jennifer waited for the sentencing.

"Just have her wait in the damn study if she wants. I gotta have my bath." It was as if the house, itself, were protesting her arrival.

"You can wait in the study. I'll be done with him in about twenty minutes. I'll bring him in. You can meet with him while I make his dinner—*if you want*." She stressed the latter as if no one had ever been that desperate.

"Sure, thanks," Jennifer said. "That would be great."

The aid opened the door all the way, and Jennifer stepped into the foyer. The place was old. Jennifer felt the age of the place as entirely palpable from the stone floor to the massive oak staircase in front of her leading to the upper floor. There was a colonial bench seat under a large gold-framed mirror against the wall next to the door, and Jennifer went to it, thinking it best to sit there and wait for Robert Maddock.

The place was filthy with dust and cobwebs, but the nurse offered no explanation. She only pointed to the right, to a door that looked like the front door, but single and smaller. It was slightly ajar, and Jennifer couldn't make out what hid beyond it.

"That's the study," The nurse said flatly.

"Oh, I'm sorry. Okay, I'll just wait in there." Jennifer got up from the bench as the nurse turned away and went up the stairs without absolving her. Jennifer's pumps sounded like horse hoofs as she walked across the stone floor to the study, but when she entered it, she was immediately taken aback.

The room was more than a study, it was a library and an office, and at the far end from the door was a large window that looked out over the west side of the property. The center of the window was clear, but thick along its edges was ornate stained glass that created a frame. From the door, it appeared to Jennifer as if she were looking through a window that was also a painting of the landscape. "Fantastic," she whispered.

There were floor-to-ceiling bookshelves along the walls, and facing her, sitting in front of the window, was a heavily engraved redwood desk with a high back leather chair. In front of the desk, covering most of the stone floor, lay a rug with Islamic patterning.

On one wall, a massive fireplace interrupted the bookshelves, and in it sat three logs on an iron grate with straw underneath them waiting to be lit. A dramatic pair of gargoyle andirons in front of the logs sat behind a black metallic screen. It was plated with reliefs of angels and demons apparently fighting one another. Jennifer marveled at what the whole thing would look like with a blaze illuminating it from behind.

The entire study was an antique store, and a buyer's panic seized her as reality clashed with her desire: he couldn't have meant the numbers he quoted on the phone. It would be insanity, or the place would have to be sinking into the monsoon mud. This was a multimillion-dollar estate. This was no hundred-thousand-dollar fixer-upper.

In front of the desk to each side, facing it at forty-five degree angles were two smaller high back leather chairs. Jennifer sat down in one and gazed out the window. It made her stare; she couldn't help it. The window was a *trompe l'oeil*, and it hypnotized with ease.

She felt out of her depth. This may not be the best first property for Call-It-Home Realty, she thought. Even if they finagled a five thousand dollar knock-off for all the dust, they couldn't come up with the cash for this kind of property, and cash was all Robert Maddock said he would accept.

She placed her briefcase on the desk and took out the notes she made during their initial conversation. A mistake was made somewhere, and they were back to square one—no doubt about it. An entire day wasted for sure, but they had no other deals in the works, so what else could she do but check it out? She pulled her cell phone from her purse to ring Mike and let him know the new and unfortunate status. She was interrupted, however, and it had only been five minutes.

"Jennifer Dickerman?" an old man barked from the study's doorway.

THREE

Jennifer stood and turned to see Robert Maddock being pushed into the study in a wheelchair by the aid. He was scraggly with a white beard and white hair around the rim of his head. Wearing a plaid, cotton shirt and denim overalls, he looked every bit the farmer and nothing like a winegrower.

Jennifer smiled widely, "Hello Mr. Maddock. I'm soooo—"

"Call me, Bob," He cut in complaining. "I told you to call me, Bob, when we talked on the phone." He raised a hand as if the aid's pushing annoyed him immensely, then stood and walked somewhat unbalanced to the desk chair, holding on to the edge of the desk as he moved. Jennifer figured him for eighty if he was a day.

The aid turned the wheelchair around and pushed it out. "I'm making your dinner; then I'm leaving," she said as she exited. Maddock didn't acknowledge her declaration.

Jennifer reached over the desk to shake his hand, and he reciprocated. "So, what do you think of my offer?" he said as Jennifer sat back down.

"I think I must have misunderstood you."

"There's no misunderstanding. I mean what I say: I'll sell you this place for a hundred thousand, but I'm only selling it to you, and I want the money in cash, hundred-dollar bills will be fine."

"What about an escrow account?" Jennifer said almost unconsciously. She couldn't think of another response to his price.

"Don't need one in Arizona."

It was true. It was a terrible idea, but technically they could do the deal without it. She leaned forward in her chair. "Mr. Maddock—Bob—I have to tell you this place is worth a lot more than one hundred thousand dollars. Even without an inspection, I can tell you that."

"I know what it's worth to some, and I know what it's worth to me. I don't want my kids to get it. They wouldn't take care of it the way it needs to be cared for; I spoiled them bad. I don't mind admitting it. Well, they live out of state now, and they'd sell the place. I need a caretaker, and that person is you—I know it's you."

Jennifer began to wonder if the aged Maddock might have mental issues, old-person mental issues. "I don't understand," she said.

"You look like a pretty serious woman to me," Maddock said. "I don't think you believe in the same things I do, but you should." He leaned back and continued; "I saw a sign in a dream, a dream I had almost a year ago."

Jennifer worked hard not to patronize him. "Bob, of course I want to buy this place at that price, but people see lots of things in dreams, and—"

"The sign was a real estate sign; it said, *Call-It-Home*."

Maddock stared intently at Jennifer. He seemed to be studying her reaction, and Jennifer felt like a mark, like one of her own clients. She didn't like the feeling of being sold. There had to be a catch, and it was always the mark's responsibility to figure it out. She was sure her look of incredulity was showing, and then as if reading her mind Maddock said, "Of course, there's a catch, Miss Dickerman."

"There always is," Jennifer said, her cynicism deliberately obvious.

"The catch is you can't sell it. This place is for you. It has to be only for you. If you're going to sell it, then you can't have it. Once I get the cash, I'm moving to Bakersfield to live with a friend of mine. We were in the Army together. He's got a ranch, and I'm going to go live with him. I don't have very long, not long at all. I saw that in the dream, too, but I don't need to tell you much about that. That was just for me to know and my kids to find out.

"When I saw your ad in the paper, your ad for Call-It-Home Realty, I knew you were the one. I had the dream a long time before you started advertising your company, and I believe in it. But no matter what you believe about it, you can't sell this place. It don't matter if you live here. It don't matter if you let it turn to dust like I'm doing; it don't matter if you burn it down, course that's been tried before, but you can't sell it, and you can't take out a mortgage against it. That'd be the same thing as selling it."

Jennifer sat speechless, staring blankly at Robert Maddock. He was insane. Did he think she was insane, too? She tried to calculate what was being offered to her, but the confusion of a multimillion-dollar estate offered for a hundred thousand was too far out to reconcile. Still, you don't think about a killer deal; you grab it. And her instinct was to close the deal, except the killer deal seemed to be closing in on her, maybe more like burying her alive.

Maddock broke the silence: "Why don't I show you around. We can start in the kitchen. Have you had your dinner yet?"

"My dinner?" Jennifer mumbled. Her mind was tied up trying to calculate capital gains, insurance costs, and profit margins.

"Mattie's making my dinner, but she always makes too much. Course she doesn't have to pay for the groceries, does she? We can split it, if you want. I think it's mashed potatoes and pot roast, probably some rolls, too." In that moment, Robert Maddock seemed like her grandfather, kind and indulging.

"Sure," Jennifer said, still lost in a fog of numbers.

At that, and without warning, Maddock began yelling, "Mattie! Mattie! Bring in my damn wheelchair. We're ready for dinner—Mattie!" The last Mattie was three times as loud as the first. Jennifer wanted to cover her ears.

"Hold your horses!" came a reply from somewhere far away.

"Mattie's a good cook," Maddock said, returning to his quieter conversational volume. "She's a good nurse, too; best I ever had. Course I don't tell her that; it'd make her weak. She'd probably stop trying if I got her to thinking she was worth a damn."

Mattie arrived with the wheelchair, and Maddock made his way to it. She wheeled him out of the library and Jennifer followed close behind.

"Up those stairs," Maddock pointed, "there's six bedrooms and three bathrooms." His voice echoed in the expansive foyer. "Two bedrooms share a bathroom. There aren't any showers, though, just bathtubs. I replaced the boiler about five years ago with a propane one. It used to burn oil. Before that it was coal, and before that there was no hot water at all. We got central air about twenty years ago, too." Maddock said it as if he'd been steadily working on the place.

Jennifer looked up the staircase that led to the second floor. Three balconies formed hallways with one on either side of the building and one facing the stairs. Each hallway had two doors, all of them with the same ancient wood and iron fittings as the door of the study.

"Just over there," Robert pointed to the room across from the study, "is the dining room, and right up here is the kitchen." Mattie pushed Robert past the dining room and stairs toward the back of the house.

As they went, Jennifer noticed a door on the right that seemed to enter into a room under the stairs. "What's in there?" she asked.

Robert paused almost imperceptibly before answering. "That's the inside entrance to the winery. The winery is in the basement. It has another entrance outside with a loading ramp so you can wheel the casks in and out."

"My God, that sounds great. I'd love to see what's down there."

"Well, you'll have to do that on your own," Maddock said. "I don't go down there anymore; the steps are too dangerous." Robert impatiently motioned Mattie to keep pushing the wheelchair forward, but Jennifer stopped and opened the basement door. All she saw was darkness and the first few steps of a staircase that led down into it.

"What say we eat dinner first?" Robert interjected. "I'll let you in on a few more details."

"Sure...sorry." Jennifer shut the door and followed Mattie and Robert into the kitchen.

Mattie pushed Robert up to a pinewood table, but Jennifer walked to the glass door at the back of the room. It looked out onto a large cobblestone veranda that extended past the walkway. There was a fountain in the center and a waist-high stone wall surrounding it. At the opposite end was a wrought iron gate barring an archway that opened up into the southern vineyard fields. Wine and cheese parties could be held out there for the buyers, she thought. The sound of a hired Spanish guitar played in her mind; she'd have to book one. She turned to Robert. "I noticed when I drove up that the vines are bare. Do you still grow any grapes?"

"They grow in the spring, and we harvest them in the fall. If they grow any other time, you've got trouble."

Jennifer chuckled politely, and then noticed he wasn't smiling.

After setting the table for two, Mattie brought out the food. "Aren't you going to eat with us, Mattie?" Robert asked as if Mattie were committing a sin.

"No, I got to get home. Caesar has a basketball game at school. I'll clean up tomorrow. Just leave the dishes in the sink."

"Well, to hell with you then," Robert said as gently as a husband telling his wife he loves her.

Mattie finished setting the table, and Jennifer walked over to it. "Thank you Mattie, this looks great." The simple meat and potatoes meal on the small wood table in the corner of the room was at odds with the size and grandeur of the kitchen. To Jennifer, it looked as if it could service an entire restaurant.

"It's a big kitchen." Robert said, as if needing to stress the selling points of the estate.

"Bob, why don't you give this place to your kids?"

"Because they'd abuse it. Don't get me wrong, I love Dennis, Kathy, and Ben, but they'd sell it to the highest bidder. It wouldn't mean a damn what I wanted. And if they didn't sell it, they'd succumb to it."

"Succumb to it?"

"Look, Miss Dickerman," Robert lowered his voice and his eyes darted from side to side, "this place is old. It's been around over three hundred years. Did you know that? And there's things about this place that can pollute a soul if you let it. I won't kid you on that. It can make a person do bad things. Did you know it's burned three times?

"No, I didn't know that." Jennifer picked at her potatoes without looking. The old guy had to be drunk. Hermits tend to drink; she'd seen it a dozen times if not more, and usually it took a special cleaning crew once you got them out of a place before you could sell it. But he didn't smell drunk, and there were no cans or bottles littering the walkway. "It looks fine, to me," Jennifer said.

"Well, someone always restores it." Maddock's voice grew even quieter, and he leaned in as if telling her a secret: "The last person was my brother, William. He restored it, but he shouldn't have. Both his daughters ended up dying out here, and his wife killed herself. Course that was back in the fifties. My own wife left me and took the kids when I moved in. Didn't see my kids again till they were grown." Maddock resumed chewing his meat as if he'd just relayed yesterday's weather.

"My gosh, It sounds like there's a lot of personal pain here for you. I can see why you want to sell it." Jennifer unconsciously cut her roast.

"I'd rather give it away," Robert pondered out loud, "but I need the money to move to Bakersfield. I don't have a lot of time left. I know that. I want to enjoy my life a bit."

Jennifer put her silverware down and folded her hands in her lap. "Bob, of course I'm going to buy this place for a hundred thousand, if that's what you're offering, but it just doesn't make any sense to me. No one takes a million dollar loss—"

"Four million," Robert cut in. I had it appraised two years ago, and with the land and winery, it's worth four million. It'd be worth more, except it's so remote."

"Okay, that's what I'm talking about," Jennifer continued, "It doesn't make any sense."

"But I'm not taking the loss alone," Maddock said foxily. "We are. Because, unless you promise you won't sell it, I won't sell it to you. See, it's a four-million-dollar loss to you, as well." Robert dug into his mash potatoes and ate. Jennifer lost her appetite.

"When you're finished," Robert said with his mouth full, "you should take a look around for yourself; take some time to think about it. It'll grow on you. I can't get upstairs too much or down to the winery, so I'll let you look at those things for yourself. My bedroom and bathroom are just across the hall just past the kitchen, and there's a living room down the hallway, too, if that's what you want to call it. That's where I spend most of my time. I got a television in there, and I'll throw it in if you want it. I can show you all that when you're ready."

Jennifer took another bite out of politeness, and when she'd swallowed it, she wiped her mouth with her napkin and got up from the table. "I think I will have a look around, Bob. This place is fascinating." She took her cellphone out of her briefcase. "Do you mind if I take some photos?"

"Go right ahead, Maddock said, "You know, this can be a good home if a person lets it be."

FOUR

———●●———

Jennifer walked out of the kitchen and turned down the hall toward the foyer. She climbed the stairs and made her way to the first bedroom on the east side of the upper floor. It was larger than the bedrooms of the modern homes she sold in Phoenix, and though she was a master at making small rooms sound large, at convincing people of the spaciousness of a room even when they were standing close enough to smell one another's body odor, she wouldn't have to sell the size of these rooms at all. They were big.

She beheld a freestanding wardrobe. It has to be a hundred years old, she thought. In fact, all the furniture seemed to be original antiques, but none of it looked worn out. There was a thick layer of dust on all the surfaces, cobwebs in most of the corners, and they would have to be cleaned before the place was shown, but underneath the dust, the quaint nineteenth-century authenticity was priceless. There was no need to sell Eternity Vineyards at all—she'd have to hold an auction!

Looking through five of the bedrooms, she discovered the two along the front hallway were the largest. She'd call these the king and queen suites. They both had four-poster beds, and when she walked through, she found herself wishing she could live in the house, herself, just like Maddock was insisting on. But living in the house was impossible. She banished the thought; it was dangerous thinking. She didn't have a hundred grand to throw away, and if she and Mike were going to put it together, they'd have to get a quick return on their investment. It's possible for Maddock to sell the place for any price he wants, she reasoned, but he can't stipulate a new owner never resell it. Apparently, he didn't know that, and she wasn't about to tell him.

When she entered the last bedroom at the end of the west hall, something struck her as sad and beautiful all at once. The sun was setting, and its orange light fell through the window like a dying hope, and Jennifer sensed a kind of loss she didn't understand. The room possessed a heaviness that lingered in the air. It wasn't at all like the other rooms.

In it was a queen-sized sleigh bed against the north wall, a freestanding wardrobe across from it, and a French writing desk and chair against the wall by the window. In one corner sat a vanity with a mirror and a stool. Like the other rooms, a heavy layer of dust settled on all the horizontal surfaces as well as the hardwood floors. Jennifer saw that where she walked, her shoes left footprints in the dust on the floor.

Being in the room began to feel like violating a space that had been left alone for a very long time, and maybe for a very good reason. Jennifer walked over to the writing desk and ran her finger along the top of it. She rolled the dust on her finger into a tiny tube and let it fall. Definitely professional cleaners would have to be contracted before she could ever sell the place. Fortunately, that would give Maddock a chance to clear out to Bakersfield and forget about whether or not it was being resold.

She went to the vanity and opened the drawer. It was barren except for a pair of barrettes, and seeing them brought about a wave of what she felt when she first entered the room: an ancient overwhelming sadness and loss, as if it were part of the atmosphere she inhaled.

Lost for a moment in her emotions, she sat on the vanity stool and didn't consider that her skirt might be getting dusty. She picked up a barrette and examined it closely; then she looked in the mirror and saw the figure sitting on the bed behind her.

Jennifer let out a quick and startled scream and put her hand to her mouth to control it.

Reflected in the mirror was a young girl sitting on the bed. Her complexion was ashen, and she wore a light blue nightgown. Her black hair hung down past her shoulders, and she stared straight ahead with her hands on her knees as if looking at something approaching from outside the window.

Jennifer brought her hand to her chest. "Oh my God, you scared me," she said. "I didn't realize this was your room." Jennifer stood and turned, ready to introduce herself as <u>Jen</u>, but when she did, the room was empty. There was no girl, and the quilt on the bed was undisturbed.

Confusion flooded her. It must have been a trick of the light. Surely it was a trick from the setting sun, but she was certain it was a girl.

Jennifer instinctively dusted the back of her skirt with her hand. She felt anxious, like she'd just seen a snake that slithered away and now it could be anywhere. She left the room straightaway, not wanting to be in it alone.

At the bottom of the stairs, Robert Maddock sat waiting in his wheelchair. "So do you like what you see?" He wasn't smiling.

Jennifer paused on the steps and thought of mentioning the girl but feared sounding ridiculous. She was, after all, trying to control this deal. Control was the key. The place was a gold mine, and if Maddock was crazy enough to believe in a dream that told him she was the new caretaker for a hundred grand, then by God she was going to get that gold. She decided in that moment to tell him anything he wanted to hear, anything at all. She smiled and walked down the steps. "I do like what I see, Bob."

"So, all we have to do is sort out the details," Maddock said. "The first is your intention: Are you going to keep this place and not sell it?"

"Yes, I am. I would love to have this place, but if it's so wrong to sell it, what about you? You're selling it."

"I need the money," Maddock said indignantly, "and I know you're the right person to pass it on to. If it gets into the wrong hands, and there aren't no hands living today that are the right ones except yours, we'll all be sorry—you'll be sorry."

"Then I won't sell it." Jennifer smiled at him with her straightened teeth. Whatever the paranoid old man wants to hear, she thought. "I think it would be a great place to have for a home," she lied.

"Do you promise—do you swear—you won't sell it?"

"I promise you; I will not sell it." Jennifer stopped smiling to assure him he could trust her. She knew that too many sales-people don't know when to stop talking, and they sure don't know when to stop showing teeth. They lose deals that way, because their performances are out of control.

"Then since you've promised for all to hear...," Maddock continued glancing around at the various corners of the ceiling as if some hidden camera were recording them. "Since you've promised, I know you'll end up keeping your word." Robert wheeled to the front door, and Jennifer walked down the stairs and stood beside him.

"I wouldn't ask you to leave so soon, but I know you don't have the cash or the paperwork with you, so come back when you do. It ain't like I got anyone else looking at the place. Besides my TV show's on in five minutes. I got a satellite dish out here, you know? I'll leave it for you when I go."

"Thanks," Jennifer said. She felt corralled through the front door.

"Take care on the highway," Maddock warned. "It's narrow, and it can be dangerous at night. And keep it slow through Sonoita; it's a speed trap."

They shook hands and Jennifer said: "I'll get the paperwork together for a sale-by-owner, and we'll get together next week to go over it, but call me if you have any questions before then...or if you change your mind, you can always—"

Robert looked stern, and his eyes locked onto hers, "I won't be changing my mind, Miss Dickerman, will you?"

"No," Jennifer said, and for a moment wondered who closed the deal. Willing to take such a huge loss, Robert Maddock held all the cards. With that kind of sacrifice, he could dictate any terms he wanted.

* * *

She navigated her Dodge over the dirt road leading to Highway 82. When she got to the junction, she turned left and began the hundred-and-sixty-mile trip back to Phoenix. Traveling in a field of black, she perceived only as much of the road as the headlights would reveal. It was a thin highway, and with no other cars or lights from any civilization, the night enfolded her and uneasiness set in. It wasn't so much the dark that spooked her as it was what Robert Maddock said before she left: *Since you promised for all to hear, I know you'll end up keeping your word.* Who was *...all to hear?* And who or what was that damn girl she'd seen—or thought she saw? Maybe the place was haunted. Maybe spirits were lurking about. Maybe they were the ones who heard *the promise.*

She laughed. The old man's lunacy must be contagious, she thought. Besides a good haunting was a selling point. She could spin it as an interesting legend. People love that sort of thing, especially people interested in owning a winery three hundred years old. If there were no ghost, she'd have to invent one. A ghost meant more dollars, pure and simple. If that's what the old man was talking about, then his loss was her gain. She wouldn't be taking any four-million-dollar hit with him—that much was certain.

Her excitement grew as she drove. The deal was going to show everyone at McWilliam's that she was the real success in this racket. She was the boss. When she grew Call-It-Home Realty into a multimillion-dollar agency practically overnight, they'd all have to eat their words, especially Joel; he'd be eating his for damn sure.

Joel, her ex-boss at McWilliam's Real Estate, was obnoxiously nine months younger. That meant when she turned forty, he was still thirty-nine for far too long. It was on her fortieth birthday when he said: "*It's a whole lot easier to sink than swim out there. Most people need the structure of an established business to make it. I think you're one of those people, Jen— and there's nothing wrong with that.*"

She hated him. She hated McWilliam's Real Estate, and she knew they were all watching for her to come running back. They laughed when Mike went with her, and it seemed to soothe their jealously that he was the only one to fall for her arrogant scheme of an independent agency. He wasn't even a Realtor, so to them he was a joke. She'd sacrificed everything to make it in real estate. She considered the losses now as she unconsciously steered her way home.

She hardly knew her daughter, and her daughter hated her for it. After she and Tammy's father split up, she remained a good provider, but never a good mother. She was never at home, and now she lived alone, and her daughter lived with her ex in California. It would take a few more years in her own business, she thought, to make the sufficient dollars to work fewer hours. Then she could repair the relationship with Tammy. But if this deal worked out, she was already there.

She tuned the radio to an FM jazz station and lost herself in the music as she drove. By the time she got to the I-10, she was truly happy with the possibility of becoming rich, and with the streetlights of the freeway, there wasn't as much darkness as before. Things were better.

"Shit," Jennifer said to herself as the realization came screaming into her mind. Mike was going to be pissed. She forgot to check the basement.

FIVE

———— • ————

The guy is freaking nuts," Jennifer beamed as she walked through the door of Call-It-Home Realty. She held two lattés in a carrier and sat one on the desk in front of Mike.

"Thanks," he said. "So I take it the place is worth more than a hundred grand?"

Jennifer positioned herself at her desk and dislodged her own latté. "Mike," she began, struggling to harness her enthusiasm, "the place is a four-million-dollar estate."

Mike eased back into his chair and smoothed his tie down the length of his shirt, his expression a question mark. "So, no deal then?"

"Yes, deal; he's going to sell it to me for a hundred thousand dollars, and get this: because he saw Call-It-Home Realty in a dream." Jennifer spit out a sarcastic laugh. "He thinks I'm some chosen one to be the new caretaker of the place." "Can you believe it? He says he won't sell it to anyone else. He said he'd give it to me, but he needs the money to retire to Bakersfield or some damn place."

"The caretaker?" Mike sipped his coffee. "That's ridiculous. What's the catch?"

"I don't think there is one, not a real one anyway. Maddock is totally convinced by his dream. He says he had this dream nine months before we even opened up shop."

"I know you're not that naïve. This is not a possible deal, Jennifer. Is the place dilapidated? Condemned? What?"

"No. Near as near as I can tell it's in great shape. It's dusty. I mean it's really dusty, cobwebby, too. We'll have to get it cleaned, but I don't get the impression he's withholding any-thing—not this guy. I don't think money means that much to him."

"Money means everything to everyone," Mike said.

"I don't know," Jennifer said. "If he wasn't in a wheelchair, I think he'd be pushing a cart on the street. Oh, and get this: I can't resell it. He says the deal is only a deal if I don't resell it—that, and he wants the hundred grand in hundred-dollar bills."

Mike considered before he spoke. "Jennifer you're a Realtor. That's what you do. You buy and sell real estate."

"Don't worry; it's not binding. I didn't sign anything, and I won't. I just gave my word, and he seems to think that's good enough. Like I said the guy's a crackpot."

Mike walked to the front of the office and looked out the window at the strip mall parking lot and the Phoenix morning sun. Heat radiated through the cold windowpane. "If he's nuts, then the deal won't be valid. His relatives will come back on us."

"We'll flip it before that happens." Jennifer said. "It'll sell instantly. His kids can fight the new owners if they want."

"What's the basement like?" Mike asked.

Jennifer didn't skip a beat: "It's great. It's in great shape. There's no water, cracks, nothing. But that's just my assessment. You should really take a look for yourself when we go out and close the deal." She felt uncomfortable lying to him, but it didn't stop her either.

Mike raised his hands in capitulation. "Fine; I hope it's real. What can I say? Good God, Jennifer, this is a lottery if it sticks. But I still won't believe it until the title is transferred and he's out in Bakersfield with the cash. You do realize that's about all the cash we can muster?"

"Don't I know it," Jennifer said, "but I have a good feeling about this place. I think it's going to put Call-It-Home on the map. The profit from this sale could multiply over and over."

Jennifer took out all the notes she made at Eternity Vineyards and handed them to Mike. He looked through them briefly. "OK, great," he said. "I'll start the tax and title search today, check for encumbrances. You should start the purchase agreement and disclosure. We'll get the septic guys out there, and get the affidavit of legal value drawn up. It's not subdivided or incorporated, so it should be pretty simple. The sooner we close and ship this guy off, the better. I just feel like it could go sour. Any one of these could go bad. I'm not saying they will; it just has the potential, that's all. And don't forget to call your daughter."

Jennifer sat staring at her coffee as if she didn't hear him. "Damn," she finally whispered, picking up the handset of her desk phone. "Please God; let it be the answering machine." Jennifer listened to the ring tones from the California end, and Mike waved goodbye as he walked into the back room of the office to give her some privacy.

"Hello," a young woman's voice came through.

"Hey, Tammy. It's your mom."

"Helllooo," Tammy said, "I tried to call you yesterday, but you were already gone. I was wondering if I could come out on the fifteenth. I could stay a couple of weeks, and then come back and spend some time with Dad before next term." Her voice was optimistic.

"Yeah...hey honey, that's something I wanted to talk with you about. See, I moved out of the house..."

"You moved out of our house?"

Her daughter was born in Phoenix and raised in their suburban bungalow. Eight years ago, after the divorce, Jennifer retained the house when her ex- moved out to California. Even though it meant changing high schools mid-year, Tammy moved with her dad. Jennifer never tried to fight for custody. It was an arrangement that worked out for all of them.

"Why did you move out of the house?" Tammy asked.

"Actually, honey, I sold it."

"You sold our house?" A whine was developing in Tammy's voice. "What are you talking about? Since when did you sell our house?"

Jennifer wanted to correct her. It wasn't *our* house. Since the divorce, it was all *her* house. She could sell it if she wanted to. But she held her tongue. "Well, one reason was I needed the seed money for Call-It-Home Realty, and there was no other way to raise that kind of capital without taking a huge credit risk, and—"

"What about my room? Where will I stay when I come to see you? What about our get-together?"

"Actually, honey, I might need to postpone that a bit. See, I have this deal I'm working on, and I think it's going to make a lot of money for us. Think about it: here real soon your room is going to double in size, because I think I'm about to close on something really big."

There was silence on the other end.

"Tammy?" Jennifer inquired into the void.

"So, we're not going to spend any time together," Tammy said.

"Sure we are, honey, but maybe around the end of your next term. By then I'll have Call-It-Home Realty off the ground, and I'll have so much more time to spend with you. If we can just put it off this time—"

"This time, Mom? It's always like this. It's always about you getting rich, isn't it? It's all you ever talk about. I can't believe you sold our house."

Jennifer could hear the anger growing in her daughter's voice—years of hurt coming out to take vengeance on a mother who never had the time for a daughter's first grade play or her high school prom.

"Now, take it easy, Hun. It's not about me being rich. It's about *us* being rich. This is going to be good for *your* future, too. I just need you to understand and have a little patience with me...this year." Jennifer was switching into closing mode. *Make it impossible for them to disagree without sounding rude or unreasonable.* "Next year, everything will be different and better."

But there was silence on the other end again, then a small voice that seemed too small for twenty years old, "So, no visit?"

"Tammy, it's just that I live in a very small apartment, now, and I'm not around very much."

"I can't believe this."

"Now, Tam, try to be fair. I'm working for us, not just for me; you know that. You have to give me a little room on this, because—"

"I've never stood in your way. Jesus, Mom, I've never even been in your line of sight." She no longer sounded so small.

"I have responsibilities to us as a family," Jennifer tried to sound indignant.

"No," Tammy said, "you don't have any responsibilities anymore, do you? It's just you now, isn't it? Just the way you always wanted it. You don't do anything for anyone but you!"

"Tammy—" But Jennifer heard the disconnect in her daughter's voice and in the phone line. "Tammy...Tammy—God damn it!" Jennifer yelled into the dead handset. Then she slammed it back into its cradle, and shielded her eyes while raising her elbows onto the desk. Her back jerked as she caught her breath between the silent crying that overtook her. She hated her tears.

Without warning, a box of tissues came into her periphery. "Sounds like she didn't take it so well," Mike said.

"She doesn't understand," Jennifer plucked a tissue from the box. "She's had it all handed to her. We spoiled her, Dan and I. We gave her everything, and we never let her know what it took to get it. We hid our sacrifices from her. But I failed, Mike; I failed."

"Sounds to me like you did a pretty good job," Mike came around the desk and put his thin arm around her. Sometimes he was the perfect mother she never had.

"But she's spoiled, Jennifer said. "Or maybe she just sees through me; I don't know. I had to work. Now she hates me."

"When this deal is done, you'll have time for her. She's only twenty. She'll forget it this one time. She'll come around, again; you'll see. It's going to be alright." Mike stroked her hair.

"Sure," Jennifer reflected cynically, "she'll come around, and I'll write her a bigger check." Jennifer dabbed her eyes being careful not to smear mascara. It was one thing to cry. It was another thing to look like you've cried, or to seem capable of it in the first place.

Mike only watched, leaving space in their conversation for her to speak, but when she quickly threw the used tissue into the wastebasket and pulled out her appointment book from her briefcase, he interjected: "Look, I want to take you out tonight, and show you a new place I found. It's a wine place. It's just the distraction you need, and I don't want to be alone in there should things go bad. Besides, it's all about wine now, right?"

Jennifer let out a short laugh through her recovering sob. "I take it you've found a new love interest."

"Honey, I'm always finding a new love interest," Mike said without apology, exaggerating his natural swish.

"Then, I better bring my own car." She said mockingly, and reached out to squeeze Mike's hand. "Thank you for always being on my side."

"We go back a long time," Mike said, as if fondly recalling the past, "and I know what you're capable of."

SIX

Fifty-Five Degrees was off the 101 in Tempe. Jennifer pulled in to the wine bar's parking lot that was surprisingly full for a Tuesday night. She went back to her apartment before going out, but didn't change from her business clothes; there was no need. It had been an easy day, and she wasn't haggard like after a day at McWilliam's.

She reflected on the reason for her kept appearance and worried about it a little: they didn't have any other deals to work on. All their eggs were solidly in one basket, and a demented farmer was swinging it by the handle.

The title search and paperwork for Eternity Vineyards were going smoother than expected. Mike had been working on it all day. It made her uncomfortable. It was one thing to railroad a client into buying a bad deal, it was plain scary to be hurtling down those same tracks on a deal that was too good to be true—or even possible.

The front door of Fifty-Five Degrees opened up into a wine store with various brands and varietals from all parts of the world. A young man, an ASU student she thought, looked up from the counter. "May I help you?" he asked.

"Yes, I'm meeting a friend. I thought this was a restaurant." She couldn't keep her eyes on the cashier. They wandered around the store and over the nearly endless selection of wines.

"Oh, it is. It's right through there." The young man pointed to an entranceway closed by two red velour curtains.

"Thanks," Jennifer said. She took another moment to look at some of the bottles as she made her way to the curtains. One Pinot Noir at the top of a rack was selling for $350. A few levels down, there were Pinots for a mere $120. She shook her head. How could wine ever be worth that much?

When she parted the curtains, there was an elegant restaurant and bar with a slightly Asian theme. Contemporary jazz played through speakers hidden throughout the spacious room, and the tables, of which more than half were occupied, glowed softly in red candlelight. Some of the customers sat at the bar with goblets of wine before them, sniffing the wine, tasting it, and talking casually. She scanned the room for Mike's familiar face, but didn't see him. A young woman approached holding a menu. "Welcome to Fifty-Five Degrees. Do you have a reservation?"

"No," Jennifer said, "I'm meeting a friend here tonight—" She saw a hand rise from a set of couches at the far end of the bar. "Oh, there he is."

Mike sat with two other men and a woman. The man closest to him wore a loose white shirt buttoned down a hole below modest. He was stunning with extra-short black hair and the slightest mustache trimmed tightly. He had an arm over the back of the couch where Mike was planted close to him, but they seemed to be talking like colleagues. Still, Jennifer noticed the subtle cues of a relationship. She guessed he was in the military. What a terrible loss to her gender worldwide.

Walking over, she sat on the other side of Mike.

"You made it, finally," Mike said. "Everyone, this is Jennifer, my business partner. Jennifer, this is Stephen. He's a friend of mine from the...well, he's a friend of mine."

The other two chuckled appreciating the humor Mike built his popularity on. Stephen reached across to shake Jennifer's hand. "I run the firing range out at the base," he said without apparent concern that anyone would ask or whether he should tell.

"It's true!" Mike blurted out like a desperate confession. "Stephen's teaching me to defend myself. Last week we went to an indoor range and I shot a...what was it?" He looked to Stephen for the word.

"A .357 magnum," Stephen said.

"Oh, my God," Mike looked to the group and put his hand on his chest, "I felt just like Dirty Harry." Another round of laughter broke out. Two drinks in him and Mike flamed brightly.

"Oh, and Jennifer, this is Susan Blake and her husband Jeff," Mike motioned to each.

Susan looked to Jennifer like an old hippie. She had to be forty-five if she was a day, but she wore her blonde hair unprofessionally long, and the simple flower-patterned skirt topped with a burgundy sweater made her a stay-at-home mom, for sure. Probably didn't get out much, definitely not successful, though her husband in a sport coat and wire-framed glasses might have been an attorney. Jennifer shook hands with everyone, and then jokingly with Mike.

"We've already ordered, but what are you drinking?" Mike asked Jennifer, apparently ready to pick up the tab. He waved his hand to signal the waiter.

"Well, wine, I suppose."

"Then I'll bring you our menu," a dignified voice spoke from behind her couch.

"Okay, thank you." Jennifer twisted to look behind her at a lean, tall waiter in a black suit smiling back at her. He looked older than she expected for a waiter, given the relative youth of the other wait staff. He had to be her age, if not a few years beyond, maybe even five. He walked to the bar, and as he went, she saw that his slightly graying hair was slicked back and tied in a short ponytail. And when he reached for a menu, she noticed the heavy gold watch he wore that even from a distance said expensive. *Rich waiter*, she thought.

He returned with the menu and handed it to Jennifer, then automatically withdrew a lighter from his pocket and lit the candle on the coffee table in front of them. The watch was unmistakably Rolex. "My name is Samuel, and I'll be your server tonight."

Jennifer held the menu but without looking at it admitted to him, "You know, I don't really know that much about wine. What do you think would be good?"

Mike snickered, and she gently kicked his ankle with her pump.

"Well, do you like red or white; do you like sweet wine or dry?" Samuel asked her.

"I think somewhere in the middle."

"I see," Samuel said, "not given to extremes. Then might I suggest the Foxglove chardonnay? It's a good California white without a lot of pretensions. It's a popular choice.

"Okay, I'll take a glass of that." Then curiosity got the best of her, "You're not really a waiter, are you?"

"Well, most days I'm the manager," he chuckled, "but one of my servers called in, so tonight I'm a waiter. I'll be right back with your order." He smiled.

There was a spring in his step suggesting more energy than his job required, a man obviously physically younger than he was chronologically. Jennifer felt disappointed that he rushed off so fast. She turned to Mike, "One of your friends?"

"I wish," Mike sighed. "Unfortunately, he's straight. Grieve for me." Then Mike continued to the rest of the group, talking more freely than Jennifer cared for, "Jen and I are buying a winery, and we're about to make a serious killing."

Jennifer glared a quick *shut up* to Mike, who suddenly showed a realization of his slip of the tongue. Until the deal was done, it wasn't even close to done. Anything could pop the soap-bubble contract they had with Maddock, especially if he really was insane.

Susan asked, "Oh really? A winery? Where at?"

"Down south," Jennifer said, as if it were another country hardly worth considering. She hoped to take control of the conversation and steer it away.

"There's a winery in Arizona?" Jeff asked. "We were just in Sonoma last year. I think every other house outside the city limits was a winery."

"It seems counterintuitive, doesn't it?" Jennifer deliberately paid little attention as she spoke. If she sounded bored with it, they might change the subject. She watched Samuel carrying the glasses of wine toward them on a tray: three reds and two whites.

"I wonder how the wine from Arizona tastes." Susan said.

"Either very good or very bad," Samuel interjected as he set a glass before each of them. "I apologize. I couldn't help overhearing. Which winery are you buying?"

"Eterni—," Mike started, but then stopped himself. Jennifer noticed the expression on Samuel's face suddenly drop, as if hearing bad news.

"Eternity Vineyards, Robert Maddock's place," Samuel said.

"You've heard of it?" Jennifer asked, wishing Mike would control his liquor better.

"I have. And good luck with that."

"Thanks," Jennifer replied. No one else at the table seemed to notice, but Jennifer was sure Samuel stumbled slightly when he backed up from their table, as if trying to get away.

She thought about the basement she never inspected. Maybe the place was a wreck. Maybe everyone into wine around here knew it. Maybe Maddock hadn't disclosed the problems with the basement to her. But that was impossible. He freely told her to go down and look. He wouldn't have said that if it were crumbling.

The conversation on the couches continued as Jennifer finished her glass. The warmth of the alcohol began spreading throughout her.

"Susan," Mike said. "Tell Jennifer what you do for a living." Mike sounded excited, and then couldn't wait: "Susan's a medium."

"A medium?" Jennifer asked as if not understanding the term.

"Technically, I'm an astrologer, but I do tarot readings and private séances on occasion."

Jennifer wondered how she could talk so seriously about such a ridiculous profession.

"She does my chart at least once a quarter," Mike interjected. "You should see her shop in Scottsdale; it's gorgeous. It's full of books and all kinds of fantastic new age stuff. She must have fifty different crystal balls. I love going in there. I love your incense," Mike said directly to Susan.

"Thanks." Susan lifted her glass to Mike in a slight toast and took a drink.

Jennifer tried to keep from laughing or shaking her head in disbelief. Phoenix was a big place, and all types found their place in it. Her one frustration with Mike was how easily influenced he was by such things, but she feigned fascination with Susan's work, following the time-tested sales rule: You never know who your next customer might be. "How intriguing," Jennifer said. "So how's business?"

Susan reached in her purse and handed Jennifer a card. "It's booming actually. I usually have appointments scheduled for a month out or more."

As if the greatest idea had just dawned on him, Mike said, "You should have her do your chart, Jennifer. She's fantastic."

Jennifer manually constructed an expression of interest: "Maybe I should," she said, putting Susan's card in her handbag without looking at it. "So, Susan, what does a typical chart run?"

"Well, you're Mike's friend," she waved her hand dismissively, "so I won't charge you anything. Just come by the shop sometime, and we'll see what we can do."

Susan seemed too sincere for a phony. "Maybe I will," Jennifer said using her well-practiced sweetness. She thought about the vision of the girl at the winery the day before and was going to add it in for fun, but there was no way she was going to bring up Eternity Vineyards now that the topic had drifted away, and no way some phony psychic was going to make more out of a trick of the light than it was worth.

As he immodestly imbibed, Mike's inhibitions began to fade. He whispered something in Stephen's ear, and then nibbled the man's earlobe. Jeff looked away and swigged his wine. Suddenly Mike broke free, his speech trending towards a slur. He raised his glass for a toast. "Susan's the best psychic in the world, and if you want to buy a mansion south of Sonoita, see Jen!" Everyone laughed, as he took another gulp of his Merlot.

Jennifer smiled in pain, and then excused herself to use the restroom. She hoped her absence would extinguish Mike's verbal diarrhea regarding their deal. Hopefully, no one was within earshot that would actually care, but she half-expected Robert Maddock to suddenly spring from one of the glowing tables in the dark and shout out, *Remember, you can't sell it!*

When she returned, she stopped at the bar where Samuel was polishing wineglasses and suspending them in a wooden holder that hung above the bar. "Can I get another glass of that same chardonnay?" Jennifer asked. She smiled so he could see the perfection of her teeth.

"Of course." Samuel retrieved a bottle of white wine from the cooler behind him, and then took a glass from above and poured. "So, you know more about wine than you're letting on. Will you be making wine at Eternity?" Samuel asked.

"No, I sell real estate. I really don't know a thing about wine, but I suppose I should learn. You see I won't actually be reselling this place. I intend to live there," Jennifer hoped her lie would sell. She had to counter the *make-a-killing* remark from Mike that could easily threaten any deal with Maddock if it got back to him. And Samuel was obviously fishing.

"If approached correctly, some really fine berries can be grown out there, cabernet sauvignon anyway."

"Is that right? Well, I doubt I'll be making any wine. Raising living things is definitely not a talent of mine. I have one houseplant, and it's not doing so well. But who knows?"

Samuel poured a glass of the same chardonnay for himself. "If you change your mind and need any tips, I know grapes, just give me a call." He reached over to a holder containing business cards for the wine bar and wrote his name, Samuel Ansell, on the back.

Jennifer took the card, "Thank you, Samuel." She reached in her purse and gave Samuel one of her cards. "In case you're ever in the market." It was a night for cards, she thought.

"So, are you Jen or Jennifer? Your card says, Jen, but everyone seems to call you Jennifer."

In a short circuit of honesty brought on by the growing influence of the chardonnay, Jennifer replied, "Well, typically, my customers just call me, Jen...so make it Jennifer."

Samuel laughed. "Well, okay, Jennifer. It's good to meet you."

They shook hands, and Jennifer noticed his grip was confident, like the men she'd met in real estate, but unlike them, he didn't dominate her hand. She also realized they'd just exchanged phone numbers.

* * *

Robert Maddock sat in his living room down the hall from the kitchen. The sun was just disappearing behind the mountains and shadows within the house disappeared in the gray that overtook it. Every minute that passed, the house grew darker. Maddock kept two lamps on in the living room. He always did. He watched TV and ate a slice of the cherry cheesecake Mattie made two days prior, but when he heard the young girl crying, he dropped his fork in his plate.

It was just a whimper at first from somewhere on the second floor, and it had been years since the last visitation.

"I got a right to leave this place!" Maddock shouted into the air of the room. His voice quivered with anger and a bit of cheesecake fell from his mouth and lodged in his beard. "I've paid for his mistakes with the whole of my life!"

The crying grew louder.

"She's the one. I'm honoring my responsibility, damn it!"

The crying grew even closer, as if moving down the stairs.

"There's nothing more I can do for you, Whitney. I'm an old man now, and I'm not going to die here. All I have to do is pass it on to the right person, and I've done that."

The crying returned to a hopeless and terrified whimper, it became the sound of prey before an attack, but it was closer now. It emanated from just behind him. Maddock didn't turn to look.

"I'm an old man, Whitney." His tone became a resignation. "I have to pass it on, or it'll be too late."

The gray hand of a dead preteen rested on his shoulder. He didn't turn to look, but he felt the coolness of it through his flannel robe.

SEVEN

———— • ————

I think Robert Maddock was too eager to sell," Mike said. "He called every day the week before we closed to see if you were ready to move in. I've never known anyone so eager to take a four-million-dollar loss. I hope we aren't getting fucked on this one."

"You should have come out with me. You should have seen it for yourself," Jennifer said.

"Everything went so fast, so smooth; I never had the time." He reached forward and searched for music on the radio.

Jennifer signaled and exited at 281 off the I-10 onto highway 83. Clouds were moving in from the south, gathering for a winter rainstorm on the Friday afternoon. "We're not getting fucked. Wait until you see the place. Last time I was out, it looked even better than it did the first time."

Jennifer considered the fact that she still hadn't looked in the basement herself. Why not? Both times she went out, she reinforced the importance of it to herself, and yet forgot both times. She tried to brush it off. The inspector had been out there and gave it a clean bill of health, and she had the disclosure statement. Whatever it looked like, she could just tell Mike it wasn't that way before. She'd make up something.

But she did have doubts. Robert Maddock, in fact, was too eager to sell. He didn't even want to talk when she showed up with the documents. He just wanted to sign, like a man desperate for drug cash. "You can look around later," Maddock grumped. "Let's get this paperwork out of the way. You act like I'm ripping you off or something."

She wanted to close the deal as much as he did and get him off to California as fast as he wanted to go, but when the papers were signed and she took the ten wrapped bundles of hundred-dollar bills out of her briefcase, expecting him to grab at them, Maddock didn't even look; he left them sitting on the desk. Instead, he spun slowly around in his chair and stared out the picture-frame window of the study.

He was miles away, as if he were in Bakersfield already, or maybe it wasn't distance, but decades away in the past. "You can make this a profitable vineyard, you know," Maddock said. Might not get rich, but I'll bet you can make a living. I'll bet you could make a life."

"I hope Bakersfield is good for you," Jennifer said to his back.

"Me, too, Miss Dickerman...I'll be out of here in a week; you can start moving in then. The key for the bolt on the front door will be under the mat. The other keys will be on the kitchen table." Maddock seemed more reconciled than depressed, but Jennifer felt sorry for him, for no good reason she concluded. He was getting what he said he wanted, and she had what she fought her entire career to get. They should be popping a cork on a bottle of Eternity's best champagne, but Maddock only stared out the window. He didn't even walk her out.

* * *

Mike and Jennifer turned onto the dirt road that led up to the house. "Oh my God," was all Mike said as they approached.

"I told you you'd like it." Jennifer parked the car next to the house and noticed the same old Range Rover was still there. "I think that's Maddock's car," Jennifer said.

"I thought he already cleared out."

"He's supposed to have. Maybe it's not his." Jennifer got out of the car and walked to the Range Rover. The fast, cold wind bit at her face and knifed easily through her dress coat and nylon stockings. Mike came up behind her holding his arms tight across his chest. He looked into the passenger compartment. "It doesn't look abandoned. It looks in good shape."

"Forget it," Jennifer said. "Let's get in, or I'm going to freeze to death."

They went to the front door, and as Maddock promised, the key was under the mat. Mike looked behind him at the mountains on the horizon, braving the wind that hit his face. "Doesn't seem like a lock is really needed out here. I can't see another house."

Jennifer unlocked the door and they stepped in. The house wasn't heated, but they escaped the wind.

"Oh God, I think I'm going to throw up!" Mike said as he covered his nose and mouth with his hand and tried not breathe.

"What the hell—" Jennifer began.

"Something died in here," Mike said.

"An animal must have got in. It must have got trapped. Open the door. I'll open the back door in the kitchen. I'm sorry, Mike."

"Not your fault," Mike said quickly and unconvincingly. He looked at the surroundings. "This place really is a mansion."

They walked past the stairs together to the kitchen. "I think it's coming from up there." Jennifer pointed up the staircase as they walked by it. The basement door was open and a light was on over the stairs that led down into it.

"No, I think it's coming from down here," Mike said. Jennifer opened the door to the veranda and wind raced through the downstairs interior. "Oh shit, it's cold," Mike said.

"Yeah, but the smell's going away. I'm going to check up stairs." Jennifer walked back to the staircase.

"I'm going to check in the basement!" Mike shouted after her.

"Oh, hey, Mike, I—" Jennifer's first instinct was to stop him, stop him from finding the water or cracks in the walls she'd previously denied. Why hadn't she checked the basement? Part of the money she used to buy the place was his. She heard Mike's footfalls on the basement steps. It was too late.

"Oh, my God!" She heard Mike shout.

She froze in the middle of the staircase. "Crap," she said emphatically but silently as her heart pounded in her chest. Mike was probably knee-deep in festering water. She had been too hypnotized by the grandeur of the place. It was a damn rookie's mistake. She'd fallen for the cosmetics of the upstairs as much as the cosmetics of Maddock's honesty. She felt like a first-time homebuyer. She felt like an idiot.

"It's fantastic! This is fucking great!" Mike yelled.

"I told you so!" Jennifer shouted back even as she gave thanks with an insincere prayer, but then she realized the source of the rotten sulfur smell of death was even closer. She prayed more sincerely, "God, no, please..." but the inevitable truth was unfolding before her.

At the top of the stairs, it was obvious the stench was coming from the same room. As if under a spell, she walked slowly to the last room down the hall, the room where she saw the vision of the young girl in the mirror. She could barely hear Mike yell: "Jennifer, you won't believe what I've found! I'll bet you never saw this." But she didn't turn around, even though the primal need to run away overwhelmed her.

She didn't answer Mike's calling but kept moving under the influence of the need to know the truth beyond the bedroom door. She could hear Mike running up the basement stairs, and then up the staircase.

Jennifer turned the doorknob and slowly opened the door. The pungent odor flowed over her, tainting her, stopping her breath.

"Jennifer, guess what I found," Mike said at the top of the stairs.

In the room, someone was in the bed, half under the covers but she couldn't see the face, because the young girl with the thin blue nightgown stood at the edge of bed obstructing her view. The girl was looking down at the figure in the bed, like a nurse holding the hand of the dying—or holding the hand of the dead. She recognized the girl from before. "What happened?" Jennifer asked softly.

"Hey, Jennifer!" Mike was just behind her now in the hall.

The girl turned and looked at Jennifer. Her eyes and mouth were completely black, as if missing and replaced by some dark universal void. Her skin was nearly white, and she looked frozen in the cold. Jennifer stared transfixed, and then in the time it took to blink, there was nothing. The girl was gone, as if she was never there, but Robert Maddock was.

"Hey, Jennifer, guess what I found—oh my, God." Mike stopped. He covered his nose and mouth again and began to convulsively heave. Together they stared at the figure lying in the bed. Robert's mouth and eyes were open but there was no longer any color in his lips or skin. He was still, like the furniture in the room. "I think I'm going to be sick," Mike said.

Jennifer continued to stare at the body, even as she pointed to the door on the right. "The bathroom's in there," she said, remaining distant and stunned. Once again, she stopped before mentioning the girl. Who would believe it? She couldn't even be sure it was real. The idea of the girl was in her mind like an image one remembers but can't say if they saw it in a dream or in real life. The girl made her feel unbalanced.

Jennifer listened to Mike puke in the sink, regurgitating in waves of retching as she walked over to the bedroom window and opened it. Freezing wind blew in immediately, blowing her corporate hairstyle beyond repair, but she had no concern for it. The smell in the room dissipated by half almost immediately as the frigid wind rushed through to the open door.

"We're going to have to call the police," Jennifer said. Mike came out from the bathroom wiping his mouth on a dusty hand towel. Neither one could take their eyes off the corpse in the bed.

Mike was first to notice. "There's a piece of paper in his hand. Did he...kill himself?"

Jennifer went to the corpse of Robert Maddock, being careful not to touch the decaying skin as she leaned over the bed and reached for the note. For a grotesque moment she felt how close the side of her face was to his gaping mouth. She expected to feel his breath or hear him gasp in her ear, but there was only the cold wind in the room. She pulled at the wedged paper; his stiff arm rose. Finally the paper freed, and the arm sprang back to the mattress, hitting with a dull thud.

"I think I'm going to be sick again," Mike announced.

"Hold on," Jennifer said as she read the faded black words on the ancient paper. "I don't think this is a suicide note, or at least not his suicide note." Jennifer read the words out loud: "I gave her to him. Whitney, 1957."

"Who's Whitney?"

"I don't know," Jennifer said. "He never mentioned her. I suppose he must have died after letting Mattie go, or she would have found him."

"Well, I'm cold as hell. Let's leave the window cracked, but let's get out of here."

Mike was out first and Jennifer closed the door behind her. "We have to call the police," Jennifer said again.

"We can't have any bad press, if we're going to sell this place." Mike sounded worried and looked more frightened now than sick.

"What bad press? Old people die in their beds all the time. That's how property gets sold. It's not even news."

"It will be if they see this." Mike motioned with his finger for Jennifer to follow him.

EIGHT

———— • ————

Together they descended the staircase, and Mike led her to the basement. "I'm not surprised you missed this," Mike said. "I almost missed it myself, and it was probably closed when you were here last."

The basement was a cavernous space with walls created from red brick, and the concrete floor sat at least twenty feet below the floor beams of the house. Two massive racks of oak wine barrels, three barrels high, ran the length of the room with an aisle separating them, and though the plain light bulbs in sockets throughout the cellar provided enough light for Jennifer to see her way, the shadows cast by the barrels kept the room looking dim. She noticed it was warmer than upstairs, but it was still very cool; a white-faced thermometer on the end of one of the racks read fifty-eight degrees. She took in the vastness of the room, but withheld her surprise at the near perfect condition; it couldn't seem like she'd never been in it before.

At the far end of the basement a concrete ramp led up to a pair of double doors identical in construction to the front doors of the house. The doors, elevated above the rest of the cellar, looked out over the entire room as if somehow supervising it, but Mike led her to the other end toward a different door.

At the opposite end of the cellar was an entire wall dedicated to a wine rack. It had slots for hundreds of bottles of wine, but most of the holdings were empty, only a few bottles dotted the rack. In the middle of it, a door opened up into a dimly lit room. Jennifer could see the door was part of the rack, itself, and made in such a way that if it were closed it would be nearly impossible to detect a door was even there.

"I saw this opened when I came down." Mike was obviously excited. "You're not going to believe this."

Jennifer already felt as if bad had gone to worse. She was cold and in a house she owned along with a dead man upstairs waiting to be tended to. Where's Mattie when you need her? she thought. And of course she'd seen the ghost-girl again, or at least the hallucination of it. She couldn't determine which was worse, but as they walked through the wine rack door, she saw what was worse.

They entered a small room, twelve by twelve feet at the most. It wasn't part of the basement proper, but more of a dug out area added on. The walls weren't lined with brick but remained bare rock and dirt. Jennifer could tell the room was old. The dirt on the walls was hardened and remained fixed almost like concrete. But the wooden floor was covered with a thick layer of dust, even more than the rooms upstairs.

In the center of the room was a large wooden table. Through the dust on its surface, Jennifer could tell it was haphazardly stained, and in the center of the table, an ornate silver dagger was stabbed into it like a hatchet stuck in a chopping block.

At first she thought the staining was wine, but the dark brown running down the legs and splashed on the floor lent itself to another explanation: "Is that blood?" Jennifer asked.

"I think so," Mike said. "And look," Mike pointed to the wall at the far end where a wrought iron pentagram hung. In front of it was a small alter with a pewter candelabrum. Each of the twelve stems held a black candle, and each stem was fashioned as an upside-down crucifix. On the adjacent wall, dug out into it, was a single bookshelf with a leather-bound handmade book. There was a pewter wine goblet and a simple corkscrew, and beneath the bookshelf stood a twenty-bottle wine rack with several black wine bottles, two of them were corked; the others were empty.

"What the hell?" Jennifer said without conscious thought as she scanned the room.

"And take a look behind you." Mike nodded toward the door. On either side were chains and leather restraints of various lengths. Attached to the chains were small iron shackles. Jennifer reached out and took hold of one, examining it more closely.

"Are these for animals?"

"I have no idea," Mike said.

Jennifer continued to stare at the sights as Mike went over and took the book from the bookshelf. "I don't think I like it in here," Jennifer said.

"Oh no—oh shit." Mike said as he thumbed through the pages of the book. "Jennifer, this can't be." Mike dropped the book onto the table as if holding it were infecting him. His face contorted with revulsion.

"What?" Jennifer went to the table and opened the book. The title page read: *Child Sacrifice to the Great Lord Satan for the Preparation of Black Wine*. "Good God," Jennifer said. She turned the pages. There were lists of ingredients, steps to be followed, and pictures to illustrate the process.

One of the pictures was a detailed illustration of a small male child lying nude on top of the very table that sat in the middle of the room. Tiny shackles and chains bound the child's arms and legs to hooks on the table legs. Another drawing showed a man in a monk's hooded robe, tied at the waist with a rope, holding an ornate dagger with both hands above his head. A close-up drawing on the same page showed the correct positioning of the man's fingers around the handle of the knife. Another was of a hand holding a wine bottle collecting drops of blood as they fell from the table. Toward the back, an illustration showed a figure of another hooded monk walking down a road with a disheveled man crawling behind him trying to hold onto a bottle.

"What went on here? What is this place?" Jennifer said.

Mike spoke quickly: "We got to get out of here, right now. We shouldn't be here."

"We have to call the police," Jennifer added.

"Fine, but let's do it from the road," Mike said, already heading for the basement stairs. Jennifer followed so closely she nearly pushed Mike up the steps.

* * *

They left Eternity Vineyards, not even bothering to lock the front door. They drove the narrow highway north for twenty miles before either of them said a word. When Jennifer finally spoke, it was to provide a half-lie: "I never saw that room when I was down in the basement. I looked all over that place and never saw that. Maddock never told me a thing about it. He certainly didn't put it in his disclosure statement."

"When that wine rack door is closed," Mike said with a slight tone of awe, "you wouldn't suspect a thing."

"We should call the police. We have to report this, not to mention Maddock's body."

Mike raised a hand as if trying to slow Jennifer's rate of thought. "Jennifer, you've put in seventy thousand dollars of your money. What do you have left, maybe six months living expenses?"

"Four," Jennifer specified.

"I invested thirty thousand, and I'm living off a second mortgage on my condo. All I have is the promissory note you gave me for my percentage of the profit. Without even raising so much as a feather duster, that place is worth an easy four million. We could sell it for three just to move it fast."

Jennifer got the feeling Mike was closing, selling her on something. "So, what's your point, Mike?"

"My point is this: from the minute you dial 911 on your cell phone, our potential to be rich ends. They'll come and find Maddock; they'll investigate his death and search the house. If we don't tell them about the cellar, they're going to think we're involved with it when they find it. If we do tell them about the cellar, then the cat's out of the bag. Either way, we're fucked, because it'll be the biggest news story of the year, especially in this Podunk part of the state. It might even go across the nation. We won't have a product to sell; we'll have an oddity that everyone will expect us to tear down. Remember that Amish school where the gunman killed all those kids?" Mike pointed his finger at her, "That was good real estate, but what did they do? They tore it down."

Mike was coming in loud and clear. She could feel the loss, the mistake, the guilt, and the failure beginning to mount in the situation. Things were spinning out of control, things that only twenty-four hours ago promised so much hope and happiness. Jennifer's voice quivered as she spoke: "We can't just leave Robert Maddock lying in his bed while we show the place. We can't hide what we know. We have to tell someone."

Mike shook his head: "It's like you said, who cares if an old man dies in his bed, but a cellar for sacrificing kids...? Maddock's dead. If anyone knew that place existed, it would already have been all over the news. No one knows about that room. We have to make sure no one ever does--especially a buyer."

They approached a long stretch of highway that fell before them without any curves. The gray overcast day left no shadows or contrasts in the passing landscape. Jennifer thought about turning off, getting out, and running away. She felt like hiding, like forgetting she'd ever seen Eternity Vineyards "Shit." Jennifer said and hit the steering wheel with the palm of her hand.

She put her Bluetooth headset in her ear and turned on her phone. Mike looked at her with a mixture of horror and concern at what she was about to do. She tapped nine, then one, and then turned the device back off.

Mike gently took the phone from her hand and laid it on the center console. "If the damage has already been done," he said, "what good can we do? Whatever happened in that room isn't happening now. We can't change what happened; we're only going to change our futures from really good to really bad."

"I can't believe Robert Maddock was involved in that," Jennifer said.

"Maybe he wasn't. Did you see all the dust? How long does it take for that kind of dust to accumulate? I have a feeling the door wasn't left open too much. According to the title search, Maddock took ownership ten years after his brother's death in 1964. Decades of dust? It sure looks like it to me. Even if the old man knew about it, I don't think he ever stepped foot in there."

"Oh my God," Jennifer said. "Robert told me his brother's two daughters died there and his wife, William Maddock's wife, killed herself. His brother must have been into it. His wife must have known, or been part of it, herself. I wonder what happened to his kids." Jennifer wanted to tell Mike about the girl sitting on the bed when she first came out to the place and then again sitting with Robert Maddock, but not wanting to add crazy to trouble, she kept it to herself.

"Jennifer, we have a real problem here. If we're going to sell that place, we have to act now. We have to fix this problem now. Because, you're right: we do have to get the cops out there about the late great Robert Maddock. Whatever happened in the 1950's has nothing to do with us, you know."

"I want to do the right thing, Mike."

"If you didn't do the deed, then you've done nothing wrong. That means you're in the right."

Jennifer considered his moral reasoning and found it wanting, but she knew he was correct. Their actions at this point were multimillion-dollar actions. What they did from this point would have serious consequences for their lives at present and for their futures.

"So what do you suggest?" Jennifer asked.

NINE

From her window, Whitney watched Jennifer and Mike drive away from Eternity, and as they went away, her loneliness crept back. She drifted from the window and returned her awareness to Robert's deathbed. Except to watch the two of them go, she hadn't moved from his side since he died two weeks earlier. She was with him when he passed, but saw nothing of him after it was all over. He moaned, rubbed his fist on his chest—the one that held her note—then drifted away. He was alive, and then he was dead, and that was it. In that moment, she knew her wish wasn't coming true: he wouldn't continue, not like she continued.

Listening to the wind coming through the window that Jennifer left open, she thought back to her own death fifty years before. After the confusion of dying cleared, she still didn't understand how it all worked. All she knew was that ever since that day it was only her alone in the space surrounding Eternity Vineyards. People who died didn't join her, and she never found her mother or Kerrie waiting for her like she hoped she would.

What she found instead was that she never grew up. Time passed on the kitchen clock, and then in the sunsets and seasons, but she no longer followed its course. It no longer affected her, any more than she could affect the physical objects within the house. Her consciousness simply moved from one point of view to the next, day after day.

And as she sat watching her uncle's clay-like skin rotting, she felt sad for him and for herself, too. They'd grown closer as he got older, and she wondered when he'd be taken out and buried like she was taken away and buried, though she never learned where that was.

The early years were admittedly difficult for the two of them. She'd been alone for so long that when he first moved in she didn't recognize him as her Uncle Robert. She just watched him. Sometimes he'd catch a glimpse of her, and it startled him. His startling would scare her, too. Then she would scream, and he'd cover his ears like a madman trying to exorcise the voices from his head.

He'd be shaving, or working in the vineyard, or fixing his car, or shooting his gun—*the gun*—and he'd see her watching. She knew he saw her, because he'd stumble backwards and try to run. He even shot her once, but the bullets no longer mattered the way they used to. What mattered was that he suffered on her account, and she didn't want that at all. Eventually, she learned not to follow him when he ran from her. She learned to just let him get away.

Later, when he'd grown old and no longer left the house, he began talking to her. "I know what happened," was the first thing he ever said, and it made her cry for over an hour. She knew he heard her crying, but he didn't go crazy about it. He just listened to her, and then he cried, as well.

That night he made a vow to her while looking through a family photo album. Speaking into the atmosphere of the study, illuminated only by the fireplace, he said: "Never again, Whitney, not while I'm alive. I'll keep this place safe. That's all we can do now. We can't change what happened, but we can be good caretakers today."

When he died in her bed, he wasn't tortured to see her at his side. He seemed to be comforted by her presence while he passed on. She was happy for that, but she cried for days after he went. She knew she was going to be alone again, maybe forever if Jennifer didn't keep her word.

Whitney watched her curtains billowing in the cold wind. She tried once more to hold Robert's rotting hand. It still wouldn't work. His hand was like a mirage to her, and her own hand acted like a mirage when she placed it on his. Their hands passed through one another, as if both were illusions.

Meeting Jennifer for the first time was a thrill. Almost no one came to the vineyard to see Robert except for Mattie, and Mattie always crossed herself whenever she saw her. Then she'd rattle off a rosary in Spanish. Eventually, she stopped appearing for Mattie. Robert needed his nurse, but now Whitney didn't miss her at all.

When Jennifer arrived, though, she watched her from her bedroom window as she drove up the dirt road in her beautiful blue car. Robert told her that Jennifer would take over for him, that God had sent him a dream about her; he was sure of it. And when Jennifer spoke to her in her bedroom, just like she was a real person, she was certain, too. And she liked Jennifer from then on.

Whitney drifted back to the open window and looked out toward the highway. She watched for Jennifer to come driving back. It must be great, she thought, to be a successful grownup working and making her own way in the modern world. Jennifer was so confident, and she had never felt very confident, herself. She only remembered being afraid when she was alive.

Whitney let her awareness drop from the open window and glide close to the floor, then accelerate up to the ceiling of the hallway as she exited her room and left the dead Robert Maddock behind. She descended the stairs perceiving them only an inch away from her face as she sailed across their wooden surfaces, and then she ended her movement in the middle of the foyer, watching things from the height of a twelve-year-old girl.

The foyer was cold and drafts blew through it, but that didn't matter. What if Jennifer never came back? That mattered. What if she spent years again watching Eternity by herself? She sailed back up the stairs, into her room and to the side of her uncle's corpse. She had nowhere else to go. She cried again, and the sounds of her weeping echoed throughout the house.

TEN

It was near five o'clock and getting dark. At Casa Grande, Mike directed Jennifer to exit the freeway and enter the parking lot of the Camp Town Inn.

"A cheap motel? Is this how you propose to a girl?"

"This is my proposal," Mike said. "The doorway of that antechamber is small. In the morning we go into Casa Grande and get enough bricks, a bag of concrete, a couple of buckets, whatever, and we brick up the entrance to that room. We close the wine rack door, and we never mention it again. No one will ever know it's there. I'll even remove the electrical wiring leading to it. Absolutely no one will ever know it existed. I highly doubt it's on the original blueprints."

Jennifer remained silent as she considered what he said. She kept her hands on the steering wheel even after shifting the car into park and removing the keys; she didn't want to let go of her option to drive away. "What about Robert Maddock? Don't tell me we're going to brick him up in there."

"No, no, no," Mike patronized, "We're not Edgar Allen Poe here. We're going to call the police and report his death just as soon as we're finished in the basement. Everything will happen after that exactly as it was supposed to. Then we'll flip the damn place and be rid of it."

"I'm no good with my hands," Jennifer said.

"I'll do the brickwork, you just start inventorying the place and tap in the For Sale sign on the front lawn...gravel, whatever. It won't take more than a couple of hours to brick up that doorway. Then we'll clean up everything down there and call the police. We'll act like we just came out and found him. Can you act surprised and shocked?"

"I am surprised and shocked."

They rented two rooms, and after dinner at a fast food restaurant, Jennifer laid on her rented bed with the TV off and the lights out. Only the Camp Town sign and streetlights of the parking lot illuminated her room through the gaps in the drapery. She thought about the vision of the girl sitting on Maddock's bed and tried to remember Tammy when she was that age, but she could hardly dredge up a scene or an image.

She thought about other things, too: how she was always working, always away from home, and as it always revealed itself in the dark, the truth was that she never wanted to be home. She never wanted Tammy. How do you tell someone you love her but wish she'd never existed? She made a living selling, but she couldn't sell that one.

At first it was easy: she married her ex, Dan, almost out of high school and just followed the default programming already within her. It was the easiest thing to do: fulfill the expectations of her parents, friends, and even her role as a woman. She never asked any questions; she just did what she was supposed to do. But the questions eventually found their way in.

They came up in her mind and stuck there, and she couldn't look away, questions like: How do you get your life back when half of it is already gone? How do you define yourself when your husband has already defined you? Her marriage fell apart after the questions came to live within her, and she had to admit it's what she wanted.

Now, lying on her pillow, staring at a crack in the curtain and the lonely hotel sign brightly shinning in neon out by itself in the parking lot, she turned the coin in her mind to read its other side: The identity of self and the company of family are incompatible; you don't get both. You get you and nothing more. You get loneliness.

She let Tammy down. She left her alone, and Tammy didn't need her anymore. Tammy could freely hang up the phone on her, because what good was she to her? She raised Tammy with the ability to disconnect from her.

But people don't hang up on millionaires; that's for sure. People forgive millionaires. They take what they can get from people with money, and selling Eternity Vineyards would change everything. She'd love Tammy on her own terms, and Tammy would take what she could get. She had to make Eternity Vineyards work, or she'd have no chance to love and be loved by the daughter she never wanted. And in the conflict of that dichotomy, sleep found her at last.

ELEVEN

The Durango sagged under the weight of the bricks and bags of concrete in the back. Jennifer searched the radio stations for something to listen to, anything to listen to other than the silence, or worse, more conversation about bricking up satanic cellars while an old man rots in the upstairs bedroom.

"By noon we'll be ready to call the cops," Mike said as if it were all figured out. "But I haven't done brickwork since I was a teenager."

Jennifer gave up looking for a satisfactory station and turned off the radio. "Can you still do it?" she asked.

"It's pretty much like riding a bike; it's not exactly rocket science. Not having second thoughts, are you?"

"I want to be rich, Mike. I have to be rich."

"I know what you mean." Mike put down the passenger visor as they curved toward the morning sun. "They say *might makes right.* I don't know if what we're doing is right, but I don't really care anymore, because I think they only tell the half of it when they say that. They miss the first part."

"What's that?" Jennifer asked.

"Money makes might."

They pulled up to Eternity Vineyards just after nine. The morning was still cold, but the shining sun promised a warmer afternoon.

"Pull around to the back," Mike said. "We can use the cellar doors and that loading ramp. That'll be easier than dragging this stuff through the house."

Jennifer parked at the back of the house. They got out, and she unlocked the double doors, letting the morning light spill into the wine cellar. Mike walked down and came back up dragging a wheel dolly behind him.

"Just leave the concrete in the car. I'll mix it up here." Mike said.

"Okay." Jennifer replied, "In that case, I'll go start the inventory. If it still smells, I'll open all the windows and air it out."

"Fine. I'll call you in a couple of hours to look at my handiwork, and Jennifer, when we close that wine rack, it's over; it never existed, and you won't have to worry about it ever again."

Jennifer managed a resigned smile.

Mike began loading bricks on the wheel dolly as Jennifer turned and walked away. She raised her cell phone up and shouted back without looking: "Call me if you need my help, or the devil challenges you to a fight or something."

Mike laughed, "Yeah, you can referee."

As she retrieved her briefcase from the car, out of habit, she checked her look in the review mirror. They had bought some basic toiletries at a Walmart in Casa Grande, and she showered at the motel, but she wasn't able to fix her hair as she usually did for business. It hung straight down like it used to in her youth. Without her usual make up, the contrast of young hair and an older face was startling. It was an early-morning look she may have seen before but never allowed herself to wear in public. She realized this is how she would have looked all her life had she never become a Realtor, and a successful one at that. It was an honest look, maybe even attractive, but it reeked of *unsuccessful* as much as Robert Maddock reeked of death. She wasn't used to it, and she didn't like it.

In the house, Jennifer noticed the smell had nearly dissipated. Leaving the bedroom window open must have worked better than she thought. Still, she had no intention of inventorying that room—not alone anyway. She'd do the dining room first. Entering it, she noticed the heavy oak ten-seat table was immaculately set with dishes, silverware and glassware, too, as if an elegant dinner was about to be served to guests who were a century too late.

Everything was covered with dust, and cobwebs hung from the chandelier. A spider's web stretched between a silver fruit bowl at the center of the table and a candlestick to the right of it. All of this would have to be washed, she thought as she made a clean streak across the dust on one of the plates. Maddock must have ignored most of the rooms in the house for decades.

She went to the deep purple drapes hanging over the two windows that looked out onto the front of the estate and pulled them open. Sunlight cut through the resulting airborne dirt giving the room a diffuse smoky atmosphere. She went to the china cabinet at the far end and looked at the numerous collections of plates, saucers, and delicate-looking teacups that appeared to be fine Wedgwood designs. "This is worth thousands," she said out loud.

As her eyes went up the shelves in the cabinet, she noticed her own reflection at eye level and then focused on the reflection of the table and chairs behind her. "Oh, my God!" she gasped and put a hand to her mouth as if something worse was sure to come out.

In the middle chair, on the right-hand side, the young girl sat in her thin blue nightgown. She stared ahead as if looking out the dining room windows toward the vineyards in the distance.

A surge of adrenalin raced through Jennifer's insides, but this time, wonderment overrode her panic. She didn't turn around but only stared into the china cabinet. She studied the girl in the reflection, and with the first thought that came to mind, she spoke, giving in to the madness that surely was at the root of these visions: "Are you all alone here?" Jennifer whispered to the reflection. "Who are you?" she asked.

No longer able to resist, Jennifer turned around, but when she looked to the chair where the girl was sitting, nothing was there, just as if it had never been. She put her trembling hand to her chest and stared at the empty seat. Tears formed and ran down both cheeks, not for the girl or the vision, but for herself and her state of mind. She was having hallucinations; she was talking to them, and she felt like she couldn't tell what was real from what wasn't. She felt like she was losing control, so she ran out of the dining room, through the foyer, and out the front door.

TWELVE

W hitney knew better than to follow her. She waited in the dining room moving up to the corner of the ceiling and looking down as Jennifer ran out. Then she let her consciousness drift slowly through the ceiling into her room where Maddock lay in her bed, and continuing up, she rose through the roof, and then up into the air where she looked down on the estate and watched Jennifer sitting in her car with the driver's door open.

Most of the time, Whitney had no control over what people saw of her. If she kept her consciousness out of the room, they didn't see her. If she was in the same room but perceived the room from some small place, like a corner edge of the floor or in the corner of the ceiling, they didn't see her. But if she watched them from a normal position, like sitting in a chair or standing in a hallway, they eventually focused in on her.

Throughout the decades, there were those who visited Robert and had seen her, and their reactions were always unpredictable, but Jennifer's reaction made her feel bad, just like Rob-

ert's had. She'd have to be more careful with her. She didn't
want to lose her and end up alone in the house like she was after her father died. Being alone and unperceived made her feel
unreal, and that felt like madness to her, just as seeing her made
Jennifer feel mad.

Whitney descended on the estate and accelerated through
the open double doors of the freight ramp to the cellar where
Mike was working. A stack of red bricks sat beside the open
wine rack at the back of the cellar. Beyond that, a light was on
in her father's room.

Whitney hated her father's room. During her life, she was
never allowed to see what he did when he was in there. But she
and Kerrie would hear the screams of a child every six months
or so. If they were playing cards, or dressing up, or eating dinner when the screams began, they would look at one another,
but they never spoke about it. Sometimes Kerrie would cry,
especially when she heard the screams of a baby, so Whitney
would take her outside to play hide-and-seek in the vineyards,
far away from the sounds of the suffering.

The day she shot herself, before she completely realized she
had died, she went into the room, even though she wasn't allowed to. Somehow, after the gunshot, she found the courage to
defy her father. In the room, she sensed the stink of blood and
saw her sister lying naked on the table, pinned to it with a silver
dagger through her sternum. Her limbs were clasped and
chained to the four legs of the table. Her eyes and mouth were
open, and she stared in dead horror at the ceiling. Loose stool
and urine spilled out from between her open legs, and her blood
was everywhere on the floor as well as congealed into a single
crimson glob on the table's surface.

In a dim corner of the room, illuminated by the burning candles of the candelabrum her father sat in his hooded black robe.
He drank wine from the pewter goblet while staring at Kerrie

on the table. When she came into focus, he screamed and threw the goblet at her and curled himself into a ball on the floor.

She marveled at how the goblet went right through her and hit the wall behind her. She couldn't understand how it happened, and for some reason, the goblet passing through her mattered more to her than anything else at the time. Then the realization pieced together so fast she couldn't stop it or deny it. She was dead.

As the years went on, he no longer seemed to care that she was in the room when he worked. He molested the kids before killing them and spit at her when she came into focus. She hated her father and his room, but from then on she witnessed every child he sacrificed while making his black wine. There were seventeen others before he finally died seven years after her suicide.

She only learned about his death after Robert moved in. She listened one day while he talked about it on the phone to some other relative she never knew. She remembered the day her father began to bleed into the toilet when he sat on it. After that, he got in his car and drove away never to return. According to Robert, he checked into a hospital in Tucson and never made it out. He was in too long, bled too much, and didn't have his wine.

Now, Jennifer's friend was in her father's room looking at the artifacts therein. He fingered the shackles and chains, and touched the candles in the candelabrum. He dislodged the dagger from the wood of the table and stabbed it back again. "This is incredible," She heard him say.

Whitney put herself into the corner of the ceiling by the pentagram and watched him. He removed one of the corked black bottles from the rack and dusted it off. Holding the bottle up to the hanging light bulb, he squinted and tried to see through it, but it was too dark. He set it on the table and took the goblet and corkscrew off the bookshelf. After blowing dust out of the goblet and wiping the inside of it with the tail of his shirt, he said, "So let's see what the fuss is all about, shall we."

With the corkscrew, he pulled the cork from the bottle, and sniffed the inside. He shrugged, making an uninterested face as if the bottle were no different than a million others. He poured some into the goblet and swirled it around, but it just looked black. He stuck his entire nose into the goblet and inhaled deeply in one long draw; then he tasted it.

With the smallest amount on his lips and tip of his tongue, his eyes widened. "Oh my God," he said, as if he had tasted the very passion of life itself.

Whitney moved her perception to a common position. She stood in front of him. His face had changed ever so slightly to the expression her father wore almost endlessly. She wanted him to see her. She wanted to warn him, but he quickly grabbed the goblet by the metal stem, and with the appetite of a satyr drank the entire contents in one gulp. He took the bottle and filled the goblet nearly to the top. Joy spread across his face, as he took another drink. He looked around the room as if it had become brighter with some secret sunshine, as if he were a new tenant in an apartment deciding how he should decorate.

He went to the book on the shelf and took it down. He laid it on the table and opened it to the middle. A skillful rendering showed a hooded figure holding up the goblet to the pentagram and all the candles ablaze. In the background, a slaughtered child lay skewered on the table. He chuckled and drank some more of the wine as he flipped through the pages.

When he looked up from the book, she could tell she'd come into focus, and she was close, just across the table. Her eyes fixed on him, and when she was sure he could see her, when she saw his initial shock, she opened her mouth to scream and it worked. Mike covered his ears and stumbled backward from the table. The joy in his face changed to the stress of terror. He backed all the way to the far wall. She pursued him. She accelerated until she was just at his face again.

His screaming became panicked, like a person trying to swat away a horde of bees. He swung at her image, flailing as if in a deep lake and unable to swim. He ran past her and out of the room. He ran to the concrete ramp and looked back, anxiously pouting, but she didn't follow him.

She watched as he stood on the concrete loading ramp panting and bending over with his hands on his knees. He looked back at the entrance to the room. Droplets of sweat formed on his forehead and cheeks. She moved to perceive him from the upper corner of the cellar, and for a moment she thought he would leave for good, but then he moved carefully back to the entrance. She quickly returned to the room, because he had to be stopped; she had to keep him from the wine.

She wanted her father's room to end once and for all, so the pressure had to be just right, not too much, not too little, just enough to keep him working—but working hard. She accelerated to the table. She placed her consciousness in such a way that she was looking up from the table toward the ceiling. The perspective sickened her as she realized this was her sister's last point of view, but she stayed in that position, knowing he would eventually focus on her. She imagined herself as a body. She imagined her arms and legs hanging over the edges of the table, and she remained there as Mike worked.

The speed at which he worked, the occasional whimpers he let out, the desperate way he occasionally said, "Oh God" as he slapped the concrete onto the next layer of bricks let her know that he was seeing a twelve-year-old girl lying like a sacrifice on the table. He saw her; she knew it. He even flicked off the light switch as he bricked her up in the room. He never even tried to find out if she were real. He just kept laying the bricks. He was murdering her, and he didn't care. It was the wine, and she knew it.

As the entrance was gradually sealed off, Whitney began to moan in the gathering dark. Lying on the table as if waiting for death, she realized more fully what she had done to her sister, what she had done to protect her own life, and she despised herself for it anew.

Obviously hearing her moaning, Mike began to cry with a panicky blubbering, slapping bricks and concrete even faster than before. She saw him look through the last remaining brick-sized space into the darkness of the satanic chamber, and then he placed the last brick, and it was finished.

Whitney lay in the absolute dark, listening as Mike cleaned up. He moved the unused bricks, swept the floor, and then finally shut the wine rack. She didn't want to exist any longer. She wished she could dissolve into the black. She didn't want to be conscious anymore, but she was conscious—always conscious.

THIRTEEN

———————•●•———————

After running from the dining room, Jennifer sat in her car and decided to tell Mike about the girl. She had to tell someone. She had to connect this thing to an external reality before it drove her mad, and if she could just share the experience, she could get it out of her head. In the beginning, the girl was interesting, a curiosity; now she was becoming a personal problem. If anyone would understand, it would be Mike.

She walked around the house to the back where the loading ramp doors were still wide open. Mike was rinsing out two large buckets with a garden hose.

"How's it going?" she asked.

"Done," Mike said without further comment, and Jennifer noticed his reticence.

"Everything okay?"

"Sure."

"Mind if I take a look?" Jennifer asked excitedly.

"Be my guest. Just don't touch anything; it's still wet." Mike didn't look up from his task with the buckets.

"I wouldn't think of it," Jennifer said in mock seriousness. But something was different. Something was bothering him. For the moment, she put it out of her mind and descended the concrete ramp into the cellar. At the back wall, she opened the imperceptible door in the wine rack revealing no longer a small, dirt-lined torture chamber, but instead a professional-grade brick surface. Remarkably, it matched the rest of the brick lining of the entire wine cellar. Maybe this thing was finally over after all. Maybe they could sell the house now and no one would be any the wiser. She nodded with satisfaction and walked back up to join her partner at the top.

"I used almost all the bricks. There's only a few left," Mike said.

"That's lucky. It's a long drive back to the store." She approached the next topic gingerly: "Mike, have you seen anything strange around here?"

"What's that supposed to mean?" He spat, sounding.

"Nothing," she said, taken aback. "It's just that I think I might be seeing things."

"Is that right?" he continued rinsing the buckets as if the conversation were boring him.

"I keep seeing a girl—" Jennifer halted when she saw Mike's sudden reaction. "You've seen her, too, haven't you?" She moved in closer to him. "She's a young girl in a blue nightgown, isn't she? You've seen her, haven't you?"

"I haven't seen a thing." Mike backed up, initially wide-eyed, but then irritated: "What are you talking about anyway? If you're seeing things, Jennifer, see a shrink. We need to focus on getting the cops out here and getting rid of that body—and this house."

"Fine, Mike," Jennifer said, her own irritation coming to the fore. Why was he acting like an ass? He never acted that way before. He was the most positive person she knew.

"We need to get our story straight," he said as if they had killed Robert Maddock.

"It's simple," Jennifer said, "We came out here today to take possession of the house, and we found him. We have all the documents," she said matter-of-factly. "We just leave out last night...and the room in the cellar of course. Otherwise, it's just the plain truth."

"That should work," Mike said, his eyes shifting to the cellar as if someone might be watching. "Better not tell them about the note," he chuckled dryly, "unless you want to go put it back in his hand."

"Mike, what's wrong?"

"Nothing, Jen, really, nothing. We need to finish this thing. That's all."

"Okay," she said and reached out and touched his shoulder. He didn't reciprocate; he didn't even seem to notice her reaching out to him. He walked away from her and around to the front of the estate.

Who the hell is *Jen*, she thought as she followed after him. He only called her that in front of clients.

* * *

The first emergency responder was a Santa Cruz County deputy sheriff. Jennifer and Mike gave their individual accounts of what had happened. Eventually a paramedic ambulance from Nogales arrived and removed Robert Maddock. As they carried the body bag down on a stretcher, Jennifer asked the deputy, "Will they do an autopsy?"

"Yes, ma'am. Whenever the cause of death can't be immediately determined, they do an autopsy. They'll take him to the

Pima County Medical Examiner. But it looks like he just died in his bed."

Jennifer nodded. She thought about the note. *I gave her to him. Whitney, 1957.* Was the girl's name, Whitney? Mike had seen the girl, too. She knew it as soon as she asked him. Why didn't he want to admit it, or want to talk about it? She couldn't understand him. He loved all that psychic crap, but if it made her feel crazy maybe it made him feel that way, too. Maybe he had issues with it; she certainly was developing them herself. Either way, Mike was right: it was time to get down to the business of selling the place—the sooner the better.

On the drive back to Phoenix, Mike slept most of the way. When he did wake, he didn't talk; he just stared out the passenger window. They had known each other a long time. If that was time he needed for himself, she didn't mind giving it to him. She didn't dare bring up the girl again, or the bricking of the room, or Robert Maddock. It had been too much for one day, for both of them.

Outside of Mesa, during one moment when he was awake, she tried to lift his spirits: "We're going to be rich, Mike," she said feigning excitement, but Mike only nodded slowly without saying a word or taking his gaze away from the passenger window. She let it go. It was a Saturday afternoon; things would be different on Monday.

At 5:30 it was already getting dark when she dropped him off at his condominium. He got out of the car without a comment. Jennifer got out and across the hood said to him again, "Mike, what is it?"

Mike turned to her. "You're *killing* me," he said, stressing the words like an accusation.

Exasperated, Jennifer countered, "What have I done, for Christ's sake?" But Mike just turned and walked to his apartment. "What the fuck?" was all she could mutter, and then only to herself.

She called after him, as friendly as she could make it, "I'll see you at the office on Monday, okay?"

Mike walked on without looking back.

Jennifer screamed and beat her steering wheel on the way to her apartment. He wasn't the only one feeling guilty and grossed out over the whole thing. Now, she felt betrayed, and pissed off, too. "Fucking bastard!" she shouted at the windshield, as she dropped her visor madly to block the glare of the setting sun. As usual the traffic limped arthritically along the freeway through the city.

FOURTEEN

W hen she returned to her apartment, there was one message on her landline. It was Tammy. Jennifer paused before deciding to listen. Tammy must have come to her senses, and that was good, but Jennifer wanted nothing more than to get changed, eat dinner, and watch TV. There was no capacity for emotional issues in reserve tonight, not after Mike, but she hit play just the same.

"Hi, Mom. Look, I'm sorry I hung up on you before. I just wanted to say, I'm okay with what you want to do. In fact, I think this little experiment of ours—this getting closer and all—needs a rest for a while. I guess I need a break, too, and I don't think I'm ready to leave California for a while. I hope you have a good year, and a nice life. Okay, so bye for now."

"Oh, fuck you!" Jennifer screamed at the answering machine. "Fuck you!" She screamed again, picking the machine up and slamming it to the floor with both hands as hard as she could. The plastic cover separated and a small speaker bounced from the electronic innards. A feeling of inferiority mixed with self-loathing set in, and Jennifer couldn't stop it. Mike hated her; Tammy hated her. Tears welled in her eyes. On the verge of getting everything she ever wanted, she was losing. How could that be?

Two years ago, at a sales conference, the keynote speaker reminded everyone: *For a salesperson, the key to closing, the key to getting up every morning and facing the rejection that is the hallmark of all sales endeavors is a rock solid self-image. Failure can't phase the sales professional, not if they're going to push through to success. A positive outlook is an asset, a skill, and a survival technique in real estate—no doubt about it.*

Jennifer remembered the speech, and she had a rock-solid self-image at her disposal, but it wasn't working. It fell from her like a curtain separating her from the Great Oz. It was, after all, only a façade. She wanted a drink. She wanted to feel different. Obviously, Mike was blaming her for the cellar. That's why he was so pissed off. Tammy had obviously cast her final judgment on her as a mother. Her ex had obviously won in the war of who would get their daughter's love and affection. She could see the two of them talking about her, commiserating over what a bitch she was. And no doubt about it, the assholes at McWilliam's Real Estate were waiting for Call-It-Home Realty to fail, waiting for her to come back and work for them. "Well, fuck you!" she shouted into the air of her empty living room.

The idea of drinking at home alone in her state of mind scared her. One drink in her tiny apartment with her present thoughts, and she'd be writing: *I gave her to him. Jennifer, 2015.* So, she dried her eyes delicately with one finger, pointlessly trying to avoid smearing mascara. Then she removed all her makeup and showered. After forty minutes, she had built her appearance back up, and within the next twenty minutes, she arrived at the parking lot of Fifty-Five Degrees, her façade fully functioning.

She held no illusions; he couldn't work every night, but Samuel might be there, she thought. A friendly face and someone to talk to would be better than focusing on the condemnation from those close to her. Even if it was only the small talk of a bartender to a patron, she wanted to connect to another person in some way other than as a partner in bricking up hell. God forbid Mike was there, but it was better than drinking at home.

She walked through the wine store and stopped at the counter where the same young man she'd seen before stood waiting to assist her. Apparently, he didn't recognize her at all. "Can I help you find something tonight?" He asked.

"Actually, I was just on my way into the restaurant."

"Certainly," the young man pointed, "right through those drapes."

"Oh yes," Jennifer said, "I was here about a few weeks ago."

"Of course; welcome back," he said in the language of rehearsed customer service, but she knew he didn't recognize her. Samuel probably wouldn't either.

"Tell me, do you have any wines from Eternity Vineyards?" Jennifer asked.

"Is that a California wine?"

"No, it's right here in Arizona."

The clerk looked stumped. "I'm afraid we don't carry that. I can look into ordering it, if you'd like?"

"No, that's okay, I was just curious. Thanks anyway."

"Hello, Mr. Ansell," The youth said over Jennifer's shoulder. Jennifer turned to see Samuel walking up from the curtains to the counter.

"Hello, Travis." He extended his hand to Jennifer. "Hello, Jennifer, long time no see." Samuel was dressed in black again: black turtleneck, black slacks, and a black sport coat. Seeing him felt great in any color.

"Samuel!" she replied, trying to hide the desperate relief in her casual surprise. She took his hand.

"Actually, Travis," Samuel said, including Jennifer in his reply, "you can't order Eternity Vineyards, either. It's not for sale. There hasn't been any wine produced from there in decades." Samuel smiled at Jennifer, "Maybe you're going to change that?"

Jennifer began to feel uneasy. Again, she wondered how much he knew about Eternity. Why was he smiling? What did he know about the cellar? What if she and Mike were nothing more than latecomers who were keeping a secret everyone already knew? "I don't think so," Jennifer laughed. She tried to suppress her suspicion for the sake of a possible good time.

"Will you be dining with us tonight?" Samuel asked.

"Yes, I suppose I will," she said after rejecting, *No, just drinking*, as a good reply. It had been almost a full day since she'd last eaten. Then she stepped out on a ledge, the words coming out of her mouth in her usual confidence, even before she realized in the present situation she had none: "Have you eaten yet?" she asked him.

Samuel glanced at Travis who was smiling and then quickly pretended to work. "No, I haven't, now that you mention it. Perhaps we could share a table?"

"That would be great," Jennifer said.

Samuel motioned for her to follow him toward the restaurant. A young hostess greeted them at the entrance. "Lacy, is fifteen reserved tonight?" he asked her.

The girl consulted a reservation book: "No, Mr. Ansell, fifteen is open."

"Great. Would you seat Ms. Dickerman at fifteen, and I'll be joining her."

"Certainly," the young woman said.

Samuel turned to Jennifer. "I'm just going back to the kitchen for a second to let my assistant know, and I'll be right there."

"Okay," Jennifer said, smiling like a young teen.

She was seated at a table near a window that looked out onto the sidewalk with a view of the city center beyond that. She watched as Samuel returned from the back of the restaurant toward the table with the same confident stride she'd seen before when he waited on her, but unlike most men she met in the course of her work, his confidence wasn't a pretense. It seemed to come from within, a genuine coolness that wasn't designed solely for closing the deal. When he sat across from her and placed his napkin on his lap, he asked, "Wine?"

"Oh, God yes," Jennifer said breathlessly, and then tried to laugh it off.

"I take it you had a hard day."

Jennifer leaned forward, "We took possession of Eternity Vineyards today, and there was more involved than we expected."

"We?" Samuel inquired. "I was under the impression you would be the sole owner."

"Well, technically I am, but I have a promissory note with my partner Mike, the man I was here with last time; he gets a percentage of the equity when we sell it."

"I see," Samuel said. "So you've decided to sell it, after all?"

"It seems that's our best move at this point." With Maddock dead, Jennifer saw no more need for secrecy about the deal. In fact, now was the time to let the whole world know about it. Get it sold, for God's sake. But then she wondered if the brick wall had finished drying.

Samuel turned in his seat and made eye contact with the bartender, delicately motioning for him to come over. When he arrived, Samuel asked Jennifer: "So, are you eating red meat or white?"

"Honestly, I haven't even thought about it."

"Do you like red wine?"

"Oh sure. I completely defer to your judgment."

"Bob, why don't you bring us a bottle of the Juan Gil." Samuel turned to Jennifer; "It's a Spanish Monastrell variety. I'm kind of test marketing here; it's not at all expensive, but I think you'll find it superior even to most of the California reds. You'll have to tell me what you think."

"That sounds great," Jennifer said.

The bartender slightly nodded and went over to the bar.

"You seem to know a lot about Eternity Vineyards," Jennifer ventured. "Have you ever been there?"

"Actually I have, but it was a long time ago when I was in college. We did reports on local small businesses, and I wanted mine to be different. I heard of this Arizona winery, so I set out to discover it. Of course, all I discovered was a middle-aged man who left his vines completely neglected. It wasn't a business at all."

"You went to college?" Jennifer asked.

The bartender returned and opened the bottle of Juan Gil. Samuel motioned for him to go ahead and pour rather than start the smell-and-taste ritual some customers preferred.

"Yes," Samuel perked up. "Arizona State, actually— majored in agriculture with a minor in business.

Jennifer raised her glass of wine, and Samuel returned the gesture, tapping her glass with his, both of them toasting to nothing in particular.

"By 'middle-aged man,' you must mean Robert Maddock."

"That's right," Samuel said.

"He's dead now, you know." Jennifer noticed that Samuel stopped drinking his wine mid-sip. "In fact, that's one of the things we were dealing with today. We went out to take possession of the place, expecting him to have already moved out to Bakersfield, and we found him dead in his bed." This was the version of the truth Jennifer decided to cling to.

"Good Lord," Samuel ran his hand over his mouth and chin.

"Did you know Robert Maddock well?" Jennifer asked.

"Not at all, just his name really, from the one time I met him. It's funny how you can hold things in your mind that seem permanent, and then they change on a dime."

"I know what you mean," Jennifer said thinking about Mike.

Samuel joined her in ordering the Chicken Caesar salad. When she raised the question of red wine with salad and white meat, Samuel absolved the situation by leaning in with a friendly tuition: "A real wine connoisseur drinks what he or she likes and wants. It's the confidence to be the master of the wine, rather than being manipulated by popular opinion." He leaned back, "Too many academics and experts pretend there're rules to be followed, you know, but when it comes to wine, the truth is there are no rules. You drink what you want."

An hour passed as they ate and drank. Occasionally, an employee would come to Samuel and whisper something, and he'd give a verdict or suggestion. He never seemed impatient, never unwelcoming, or even directive. To Jennifer, it seemed as if the place were running without a hierarchy at all, so much different than her experiences in real estate. If one salesperson sold two houses one month and another sold three, the one who sold two was a loser, and the one who sold three a winner. It was cutthroat, completely unlike Samuel's restaurant.

"So, Samuel," Jennifer said, "this place is great. Everything seems to run so smoothly."

Samuel barely contained a laugh. "I don't know if anyone around here would agree with that, but if I do, I assure you it's out of total desperation. I'm actually a partner here—like you and Mike. My partner, Gene, the lucky one, is a silent partner, just an investor really, but this place *is* my life." Samuel looked around as if viewing the totality of himself.

Jennifer hated the question she had to ask next and almost didn't care to know. But a man and woman can't have dinner together and not know, she thought. It's the cards that have to be laid on the table, always and right up front: "So, are you married? Kids?" she asked.

Samuel shook his head: "No, not anymore. I was, though. I was married in college. God, we were so young then," Samuel said looking back in time. Sandra and I were married for almost two years, but she passed away."

"Oh my, I'm sorry to hear that," Jennifer lied and felt terrible for it.

"Thanks, but that was a very long time ago. Almost twenty-five years now.

"So young. Way too young to die," Jennifer observed.

"It was an accident after a party. She was a passenger in a car driven by a drunk." Samuel paused. "Of course, they were all drunk, so was the driver of the car that hit them."

"Dear God," Jennifer said softly. "You never remarried?"

"No. I've been close to it a couple of times," he said it as if attempts counted. "It just never seemed to work out. A marriage defines a person, I think. And I just don't know who I'm supposed to be, or maybe I just haven't met Ms. Right yet. Who knows? What about you?"

"Divorced, eight years." Jennifer took a slug of her wine. "I have a daughter in college, but she lives with her father in California."

"Oh really?" Samuel ventured. "Do you see her often?"

"Not too much," Jennifer replied without adding to it.

Samuel said nothing, but left the silence for Jennifer to fill.

"We're trying to work things out," she eventually offered. "It's not going so well. We've never been really close. She's always had a better relationship with her father, I think." Jennifer took a noisy bite of salad and tried to look away. "I'm always working."

"I know what you mean," Samuel said. "I don't have any children, but I think my work is why I haven't ever remarried. Work can be a lover it seems."

His observation hit hard. "But I don't want it to be, you know?"

Samuel nodded.

Dinner continued and Jennifer was surprised how easy their conversation flowed. She liked talking to Samuel. He listened to her genuinely without simply waiting for his turn to talk. When he did talk, he was smart and passionate about the things that interested him. Sometime after their first bottle of wine and into the second that followed naturally, he said jokingly: "It's a good thing you're selling that vineyard."

"Oh?" Jennifer tried not to choke.

"It has a history, you know—or so the legend goes." Samuel was smiling and seemed over-eager to tell the story.

"Do tell," she said and felt the unmitigated horror of the market knowing they were selling a bona fide center of satanic worship.

"Well, it's not very wide-spread. I mean ask anyone in here, and no one even knows what Eternity Vineyards is. But I came across the story way back in school, and then only because I read up on the place. I actually found an article in some newspaper microfiche at the public library. It's haunted, you know."

"Really?" Jennifer took another long draw of her wine. She had a plan: Just look shocked when he mentions child sacrifice.

"Oh, yes!" Samuel began. "A young girl back in the fifties, Whitney Maddock, killed herself with the same gun, in the same field, as her mother who killed herself a year before. They did it in one of the vineyards."

"Whitney," Jennifer said softly as everything fell into place: The note in Robert's hand, his brother who lost his wife and kids, the girl in the blue nightdress. Her madness had a name; it was, Whitney.

Then Samuel's voice turned theatrically spooky, "Now, during full moon's you can see her watching from the windows."

Jennifer pretended to laugh. "I wish that were true!" she said, knowing that beads of sweat must be forming on her upper lip. "If it were, I could sell it for even more than it's worth. People love a good haunting."

If only Whitney was seen on the full moons from the windows, Jennifer thought. That she keeps showing up in the daytime in mirrors and on bedsides was the real problem. But now, rising at the back of her mind, the idea that a young girl, her young girl, the one she bought with the estate, killed herself with a gun that her mother also killed herself with pricked at her. Sadness came over her at the thought of the abandonment, the loss. At once she felt guilty for hiding behind some bricks the awful truth of a corrupt family secret, one that took the life of a woman and her child so horribly. It had to be all connected.

"Maybe you should advertise it as such," Samuel added. "I'd buy it. By the way, how much is it selling for?"

Jennifer snapped out of her thoughts and half-heartedly into her selling mode. She was thankful for the sanitary tale of Eternity Vineyards' innocent haunting: "Well, Samuel, since you're asking, we're letting it go way below market value, because we want it to move right away. It's worth four million, but we're letting it go for two-and-a-half. Call me Santa Claus."

"I take back that bit about buying," Samuel laughed.

"Seriously, though," Jennifer continued. "It's going to move quick. We'll have it sold in a month; I have no doubts. I wouldn't be surprised if we have to hold an auction. It's a beautiful place. It has over a hundred acres with it."

Jennifer decided to carefully test the waters. She figured if Samuel knew about the cellar, which had to be at the root of the suicides, then others might know, too. She might as well find out now. "Tell me, Samuel, in the legend, did you ever hear why the mother killed herself?"

Samuel thought about it, "No, actually. The story was always just about the sightings of the girl. You never saw her when you were out there?" Samuel smiled when he asked, then sipped his wine.

"No, never," Jennifer lied, trying hard to hide a raging paranoia. She would have loved to confess the truth, but she couldn't be certain where her culpability began or ended.

FIFTEEN

———— ◗ ● ◖ ————

Whitney looked out from her bedroom window at the darkening landscape of Eternity Vineyards. The house was empty now.

She had watched from her usual hidden perch in the corner of the ceiling as the ambulance men zipped Robert's pale, stiffened body into a black plastic bag and wheeled him out of the room. First the ambulance left, then the police, and then Jennifer left with Mike.

The last time the house was this empty, it was ten years before another foot stepped beyond its front door. Whitney began to moan, but without anyone to hear, her moaning didn't count for anything, not even to herself. She hated being alone.

It was the lack of time that came with an infinite lifespan that made being alone so horrible. Nothing had a natural course anymore like it did when she and Kerrie played in the vineyard, or in the office, or when her mother was alive, or even during the good times she had with her father before he changed, before he found the hidden room in the cellar and drank from the wine bottles. Now, there was no difference between a minute and a year. If she wasn't watching the actions of others, her actions no longer meant anything. She was conscious, but she didn't exist.

A long time ago, she gave up hoping her mother would come to her. The two of them must be in different worlds, she thought. She was certain if she imitated her behavior in the end, she would join her wherever she was. But when the bullet ended the life of her body, when her consciousness saw herself lying in the dirt between the rows of grapevines, she immediately felt a loneliness that would haunt her, even as she haunted Eternity Vineyards.

Whitney let go of her attachment to the bedroom window, and her consciousness began to drift on an ethereal tide that ran through the domain of the estate. She passed lazily though her wardrobe and floated just below the ceiling of the next bedroom. She hated her memories, but she found herself unable to stop them.

The black wine changed everything. When her father found it and tried it, he changed in that instant, just as she knew Mike had changed. Her father became dark at first, depressed and irritable. Before the wine, he was a friendly man, caring and loving; but after that first taste, he only wanted to be alone. When being alone wasn't possible, he began to beat her mother.

She thought about how she and Kerrie left the house by her mother's command whenever her father's violence started up. Her mother didn't want them to see her being kicked as she lay on the ground at his feet. Instead, they sat outside the front door listening as household objects crashed within. Her mother would scream, and her father would shout insanities at her: *I know you're fucking around, you fucking whore!*

Even at twelve Whitney knew what he meant, but she couldn't understand him when they lived in the middle of nowhere. Her mother rarely left the house, much less traveled away from the property.

One day her mother ran out of the house. She and Kerrie were sitting on the ground against the family car playing gin rummy, and her mother glared at them both, her eyes wider than Whitney had ever seen them. She bared her teeth as she ran toward them screaming, "He's going to kill us!" She flailed about, stumbling and slipping on the loose gravel. At one point she fell, badly skinning her knee, and Whitney watched the blood run down her leg as if her father were hurting her from a distance. "We have to run! Hide! Come on! Hurry!" she screamed at them, but she was already running away.

They ran behind her toward the maintenance shed at the bottom of the dirt road. Kerrie cried loudly, not wanting to be left behind, but she was unable to keep up, and no one waited for her in the panic. Finally, when they were all in the darkness of the shed, Whitney huddled against her mother, and for that instant she felt as if she were back inside of her, safe and whole.

She wanted to be inside her mother now, but instead she floated haphazardly through the bedroom wall and looked down at the gravel driveway beneath her.

One day, without a note, without any excuse or explanation, Whitney watched her mother walk from the house into the vineyards. She followed her at a distance and saw her place the barrel of a gun in her mouth. Without hesitation, her mother pulled the trigger, and the back of her hair blew out, like some gust of wind had caught it. She crumpled to the soil and never moved again.

The day Whitney removed the gun from the desk in the study after betraying her younger sister, she believed she had found a way to be with her mother again, to be inside of her and whole. But when she shot herself, she felt only a jerk in her neck. And after that, forever began.

Floating now without direction, she wished Jennifer would come back to the vineyard. She wished she could watch her, and she'd be good so as not to upset her. When Jennifer was there, she was able to forget how much she hated herself. When Jennifer was there, she could forget she was in a hell for betraying her sister. Perhaps Mike already killed her. She tried to push away that possibility as she floated on the ether, waiting forever in each second that passed.

SIXTEEN

———— • • ————

The big push to sell Eternity Vineyards begins today, Jennifer thought as she drove the ten miles from her apartment to Call-It-Home Realty, but at each stoplight, the opportunity arose to think back on the quiet Sunday that followed her date with Samuel. Of course, Saturday night was only a casual dinner, a chance meeting, but then he called her on Sunday, and they talked for hours like high schoolers who couldn't say goodbye. That had to make Saturday their first date. She couldn't help believing that good things were about to happen between them, and she certainly hoped so.

There was still no word from Mike. She tried to call him five times on Sunday, but there was no answer. She thought it unwise to drive by his condo without an invitation, and maybe it was best to let him figure things out over the weekend by himself. Besides, she'd see him this morning, and things would be different now that they were on the road to a lot of money. And part of her didn't want Mike's mood or issues, whatever they were, ruining the good feelings she was getting with Samuel on her mind, so it was just as well he didn't return her calls. Why spoil a good thing?

From her parking spot in front of their office at the Hillside Shopping Mall, she searched the lot for Mike's red Honda, but it wasn't there. She felt only half-surprised. After all, what kind of statement is *You're killing me*? How much more I quit could there be in such a proclamation? But she hadn't done anything, for Christ's sake, and he was always at work before her.

She took her London Fog, briefcase, and purse and made her way to the front door of the office. She let herself in and dumped everything on top of her desk. Now his absence was becoming ridiculous. They had a lot of calls to make today, but her first call would have to be to her sullen partner. He could dodge her all he wanted on the weekends, but Monday was business—their business, and she would tell him so.

Mike's phone rang, but again only the answering machine picked up. She dropped the call without leaving a message. "Where the hell are you?" she muttered angrily.

It was no use; she grabbed her coat, purse, and keys again and made her way back to her car. Now, she'd have to go by his condo, and this was setting the schedule for the day way behind. Who knew how long the talk would take to get his attitude screwed back on straight...or at least to get him to forgive her for whatever she supposedly did. You'd think she killed Maddock and built the room just to make him cover it up. He can be incredibly ridiculous, she thought.

Dealing with his frequent high maintenance could be irksome to say the least, but then in the parking lot, halfway to her Durango, connections began to form, two plus two adding up to four. It drained her anger and replaced it with a subtle anxiety. What if something happen to him in the cellar? The thought dawned on her, and she couldn't figure out why she hadn't thought of it before. What if suicide happens to people in that place? What if, *You're killing me*, was a cry for help that she utterly ignored?

Her pace quickened. She made it to her car and pulled out of the lot.

On any street along the way where there was room, she drove fast, running every yellow light and a few reds. What if he was a corpse in his own bed? What if his mouth and eyes were open in stone-cut fashion? What if he did it right after she dropped him off? What if there was blood? With the final image of Robert Maddock relentlessly intruding, she tortured herself with grizzly thoughts of Mike holding a note in one stiffened hand. She should have checked on him. She should have sensed his cues.

Mike lived in the condominiums of the Cactus Shade Residential Estates. They were adobe style flats with manicured lawns, tanning beds, a sparkling indoor pool kept open year-round with a massive spa and three saunas. Though not advertised as such, the place was well known to the elite of the homosexual community in Phoenix, and Mike had lived there for years. If a straight person or couple wanted to move in, it was technically possible, but a poster in the office window of two men sharing a candlelight meal at a table by the pool, and another with two men smiling in a hot tub usually spelled out what to expect from the neighbors.

Jennifer wasted no time finding a parking spot. She simply double-parked on one of the interior roads nearest his door. With the driver's side left open, engine running, and purse in plain view on the passenger seat, she ran to his door as fast as her high heels allowed. When she got there, she knocked hard but didn't wait for an answer before turning the knob. It was unlocked.

Her stomach knotted as she entered his home. Surely the sulfur-putrid smell of death would be floating in the air, she imagined it as she took a breath in his residence, but there was nothing. No stench is always a good sign, she thought.

"Mike," Jennifer called out—no answer. "Mike!" She hollered again and looked in the bathroom and bedroom, but he wasn't home, and her worst fears for him returned to her earlier anger: "Where the fuck are you! What the hell's wrong with you!" Her voice echoed off the walls.

She left in disgust, slamming his door behind her, nearly disappointed that he wasn't a corpse. If he wasn't dead, then why wasn't he at work? Today they started selling Eternity Vineyards. Now she was going to have to do it herself, or at least start it.

Damn it, she thought, this wasn't like him, and they never quarreled about anything before, not even at McWilliam's. There was nothing—*absolutely nothing*—that would make him just up and avoid her. They'd been through too much together.

She drove back to Call-It-Home Realty not nearly as fast as she left. By the time she arrived, Mike still hadn't texted her or left a message , and he hadn't shown up at work. She tried to put it out of her mind. She had work to do, and whether or not Mike was where he was supposed to be couldn't get in the way of getting rid of Eternity Vineyards—*selling* Eternity Vineyards.

The first calls would be to her contacts. She had three avid investors in property she'd be phoning: Bill Mack, an investor in properties she'd met her first year at McWilliam's Real Estate, Steve Dillard, a multimillionaire who often bought and sold properties (Mike was supposed to speak to him.), and of course she'd have to let Melissa know.

Melissa was her first real mentor at McWilliam's Real Estate. She owed her for helping her with leads and tips when she wasn't selling so well at first. However, their friendship was short-lived after Jennifer won a monthly sales contest the following quarter. For the victory, she'd received two tickets to the Bahamas, and rather than inviting Melissa, she took her then-husband, Dan. Melissa rarely spoke to her after that, and over the years, like all her coworkers, Melissa became just one more jealous competitor.

Jennifer still felt like she owed her—but even more, Melissa had the funds to invest in, and re-flip, Eternity Vineyards. What greater victory could there be than to have the top salesperson at McWilliam's buying property from Call-It-Home Realty?

But she couldn't help it: Even though she tried to tell herself she didn't give a damn, that he could be as late as he wanted, she did give a damn, and it bothered her too much. Her first call was to the police.

"911. What's your emergency?" an uninterested voice asked from the other end.

"I want to report a missing person," Jennifer said.

"You need to hang up and go to your local police station to file that."

"Oh, I'm so sorry—" Jennifer began, but the operator had already ended the call. "Bitch," Jennifer said. "Fuck you, Mike; you're on your own!" She shouted to the empty office.

She sat in the ensuing silence for less than a minute before letting out a heavy sigh. Then she picked up her coat and purse again and headed out to the police station. The schedule was toast.

SEVENTEEN

———————— ◆ ● ◆ ————————

Floating on the chaotic causality of Eternity's ether, Whitney hardly realized that she was hundreds of feet above the vineyard fields looking down on them. It mattered little to her where she was when she was alone. She'd been floating without direction since Saturday, but then with a flash, she snapped back to full awareness.

That *flash* occurred at least two miles away on the highway that led to the turnoff for Eternity Vineyards. The Monday morning sun caught on the chrome of an automobile, and it signaled to her that Jennifer was returning.

Excitement overcame her. She turned and looked to the ground and accelerated at a great speed all the way down to only an inch above the vineyard soil. She pulled up just then, and along one row she raced toward the house, watching the small bits of dirt and rocks become a blur beneath her. She had to watch Jennifer's arrival from her bedroom window. That's just where she had to be. She would concentrate and try to fully form herself and maybe even wave at Jennifer if she looked up at her when she got out of her car.

Whitney shot through the wood of the front door and up into the heights of the foyer, over the balcony railing and through her bedroom door. She came to a motionless point of view at her bedroom window and waited.

But she stopped concentrating on her form when the car turned off the highway and headed up the winding driveway road. It wasn't the car Jennifer drove, and it wasn't the police. It was one she had never seen before. It was gray and polished to a high gloss finish like only a new car can be. The clean smooth lines of it were modern, even more so than Jennifer's. Even the hood ornament was fashioned into a silver peace symbol, and Whitney thought it made for a friendly touch.

She passed through her window and glided down to the back of the car to the rear of it as it came to a stop in front the house. The dust it created flowed over and through her like a fog, but on the trunk, a chromed S600 stood out clearly. Whitney looked through the back window and saw a completely bald man, his head smooth and shiny, looking through the windshield and up at the features of the house.

When he got out, Whitney saw that he was older but athletically built, and he wore a neatly trimmed goatee and a well-tailored gray suit that matched the color of his car. She stayed behind him, and from a dozen feet above, she watched his every move. He buttoned his jacket and looked around at the countryside in all directions as if he had suddenly been dropped at Eternity Vineyards and didn't know where he was. But he smiled and nodded to himself, apparently satisfied with the location.

Whitney followed as he made his way to the front door. He knocked on it and waited a short time for an answer. Looking behind him again at the countryside, he waited, and then tried to open the door for himself, but it was locked.

Whitney continued with him from above as he walked to the other side of the house. When he got to the back, he went directly to the wine cellar loading doors just like he already knew they were there. Clasped to the doors, he found a padlock barring his entrance. He lifted up the lock, examining it, and then let it fall back.

From the ground he picked up a piece of wood, a splinter of a two-by-four, and wedged it under the clasp of the lock, but when he tried to pry the clasp, the weathered piece of wood promptly broke. It fell to the ground, and he dusted his hands. Whitney followed as he walked back to the front of the estate and opened the trunk of his car. He retrieved a metal crowbar and returned to the wine cellar doors. He used the bar to pry up the clasp, and it tore from the ancient doors with ease.

She accelerated into the cellar ahead of him and placed her consciousness at the ceiling above one of the hanging lights. The man looked around the cellar at the brick walls and barrels, and for a moment seemed awestruck by the layout. Then he walked directly to the wine rack illuminated by the light coming through the open loading doors. He tugged at various parts of the iron framing and finally found the part that gave way and opened like a door. "*Was ist das?* " (What is this?) The man said out loud.

Whitney heard it as vahs-iss-dahs, and she didn't understand him, but her anxiety grew, because apparently he knew about the room, and that could never be good. How could he know? She had never seen him before, and she'd been in the house for more than half a century. He wasn't that old. Suddenly, this bald man with his blue eyes and short beard felt dangerous to her.

He let his hand run over the brickwork, and then turned around as if he might be in the wrong place. But he turned back and traced the edges of the brickwork with his finger, right along where the new brickwork came up against the old. He chuckled, and again dusted his hands. He took one last look around the cellar, nodded with satisfaction, and walked back up the concrete ramp. He closed the doors behind him, and Whitney let herself pass through the basement ceiling, up through the floors of the house, and out through the roof. She watched him from above the estate as he returned to his car. Then he left without looking at any other aspects of the property.

Whitney returned to her room and sat in front of her window watching him descend the drive and turn onto the highway. He scared her. He reminded her of her father. She hoped he wouldn't return, and so she sat watching as the hours passed, watching for Jennifer to come back, worrying that she wouldn't.

EIGHTEEN

——■●■——

Jennifer returned from filing a missing person's report at the police department, and tried Mike's cell again, but again no answer. At the police station, she gave them one of Mike's business cards that had a good photo of him on it. She described his car, and gave them the names of his friends that she knew of, not that she really ever knew any of his friends. She didn't have their phone numbers or addresses, or for that matter, their last names. They were always just Chris, John, Peter, Fredrick, and others, some with wedding bands, some without, all with a reason to remain a little distant.

Mike lived the gay scene, but she didn't fit into that. She worked with Mike, but he kept his professional life and social life separate for the most part. She knew he met a lot of men, and he wasn't careful, and more than once that gave Jennifer cause for concern. The officer who took her report told her that even if they found him, they couldn't disclose his location to her, not if he didn't want it disclosed. So because there was nothing left to do, she sat at her desk and started her ritual: phone messages, e-mail, bills, and the plan of the day, which was to sell Eternity Vineyards.

She left messages with Bill Mack and Steve Dillard, and e-mailed them photos of the place along with the basic information. Then she contacted Melissa directly.

"How are you doing, Jen?" Melissa asked with too much concern, as if Jennifer had been in a hospital for a month.

Jennifer saw herself slamming the phone down: "I'm good, Melissa. How are things at McWilliam's?" she asked instead.

"We got the Desert View contract, so we all have a lot of dirt to move, but it's moving fast. How's Mike?"

Melissa had strongly disagreed with Jennifer's decision to leave McWilliam's, and treated it as comical that Mike was going with her. Mike wasn't a salesman; he did building inspections and worked for their office as a general contractor on maintenance or repairs to properties being readied for sale. Melissa assumed that since no other salesperson was interested in going into partnership with Jennifer, Mike was her desperate second choice. He had some start-up money, but little else to offer. Melissa didn't hide her opinions from Jennifer, but Jennifer never saw it that way. Mike was her friend.

"Mike's great," Jennifer said. Lying to Melissa came easily. "He's out at our main project, right now, and that's what I wanted to talk to you about." Jennifer laid out the details of the deal, but Melissa was incredulous.

"My God, Jennifer," Melissa spoke as if Jennifer couldn't help fucking up. "Why would you sell a four-million-dollar property for two-and-a-half?" This was Melissa's trademark and power edge. Jennifer thought about how many times she'd heard it all before, and she had to admit, it worked surprisingly well in her high-dollar sales. *Keep them justifying themselves to you; it gives you the upper hand.*

Melissa once told Jennifer that when she worked for GM selling Cadillacs, the key to hooking the person who walked onto the lot was to make them feel like talking to the salesman was a privilege. You wanted to make them feel they had to prove they were uptown enough to buy. Of course, it worked better with first-time buyers than regulars.

"Melissa, I'm going to be honest with you, we need the money." Jennifer normally wouldn't choose an honest answer, but in this case, she wanted Melissa to feel superior; even more, she wanted Melissa to smell the blood and come in for the kill. If she thought Jennifer needed money, Jennifer knew full well Melissa would try to rip her off. What else were her friends for? And given the squealing point of seven hundred thousand she and Mike agreed on after finding the hellhole in the basement, selling to Melissa for two-point-five would just make the world a better place.

"That's a lot of money, Jen."

"But you have to see this place. I'm e-mailing you photos now," Jennifer said. "And, Melissa, I know two other buyers right now. I think we can auction this place given what we're willing to take for it. Of course, you'd be in on that auction, but I want you to have first dibs before we do anything like that. If you see this place, you'll know what I mean."

"Well then, I better have a look-see," Melissa said as if taking a drawing from a five-year-old.

There was silence on the phone as Jennifer let the place sell itself.

"Wow," Melissa said quietly.

"It's worth a drive out there, "Jennifer said," if for nothing else than to satisfy your curiosity and take a nice day off in the countryside."

"Who's selling it?"

"I am," Jennifer said.

"Right, but who's the owner?"

"Me, again," Jennifer countered. "I own the title free and clear and there's no back taxes, and no structural defects. No defects at all, really." There was silence again. Jennifer could hear the mouse clicks as Melissa went through the photos. Even more, she could hear the wheels turning in Melissa's head as she went through her mental Rolodex of potential buyers to whom she, herself, could flip the place.

"Well, Jen, you really dove into the deep end didn't you?"

"You have to see this place," Jennifer said calmly. "I owe you. You brought me into real estate. This is the favor you're getting back for that. Trust me; you're going to want to see this." There was more silence, more mouse clicks. Jennifer waited.

"When do you want to meet?" Melissa asked.

Jennifer smiled like a fisherman whose line just twitched. "How about Wednesday?"

"Wednesday's no good for me, I have three clients I'm meeting Wednesday." Jennifer caught the deliberate stress Melissa put on three.

"What about Friday?"

"Friday might work," Melissa said. "Let me check my schedule a little more, and I'll—"

Jennifer detested the power play, and decided to trump it. "Oh, sure, that's fine. I'm waiting on a call back from Bill and Steve, anyway, so let me see when they want to view the property, and we'll work around that."

"Bill Mack?" Melissa asked.

"And Steve Dillard," Jennifer replied.

Again, there was a pregnant silence and more mouse clicks.

"Why can't we meet today?" Melissa asked.

Jennifer smiled. The tables were turning. "Today's good for me," Jennifer said.

NINETEEN

The drive took nearly three hours, but that would still give her nearly an hour at Eternity Vineyards before Melissa was due to arrive. On the way, she once again tried Mike's cell, but as usual, there was no answer.

Her feelings about him were becoming mixed: anger and loss swirled with worry and guilt—but guilt over what? He just changed all of the sudden. In two hours he became someone else completely, and then disappeared like the earth had opened up and swallowed him.

She tried to think of other things, tried to keep her mind on closing Melissa, but pulling off the highway onto the gravel driveway, she thought about how wrong it was for Mike to be away. He knew what the plan was and how big this was for the both of them, and now she was alone without his support. It would look to Melissa as if no one was with her in her move to leave McWilliam's. How could he do this to her?

Again, she tried to put it out of her mind. Anger would only distract her, and it was time for the dog and pony show. She'd make up something to explain his absence, and eventually she'd come to some resolution with him. He was, after all, a grown man. He could do as he pleased and take care of himself.

Inside the house, the dust and cobwebs seemed to be everywhere, maybe even more than before, but there was no time to clean. It would take a month to clean and polish the place to the standard required for showing it. At McWilliam's, the job would have already been contracted out. Mike would have seen to it, but such surface cosmetics didn't impress people like Melissa who were in the business of buying and selling.

To those trained to spot a good deal, the value of a place wasn't changed by dust on the furniture or whether the lawn was mowed or the windows cleaned. Trained investors could spot inherent value right away. Surface things mattered to homebuyers only, not investors.

Cleanliness mattered to a homebuyer, because to him or her, a house is not only shelter but also a statement about who they are as people. *So what does a dead body and a satanic wine cellar say about the owner?* Jennifer thought. *How do you clean that up?* She brushed her stray thoughts aside. She wasn't going to be the owner for very long.

Jennifer looked up at the ceiling high above the balconies that loomed over the foyer; being in the house felt different this time. Not the least of which there was no longer any smell of death, but this was also the first time she'd ever been completely alone in the house. It was large, desolate, and extravagant, and it actually belonged to her. This was her house. This was her property.

A feeling arose as she took in the place, a sick loss-of-profit-feeling that said you could live here forever. This is where you belong. This is old generational money that no matter how much you earn, you can never be part of in any other way. The house tempted her to own it, to rule it.

Again, she forced her mind onto the task at hand. She had to get down to business. The house was for selling and making her rich, not for living in. She had to remain disinterested. Many houses she sold were beautiful. Many houses had the power to sweep one away into fantastic daydreams. Jennifer examined her professional look in the foyer mirror. *But back then they always belonged to someone else.* She made herself step away from the mirror. It reflected her and the interior of the Spanish Colonial mansion all in one image.

She walked into the library and moved slowly as she approached the large desk. She let her fingers run over it as she moved around and sat down in the leather chair. *Generations of owners have sat here—some good, some bad. What are you?*

She pulled her cell phone out of her purse and called Melissa. Melissa answered after three rings.

"So, are you lost yet?" Jennifer said jovially.

"Not yet, but just about," she replied. "I'm almost at Sonoita."

"Well, if you think you're lost, don't travel too far on 82. We put a 'For Sale' sign at the entrance of the road leading up to the estate. You can't miss it. You'll see the place as soon as you head up it a bit.

"Is Mike with you?" Melissa asked.

Jennifer answered quickly: "No. He had a dentist appointment and had to get back to Phoenix. You two probably passed each other on the interstate and didn't even know it." Jennifer laughed, but Melissa didn't.

"You know, Jen, I've been on the road for three hours now, and I'm in the middle of nowhere. This place better be worth it."

"You're going to be glad you made the trip," Jennifer said. "Trust me. This place is a once-in-a-lifetime opportunity. In fact, I think I can say it's a one-of-a-kind." Jennifer wanted to laugh at that, but managed to keep it to herself.

"Okay, I'll see you in about twenty minutes," Melissa said.

"Sounds good, sugar. Buh-bye." Jennifer felt sick at her own appalling pseudo-friendliness. She brushed off Melissa's arrogant whining as soon as she tapped off the call.

Sitting back in the chair, she looked out over the dark wooden grandeur of the study. She felt pressured and desperate, as if time were running out. She wanted to walk around the place alone, to experience the house as its owner. These may be the last twenty minutes she could call the place hers.

She walked from the library to the staircase, and it seemed she was noticing everything for the first time: the quality of the leather-bound books in the bookcases, the hand-laid stone floor of the foyer, the ancient but polished wood of the staircase banister. Then as she looked to the top of the stairs, there she was, the young girl in a thin blue nightgown standing at the top looking down at her.

Jennifer fixed on her, too amazed for the moment to be afraid. It seemed as if the girl belonged to the house every bit as much as the doors and windows. She felt the same feelings of confusion that had previously made her feel like she was going mad, but this time she couldn't take her eyes off the apparition in front of her. "Whitney," she said. Not calling to her but only identifying what appeared before her.

The girl turned and moved gracefully down the east hallway, almost as if she were floating over the floor rather than walking. She moved to the end of it and gradually faded from view as she approached the last door; then she was gone entirely, dematerializing back into the structure of the house.

Jennifer almost followed her, spellbound by the disturbing sight of an actual ghost, but she turned instead and sat on the wooden steps of the staircase. She wasn't going to get emotional. She'd seen this Whitney, this ghost of Whitney, this hallucination, or whatever it was too many times now to get emotional again. She couldn't follow after her; to follow her would be to give in to the madness of the impossibility of such a thing. It would be the epitome of losing control, because what she was seeing was impossible. At least if she ignored her, she could still believe she had control of her mind.

She put her head in her hands. *This is insane*, she thought. But how could she be insane? She only ever saw the girl here. And what about Mike? Certainly, he'd seen her too, and there was the legend Samuel told her about. If she was insane, why see a young girl in a blue nightgown that meant nothing to her psychologically. Tammy never had a blue nightgown.

She reminded herself she was a streetwise real estate agent, and she wasn't about to get rattled at a time like this. She had a house to sell, and if the London Philharmonic Orchestra were playing in her ears and pink elephants dancing in the vineyard, she'd worry about that after the close, pure and simple. With resolve, she raised her head from her hands, but only inches away, Whitney stood in front of her, staring at her, studying her.

Jennifer gasped. She instinctively crawled backwards up the wooden steps. Her left shoe came loose and landed two steps below. Her nylon-clad foot slipped on the smooth surfaces, and she found herself unable to gain enough traction to get away. She gaped in horror at the specter, now so close she could reach out and touch her. But it was the pale girl that reached out for her, as if she were going to help her to her feet. Jennifer tried to scream, but found herself paralyzed—then the girl was gone again, just like she'd never been there.

Confusion swirled around her, and she felt sweat running down her body inside her shirt. Finally, she could breathe, but it was quick and short, and tears formed in the corners of her eyes as she pushed a fist against her mouth to stop herself from screaming again. Looking around in all directions like a bird that just heard a cat, she picked up her shoe and descended the stairs, clutching the banister for support. She clumsily put her shoe back on when she got to the floor. Then ran to the front door and out of the house—her house.

In the front seat of the Dodge, she trembled, completely ignorant of her next move. She wanted to drive away. She decided to drive away. Fuck the sale, to hell with this house, to hell with little girls who shoot themselves! But just then, as she realized she'd inadvertently left her car keys in the library, she saw Melissa's dust plume at the distant end of the driveway. She'd arrived. "Oh, damn."

"Okay...okay." She said, motivating herself, and with every bit of will over instinct, she stepped from her car and put on her selling smile. Nothing was wrong. There were no dead bodies, no satanic cellar, no ghosts, no madness, no panic, and no suicide pacts—just a super deal to be had in real estate today! She held her hands together to stop the visible tremors.

Melissa drove an Audi A8. When she pulled in next to Jennifer's Dodge, she didn't look at Jennifer or wave. Jennifer recognized her style: *Don't look at them when you drive up, just let them look at you. The one who's looking is more desperate than the one who's looked at.* But with practiced precision, Melissa graciously stepped from her car and approached Jennifer with open arms. She was taller than Jennifer and wore a beige business suit. Her hair was done in a short, highlighted semi-spike, and today she sported her unnecessary geek-sheik glasses. She must want to look smart, Jennifer thought. Then they hugged as they always did, two inches separating them in complete pretense.

"I see you made it," Jennifer said. For the first time since knowing her, she actually felt safer with Melissa nearby.

Melissa looked around, "You can't see another house, even up on this hill."

"It's like a castle, isn't it?" Jennifer pointed in various directions to landmarks that generally indicated the borders of the property. "There's a hundred and ten acres here along with the house. Thirty of the acres over there, as you can see, are the actual vineyards. I suppose more of the land could be developed for growing, if one was so inclined."

"I must say, Jen, it is nice out here—and this house, you weren't kidding, were you?"

"Almost ten thousand square feet if you include the basement winery. But wait until you see the inside." Jennifer said trying to create a salesman's suspense.

"So, there's an actual wine cellar?" Melissa asked.

"Boy, is there ever." Jennifer stifled a maniacal laugh.

Together they walked into the house, and Jennifer gave Melissa the guided tour: first the dining room, then the study, then the back rooms, then the back veranda with its fountain.

With trepidation, and constantly glancing around, hoping to forestall any unpleasant visions, Jennifer walked Melissa up the stairs and showed her the bedrooms, grateful that all she was seeing was the house now and not its occupant.

"Jen," Melissa began as she sat on the four-poster bed in the west main bedroom, "this place is worth more than two-point-five. What's wrong with it? How'd you get it?"

"Let's just say I always had some deals going on the side, and things worked out." Jennifer shrugged: "Why else would I ever leave McWilliam's? And there's nothing wrong with it. I mean, I thought there had to be when it was offered to me, too, but there's nothing to disclose."

Melissa got up and moved to the large window that looked out over the vineyards in the distance. "It's magical."

"Strange you should say that," Jennifer said, "I've come to think about it the same way."

"If I take this place off your hands, I want a full disclosure statement, and I'm going to hold you to it," Melissa said, "big time."

"I wouldn't expect anything less." Jennifer smiled, as if Melissa hadn't insulted her at all.

"I'll need to see the basement, too."

"You're going to love it," Jennifer said.

They left the bedrooms and descended the staircase. Melissa paused and looked down at the foyer and then behind her at the second floor. "I don't get it, Jen, what's the catch? Come on, you can't pull one over on me. I trained you; remember? Why would you let this go for a million less, maybe two million less, than any real estate agent with half a brain could sell it for?"

Jennifer kept her same political smile and demeanor she trained herself to have no matter how a person responded. "Melissa, it's not a mystery. Mike and I started a new business, as you know, and we invested in this property, and we want it to move. We want to move on and do more. Right now, it's a win-win. Those kind of deals do exist, you know?"

"Do they?" Melissa asked. "I think that's something only our customers believe. I wouldn't think you'd actually believe it. Didn't I teach you anything?" Melissa looked patronizingly disappointed.

"You can't imagine the things you've taught me," Jennifer said, trying to construct a thankful expression.

At the bottom of the stairs Jennifer suggested they walk around the outside of the house to the freight entrance of the basement. "You can get into the cellar right behind the staircase," Jennifer pointed, "but this will give us a chance to see the entire perimeter of the exterior."

"We can do that," Melissa granted.

Together they walked along the covered walkway, and at one point, Melissa stopped and touched an exterior wall. "The walls are made out of stone blocks," Melissa said. "This isn't stone veneer." She sounded almost confused by the near impossibility of it. She looked at Jennifer.

"They say this place is over three-hundred years old, Jennifer said as they continued around the structure. "The Spanish originally built it but it looks almost new, don't you think? The previous owners really kept it up. I think you'll agree when you get your own inspector out here to look at the wiring and plumbing. It's all in really great shape."

"Three hundred years?" Melissa asked suspiciously as she scanned the walls further. "What do the county records show?"

"Well, Santa Cruz wasn't a county until 1899, and the house was already here."

"So, it might not be three hundred, right?"

Jennifer wondered if Melissa was deliberately obstinate or just attempting a negotiation of the selling price. "Maybe," Jennifer conceded, "I'm only going by what the previous owner said. There's probably something about it in the study. I really haven't had a chance to look, but it certainly has a timeless quality. I mean, they don't build places like this anymore."

When they reached the double wooden doors that led to the cellar, Melissa noticed it first: "Looks like someone's broke the lock."

On the ground was the clasp with the padlock still attached. From the ripped-out screw holes on the door, it was obvious someone had broken in. Jennifer kneeled and retrieved it. Had Mike been out here? What if Mike were down in the cellar right now dangling from a beam in the basement? Is this where he's been? Jennifer felt a surge of anxiety; she wasn't at all sure what they were about to find. She was slipping out of control again, and she didn't like it.

What if the room was exposed? What about Whitney? Why hadn't there been any *Whitney* since Melissa arrived? "How strange..." Jennifer looked around at the isolated landscape. "I'm sure this was locked the last time we were out here. It's not like there's vagrants out here, or anyone else for that matter."

Melissa thumbed the latch and pulled the right-side door open. Together they walked down the concrete ramp, the hard heels of their business pumps clicking in rhythm as they descended. "This is amazing," Melissa said. "This place isn't just a collector's estate, is it?"

"Not at all," Jennifer said. "It's really used for making wine. I've been told a person could actually earn a good living from it if they knew what they were doing."

"Is there wine in these casks?" Melissa asked, running her finger over the surface of one of them.

"I think so," Jennifer replied. "The ones I've tapped on sounded full." Jennifer glanced over at the wine rack. It was refreshingly the same way they'd left it. In fact, everything looked the same, except for the door lock. "You'll notice the beams and the walls are all in good shape. I don't think you'll find any signs of water damage, wood rot or deterioration. It's quite remarkable, actually, given its age."

"Well, Jen, if it's all the same to you, I'd like to walk around a little on my own."

"Absolutely." Jennifer tried not to bristle at the implied distrust.

Melissa walked to the far end of the basement opposite the wine rack wall. She glanced around her as if taking everything in and evaluating it with quick expert precision. Jennifer went immediately to the wine rack and looked through the empty slots at the new brickwork. It was still intact and covering the entrance to the antechamber behind it. *Everything is cool*, she thought, until she heard her colleague.

"Well, hello there," Jennifer heard Melissa say. "Do you live here? Where's your—oh my God—oh my God!"

Even before she saw her running from the other end of the cellar, Jennifer could hear the fast clicking of Melissa's pumps coming up the isle between the wine casks.

"Stay away from me! Melissa yelled in a deep throaty scream. "Oh no—stay away!"

Jennifer saw Melissa running toward her; blind panic had taken over. She didn't seem to notice Jennifer at all, even as she raced past her.

Behind Melissa, floating three feet off the concrete floor, the faintest image of a pale young girl with black hair pursued her only inches away. The phantom's outstretched arms reached out for Melissa's head, her black cavernous mouth opened wide in a silent scream. Jennifer covered her mouth in shock—her insanity was chasing her mark!

"Get away from me! Get away!" Melissa yelled, swatting at her meticulously styled hair as if bees were circulating around her head. She ran to the concrete ramp and slipped halfway up, landing hard on her hands and knees. Her hair fell in front of her face, and for a moment, she looked like a drunken college girl vomiting after a night of heavy drinking. She was sobbing and crawling her way up the ramp.

"Please no, please!" her voice disintegrating into hoarseness.

Before Jennifer could say a word, Melissa rose to her feet, her pumps off and lying like casualties on the ramp. She made it to the top, and ran around the side of the house. She ran for her life in bare nylons not reacting to the hard cobblestone walkway on the soles of her feet.

Jennifer followed. "Melissa, wait!"

Whitney vanished from sight when her image entered the sunlight shining down to the foot of the ramp. This time, seeing Whitney didn't frighten Jennifer at all. She picked up Melissa's pumps and stopped at the top of the ramp. She looked down into the cellar. "Fuck you!" she screamed at the spirit lurking somewhere below in the dark.

She turned and continued running after Melissa, but by the time she rounded the estate, she could see Melissa through the windshield of her Audi struggling to get her key into the ignition.

Jennifer ran up to the car and tried to speak through the closed driver's window, "Melissa, I can explain." But Melissa was too preoccupied with her personal safety to notice. *What exactly are you going to explain?* Jennifer thought.

The Audi's engine roared, and Jennifer stepped back. The tires sprayed dust and gravel into the front wheel wells as the car sped backwards. Then the dust and gravel spit from under the car as Melissa gunned the engine and headed down the driveway. She watched her go, taking her two-and-a-half million with her as she went.

Jennifer turned to the house, seething. "You bitch!" She screamed loud enough to make her throat hurt and stormed back toward the front door.

TWENTY

W hitney watched Jennifer from the dining room window as she walked back to the house. Jennifer was mad at her and called her a bitch, and it hurt. She must hate her now, and that's not what she wanted, but she couldn't let Jennifer sell the house. Robert was sure that Jennifer would be the one to keep Eternity Vineyards, and she wanted it to be just the two of them; anyone else might find the cellar. What if the bald man came back? He knew the cellar was there.

Jennifer yanked opened the front door and slammed it behind her. The mass of it produced a low boom like a distant blast. "What the hell do you want!" she shouted as she dropped Melissa's pumps.

Whitney rose through the ceiling of the dining room into her bedroom. She didn't want to hear Jennifer yelling at her, but she listened anyway.

"Where are you?" Jennifer shouted.

She heard Jennifer's shoes making their way to the top of the stairs and then drawing closer to her room. Her door flew open and banged against the wall. Whitney shot into the corner of the ceiling. Jennifer stood in the middle of the room. "I'm not scared of you anymore! I'm sick of you, and I'm going to get rid of you!"

Whitney dropped down and stood still in front of her writing desk. She held fast hoping to come into focus. She could tell by Jennifer's grave expression that she had succeeded.

Whitney focused hard on her brown hair, her lips, and her blue eyes, so Jennifer wouldn't see only black in their place. She concentrated earnestly on them, just as she had done for Robert while he died. If she didn't try to make her features so, her eyes wouldn't appear and neither would her mouth. Instead, only darkness would manifest, and her skin would be pale and her hair black. It made her look like a monster. She had seen herself in mirrors before. She was self-conscious of that possibility now.

When she thought she might be complete, she reached out to Jennifer, wanting her to reciprocate and reach out as well. But Jennifer only stared at her and backed up. She didn't run, or scream; she just backed through the bedroom door and shut it calmly, as if she'd accidentally barged in on a funeral wake.

Whitney stood alone. Her eyes disappeared along with her mouth. Her skin became pale and her hair black, and then she disappeared altogether.

She let her consciousness drift through her bedroom window and watched Jennifer get into her Durango and calmly pull away from Eternity Vineyards. She drove slowly down the path that led to the highway, and Whitney instantly missed her. She was sorry and wanted to tell her so. She wanted to follow her, but she knew that was impossible, so she gave up and let herself float around Eternity, waiting on the ether for Jennifer's return.

TWENTY-ONE

A fter Jennifer had dropped him off, Mike walked past the pool on the way to his apartment. At that time, before everything changed, he felt angry. Jennifer made him angry. Eternity Vineyards made him angry. And it made him angry to brick up the room with all that wine still in it. He wanted what he felt after drinking it in the cellar, even if it made him see little girls that weren't really there—or at least he was pretty sure weren't there. He contemplated going back and opening the room again to get to the bottles. A sledgehammer would do; he could bust down the bricks. It felt like the greatest idea he ever had.

Of course Jennifer would never allow it, but she wouldn't have to know. After all, he didn't kill the children, and if they were already dead, and the wine already made, why should it go to waste? Jennifer wouldn't understand, and there was no way to make it make sense to her. But now, nothing was making sense to him, either. He couldn't think clearly. He hadn't thought clearly for a day and a half, not since he saw the new man through the windows at the indoor pool.

He noticed him camped out by the steaming Jacuzzi. It was a cool Saturday evening, but the heated pool and spa at his condos remained popular throughout the winter. You could heat up in the spa, get out and cool down in the pool, heat up again, cool down, and repeat as many times as you could stand.

This new tenant was obviously fit and looked all the more striking given that his head was completely shaved yet he sported a neatly trimmed black goatee. Even in passing, he could see the man's tan was nearly perfect, not at all like some who overused the tanning beds during the winter. For a moment he thought he might be naturally tan, maybe Latino or Middle Eastern.

Without breaking eye contact, and as he rubbed himself with a towel, the man watched Mike watching him. He wore a black Speedo, and his unabashed metrosexuality was stunning. Mike found himself excited while examining the man, his eyes drifting down and passing favorable judgment on the impressive bulge inside the man's swimsuit.

When his restraint finally returned, Mike looked away. He continued to his apartment past the windows that enclosed the crystal blue water of the lighted pool. Yet even as he made his way, he glanced at the man, and with every glance, he found the man watching him with blue, cougar eyes. Not smiling, not scowling, just watching, the way a predator watches its prey from a distance with hunger, or maybe lust.

Then he saw what made his heart nearly stop. There was no one at the pool but the man, and he had a bottle of wine—a black bottle of wine—a black bottle of wine with no label sitting on a small table next to his towel-draped cedar chaise lounge. Beside it were two bulbous wine glasses with extra-thin stems, one filled a quarter of the way with red wine, the other empty and clean, as if waiting.

The man seemed to notice Mike noticing the bottle. He glanced at it and smiled, and then back at Mike, watching every move Mike made. Mike suddenly felt like bawling. He hurried past the pool and ran up the stairs that led to his apartment.

He entered quickly and closed the door behind him, his mind incapable of thought. He acted on instinct and reflex; reason and logic no longer applied. That man had that wine—*the* wine!

Within minutes he was changed into a swimsuit, towel in hand. He wore his earbuds for no other reason than to give the appearance of wanting to be alone. For the same reason he grabbed a paperback off his bookshelf. The title didn't matter. Of course he hoped his pretense wouldn't be *too* effective.

Briefly he considered the possibility that the man was a prostitute, that he may only be falling into his commercially insincere trap. Maybe the man's returning glances were merely propositions. That sort of thing had been known to occur at Cactus Shade before, especially by the pool. There were rules against it. He considered it for no longer than it took him to check his wallet for a sufficient amount of cash; he made sure he brought it with him.

Minutes later, Mike strolled through the glass door into the pool area. He took a chaise lounge at the opposite end from where the man was stationed and tried not to look too obvious. He aimed his charade at giving an appearance that this was his usual routine. Obviously, the man was new to the condo complex; he wouldn't know any different.

As he laid out his towel, he heard a quick splash in the water. He glanced across and realized the stunning Adonis had dove in at the shallow end. He watched him swimming underwater like a graceful frog towards the deep end where Mike stood. He remained below the surface, and Mike wondered if he ever needed air. Quickly he sat down on his lounger before the man reached his end of the pool, again not wanting to appear to be waiting.

Finally, the bald man broke through the surface of the water and supported himself with his arms crossed over the edge. He looked directly at Mike.

"Hello," Mike said, unable to do anything but stare at the blue eyes he'd seen from a distance.

"*Guten tag*," the man spoke with a thick German accent. "That means, hello, in my country."

"Germany?" Mike guessed, trying to sound fashionably bored.

"Austria," The man said. He raised himself out of the pool like a gymnast, and Mike watched as each inch of his body revealed itself. The man walked over to Mike and extended his wet hand. Mike took it. "My name is Wolfgang."

To Mike, all of the man's w's sounded like v's and his a's like ah's, so his name came across as *volfgahn*.

"Michael," Mike returned.

"I was just catching a swim and Jacuzzi and having some wine. Would you like to join me for a glass? Do you drink?" Wolfgang asked.

Their eyes locked in a silent moment, and then Mike looked over to the black bottle; he tried to keep his lips from quivering. "*Ja*," Mike joked.

"*Ah, Sprechen Sie Deutsch*? Do you speak German?"

Mike let out a nervous giggle: "God, no. I think 'yes' is the only word I know."

"Well, *das ist* a good one," Wolfgang smiled. "Come; bring your towel and sit with me. I think you'll like this particular wine." Wolfgang went to his side of the pool and didn't look back. Mike watched the way Wolfgang's wet buttocks contracted with the movement of his confident stride.

He got up, pulled the silent earphones from his ears and grabbed his towel. He followed behind Wolfgang looking around to see if anyone else was watching his easy capitulation. He spread his towel on the lounger beside Wolfgang's.

Wolfgang picked up the black bottle and the clean glass and poured it half full. He handed it to Mike who took it and examined the dark liquid with wonder as if holding a five-carat diamond. "Is this what I think it is?" Mike asked.

"*Ja*," Wolfgang said in a deviously sexy whisper.

* * *

For the last thirty-six hours, Mike had sat on the rug in Wolfgang's apartment with a black bottle in his hands. Now, he blankly watched, Ellen reruns on TV, vaguely aware that it might be Monday; it might be the afternoon. There had been nothing else with Wolfgang, no sex, no conversation. Mike hadn't even showered or changed out of his swimming trunks. He just sat with his bottle, waiting for Wolfgang to return and provide him with another.

TWENTY-TWO

——— • ———

Jennifer drove instinctively down the highway, seeing it, reacting to it, but not noticing it passing by at all. She rejoiced that Melissa saw what she thought might only be a form of psychotic hallucination on her part. But far from a quaint tale of a haunting that attracted people who liked to believe in ghosts, this thing—this entity—was going to ruin her chances of selling the place, pure and simple.

She wished her only problem was a structural defect she missed for not looking in the basement. Structural defects could be repaired, *or bricked over*. How in the hell was she going to fix this? Her world was starting to unravel as the impossibility of the situation became clearer to her.

She needed a friend. She wanted Mike to call her back. She needed his support. She needed him to help figure this thing out. But he didn't even believe her about the girl. Even if he saw her, he refused to acknowledge it. Her mind reeled trying to figure out her next move.

Start some damage control, she thought. *You have to start some damage control, right now. Call Melissa!* What if Melissa spread a bad word about the place to Bill Mack and Steve Dillard? What was she going to say when she called her? *Hey, Hon, seems you forgot your shoes?* She put on her cell phone headset, but the first number she dialed was Mike's.

Again, only the voicemail, but this time Jennifer left more details: "Mike, we're in trouble. I know you don't believe me about the girl in the house, but you're going to have to tell that to Melissa. She just ran screaming from the place. Mike, I don't know what to do here, and I don't know where the hell you are. So, please call me before we end up living in this damn vineyard on food stamps."

Jennifer gathered herself and took a deep breath. She dialed Melissa's cell. Though she worried what she would say to her, that worry was soon alleviated; she wouldn't have to say a word.

"Jennifer," Melissa said as soon as she picked up, "I don't know what kind of shit you're trying to pull, but I hope you and that faggot, Mike, got a good laugh out of it. Is this your little get even? Is this your juvenile way of making me look like a fool? Well fuck you, and I hope you don't think Bill and Steve are going to find it funny either. They barely even know you, bitch!" Then the line went dead.

"Melissa?" Jennifer covered her mouth and began to cry. She was alone and floating somewhere outside of reality. She pulled over to the side of the road, not sure she could drive and bawl at the same time. For ten minutes on an empty highway, Jennifer broke down. Not a single car passed her by.

She thought about calling Samuel, but it was so very wrong and way too early in their relationship to expect someone else to provide emotional support. No one liked hauling someone else's baggage around right off the bat. Relationships were supposed to start off bubbly and fun, not stuck in a tar pit.

She liked Samuel. She fantasized about their possible future, and now all that would be blown. For sure it would be blown, but it couldn't be helped. There was no one else to turn to. Mike wasn't calling, Melissa hated her, Tammy was a voicemail, and her ex would revel in her misfortune. Everyone else was a customer or an acquaintance. She felt isolated. She was going down fast and looking for anything afloat. Samuel still had his head above water, so she dialed his number.

He answered on the first ring, obviously witnessing her name on his caller ID. "Jennifer! He said with surprise." Then as if whispering a happy secret they shared, "I was going to call you tonight when things slowed down a bit. How's it going?"

"I'm not doing so well, Samuel. I was wondering if we could talk tonight." Jennifer knew her voice sounded shaky, and after she spoke, she heard nothing but silence on the other end. She disgusted herself. She could feel Samuel pulling away. She could almost make up an excuse for him, and part of her wanted to. The silence continued. "Samuel?" Jennifer said, wondering if the line had gone dead.

"I'm sorry, Jennifer, I was just clearing it with my assistant manager. He'll take over for me. Where are you? Let me come to where you are? Let me come and get you." He sounded like an overprotective mother, but his lack of hesitation washed over her with a compassion she had never known, not from anyone. She began to openly cry.

"Jennifer, where are you?" Samuel nearly shouted. Jennifer could hear the worry in his voice.

"I'm okay, Samuel. I'm just a little overwhelmed. I'm surprised you even want to talk. I feel like a basket case right now. I wouldn't call you like this, but—"

Samuel interrupted, "It's okay, Jennifer. It's going to be all right." His voice was deep and smooth, and she fell into it like an overstuffed pillow. "Don't worry about a thing," he said. "Tell me where you are, so I can come and get you."

A laugh broke through in Jennifer's voice, "I'm a little far away. I'm out by Sonoita. I'm just leaving Eternity Vineyards. I'm okay Samuel, really. I was just wondering if I could see you tonight. Maybe we could talk. You've been so nice in the past; I could come by Fifty-Five Degrees."

"What's this 'I've been so nice in the past'? Now I'm a stranger?" He sounded irritated, but humorously so.

Jennifer laughed again, feeling embarrassed.

"Come to the restaurant," Samuel said. "We'll have dinner. Have you eaten?"

"No, actually," Jennifer replied.

"Well then you have to eat. Are you sure you're all right. Can you drive?"

"Yes, of course. Really I'm fine. It's just one of those days, you know?"

...Like when a ghost shreds your entire client roster. Like when you find kiddie shackles in your basement.

"Sure, I understand," he said. Just get here and tell me all about it; just get here safe, all right?"

"I will."

"It's going to be okay," Samuel insisted again, "so you drive safe."

"I will."

But Jennifer drove faster than she ever did, not even watching for the police in her rearview mirror. She drove toward the good feelings she felt waiting for her.

TWENTY-THREE

H ello, Jennifer," Travis said as she walked into the store. He was on his knees stocking wine in the lower racks of the Italian section.

"Hi, Travis. Do you work every night?"

"I think so," Travis said. "Actually just Wednesday through Sunday. Hey, Samuel said you were coming, and I should bring you back to his office." Travis got up and straightened his attire. "It's this way."

Jennifer followed him through the drapes leading to the wine bar and then to the back just beyond the kitchen. He knocked lightly on a door that read, Manager, and then opened it slightly without waiting for a reply.

"Mr. Ansell? Ms. Dickerman's here." Travis opened the door all the way, and Jennifer saw Samuel coming around from behind his desk. He took off a pair of reading glasses and dumped them on a stack of papers.

"Jennifer! You made it."

"I did."

Samuel opened his arms and took her in. His embrace surprised and seemed a little forward, given that previously they only shared dinner together, but it didn't stop her from returning his gesture enthusiastically.

"Thanks, Travis," Samuel said. Travis nodded then headed back to the store.

"Come in; sit down. I thought this would be more private for us. I was just doing some ordering while I waited for you. You sounded so upset; I was worried."

"Oh, no Really, I'm fine," Jennifer waved dismissively, hoping to brush off her previous meltdown.

The office was small and adorned with the functional type of fake-wood furniture. There were stacks of papers, files and supplies in every corner. She found herself sitting on a padded folding chair next to an unopened carton of toilet paper. Across from her was a gray metal filing cabinet.

Everything was the opposite at McWilliam's Real Estate. Every office had to appear ultra-successful. It was important the customer believed you were financially successful. A successful person could sell their house for a lot of money. It was just as important your peers thought the same. She imagined that here the food, wine, and service were great right up-front, or nothing else mattered. There was nothing up anyone's sleeve. No need for pretenses.

"Nice office," Jennifer said, looking around.

"It's not even mine; see..." Samuel moved a misplaced dishtowel exposing a brass nameplate with plastic wood and engraved white letters that said Bob Wilcox. "It's my assistant's office." Then, looking around as if contemplating a glorious past: "But it used to be all mine." They both laughed, and Samuel wheeled his chair around the side of the desk and sat with Jennifer. "So, what's wrong?"

Jennifer sighed, "It's nothing really; I'm having a lot of trouble at the Vineyard, that's all. I lost a very important client today, and I can't find Mike anywhere. He's been gone for two days. I can't get him by phone, and he's not at his apartment, but his car's still there. I think he might be avoiding me, and I don't know why." Then Jennifer asked, almost desperately, "Has Mike been in here lately?"

"No," Samuel shook his head, "not since you two were in here together with Susan and Jeff and that military guy."

"Well, I don't know where to find him, and our whole project just hit a major stumbling block." Jennifer felt like crying anew as she drug up her trouble, but she fought it back.

"Have you gone to the police?"

"I went there early this morning. They took a report, but said even if they found him they wouldn't notify me, not if he didn't want them to. They'd just ask him to call. I'm out of my head, Samuel. I really am."

"If I see him, you'll be the first to know," Samuel took her hand.

"Thanks."

"So, what's wrong with Eternity Vineyards?" he asked.

Jennifer nearly choked. *What isn't?* she thought. "Samuel, I warn you, this is the crazy part. I don't think you're going to believe me, and I don't know if it's even a good idea to tell you, because—" Jennifer paused, not wanting to sound silly or somehow mentally strange. What he thought of her mattered now more to her than she wanted it to.

Samuel spoke quietly and earnestly, he leaned in closer: "I'm your friend. Whatever you have to say, I'm going to believe. I'm on *your* side."

Jennifer looked into his eyes and saw that he meant what he said. Selling as a career had taught her to fake what Samuel's eyes were saying to her now, but he wasn't faking. She squeezed his hand, then stood and paced as she spoke.

"Do you remember the legend you told me about, I mean, about Eternity Vineyards?"

"Sure," Samuel said.

"Well, I think it's true. I didn't tell you before, when we were having dinner because I thought I was just seeing things, and I didn't want you to think I was crazy, but today a big client of mine saw the same thing and it terrified her, and she's blaming me for it. She thinks Mike and I were playing a trick on her. Even worse, she's going to tell my other two potential buyers, and that means I'm going to have to go to the open market with Eternity Vineyards. That means it could take—I don't know— maybe even years to sell." Jennifer took a breath.

"What do you mean, seeing things?" Samuel asked.

"The girl. There really is a girl, but not a real girl. I don't know; I mean, she's a ghost I think." Jennifer dropped her head. She didn't want to see his look of incredulity, or maybe even pity.

"Yes, Whitney; it was Whitney wasn't it?" Samuel said. For all his poise, confidence, business sense, and middle age he sounded like a little boy who believed in ghost stories told around a campfire.

Jennifer looked at him. "You believe it?"

"I thought you were going to tell me something really insane." Samuel got up from his chair. "Jennifer, I haven't been completely honest with you either."

She hated statements that started like that. "Meaning?" she asked.

"Meaning...When you were here before, I brought up the legend about the ghost because back in college I, too, saw the ghost. I saw Whitney Maddock."

Samuel meant what he said, and Jennifer could tell he was drudging up disturbing memories, but he continued: "You know, I always believed it was a brush with, I don't know, maybe some kind of psychosis. I was under a lot of pressure in school, and it's not uncommon, I've been told, that young people have moments of that sort of thing when they're away from home for the first time, you know, in a strange place and under a lot of pressure to make the grade.

"Anyway," Samuel continued, "I was out in the vineyard, and Robert Maddock was in the house, watching me from an upstairs window. I saw him, and I remember thinking the old coot probably thought I was going to pull up a damn vine or something and steal it. Anyway, I was walking down a row, and I saw a body lying in the dirt, a pale young girl with long hair. There was blood all over her. I ran up to her. I don't know what I thought I was going to do, CPR or something, but then she stood up. She just stood right up and looked at me, and her face, I mean her eyes, they were just—"

"Black spaces," Jennifer said.

Samuel nodded slowly. "Like the whole of outer space was in her skull. I admit, I screamed...oh, I screamed, and I ran. I never looked back. The old man was watching the whole thing. I'm sure of it. I got in my car and left. I made things up on my term paper that weren't even true just to fill in the details I never got while I was out there. Last time we were together, I wanted to know if you had seen the same thing. I'm sorry I should have been more forthcoming, but I didn't want you to think—"

"I know what you mean," Jennifer said. "I didn't tell you what I knew, either. I didn't want you to think I was crazy."

"Then we're a fine pair, aren't we?" Samuel said, and at that they both laughed and hugged again, and Jennifer felt the tension of the day easing up, so when he kissed her, she let him, and when the kiss eventually ended, they looked at each other in pleasant surprise.

"I guess we *are* a fine pair," Jennifer said.

* * *

They ate dinner again at the same table as before. The amber light of the candle made Jennifer feel like she'd come from hell to her own tailor-made heaven. The contrast of the day was stark beyond understanding, but she liked the wave she was riding tonight. This time Samuel suggested Chianti, and they drank it with abandon, their fledgling romance taking flight.

Of course, she hadn't told the entire story of Eternity Vineyards. She remained acutely aware of that. But new relationships don't require un-bricking the past, she thought. Everyone has skeletons in their closet. She simply had chains and pentagrams.

"I want to see the ghost again," Samuel said suddenly like a fighter pilot wanting another dogfight. His eyes beamed with expectation. "Will you take me out there?"

Jennifer recoiled inwardly. She wasn't selling the place anymore; she was a guide at a freak show. For one sick moment she wondered if she could make any serious money that way. *Step right up folks and see the ghosts, see the sacrifices, vomit at the smell of death!* "She's somewhat unpredictable," Jennifer said. "You might not see a thing, you know, or you might not like what you see. I just wish she'd go away, find the damn light or something and walk into it." Jennifer took a large drink from her glass. Samuel refilled it.

"We should bring Susan with us," Samuel said.

"Who?"

"You know; you met her. Remember? "She's that psychic with the blonde hair. Her husband, Jeff, is my accountant.

Jennifer felt cynical, and it leaked out in her voice. "I know; I got her business card. How do you know she's not fake? I mean most of them are, aren't they?"

"She did a chart for this place before me and Gene opened it, an astrological chart. Apparently you can have one done for places, just like people. She was spot on. She said we'd be profitable inside a year. She said we'd get four stars in the paper. Critics would love us. She even predicted when Gene and I would pay off our business loan. She was right about all of it. Maybe she can give us—" Samuel recognized and corrected his error in diction: "I mean, maybe she can give *you* some pointers?

"What other kind of consultant do you get for this type of thing?" Jennifer said with resignation. "When you think about it, it's a business problem just like any other."

"True," Samuel said. "Well, sort of."

Jennifer sniggered and shook her head. "She's got to keep this thing under wraps. I don't want this ending up as her PR piece in the Arizona Republic."

"I think she will. She's not real aggressive like some of them. I don't think she even advertises her store."

* * *

After dinner, after the wine, in the parking lot by her car, she turned to him, and he took her in his arms. They kissed again, and Jennifer knew this was where she wanted to be, where she wanted to remain.

"You don't have to go home," Samuel said to her. "I can show you my place, my house. I have a spare bedroom; we can still be together and take it slow."

Jennifer fought her conflict to go or to remain. "If I went to your place, I wouldn't stay in the spare bedroom." She looked at him, unblinking. "If I went to your place, I couldn't take it slow." Her large brown eyes found his, and she didn't look away. "Will you have me over next time?"

All she wanted was for him to respect her; she had to say no the first time. She hated to say *no*. She hated walking out of heaven.

"I'd have you over any time," Samuel said.

"I like you," Jennifer said with an unfamiliar and severe sincerity. "There's going to be a next time, if you want there to be."

"I've been out of the whole relationship scene for a few years now," Samuel said. "I can wait. It's worth it for me; you're worth it to me."

They kissed again and then parted. Jennifer got into her car, and before Samuel closed her door, he reminded her: "Meet me here tomorrow at ten, and we'll go over to her store."

"We don't have an appointment," Jennifer said. "She said she's always booked."

Samuel smiled. "I have a feeling she'll make room for what we're bringing."

TWENTY-FOUR

A s they entered, a bell above the door jingled, and Jennifer heard Susan shout from somewhere in the rear of the store, "I'm in the office; come on back!"

Spiritually Speaking was mostly a bookstore for the occult. Witchcraft, spiritualism, and various other new age topics made up the bulk of her literary stock. The counter was a long glass cabinet with colored rocks, daggers, jewelry, and other offbeat collectables on display. Wafting a light perfume into the air, the incense Mike said he loved so much burned in an ornate brass holder on top of the counter near the cash register. Behind the counter, lying on the same table as the credit card reader, an obese and disinterested black cat opened its green eye's only halfway to examine the new customers. It apparently had no intention of ever moving.

As she walked with Samuel through the store to the back, Jennifer half-expected a darkened room, a crystal ball and some candles—a classic Coney Island setup, but what she found looked more like a family therapist's office. There were two stuffed sofas in the middle of the room on a large carpet, one facing the other with a coffee table between them and a matching stuffed armchair at the end.

Off in a corner was a tiny table supporting several coloring books and a bucket of broken crayons. There were plastic chairs, and next to them, an overflowing toy box. Waxy colored streaks covered the walls of that corner, and Susan had apparently given up trying whitewash them. Her own modest desk and bookshelves sat apart from the conference area in another corner like an eavesdropping reminder that the entire room was really her place of work.

"I honestly don't think I can help you," Susan said after she studied the road map Samuel gave her with the route to Eternity Vineyards highlighted in yellow. Susan was pleasant, and seemed truly dismayed at what Jennifer and Samuel were laying out to her. She leaned forward. "I would love to do a séance with both of you. And Samuel, you're right, from a purely academic stance, it would be interesting to investigate this phenomenon, but Jennifer, a ghost is not the same as contacting a dead relative."

"I'll be honest with you," Jennifer said, "I'm new to all this. What's the difference? I thought that's what a ghost was. Can't you help her on her way; isn't that what ghosts want?"

Susan removed her glasses and let them hang from the thin silver chain around her neck. She concentrated on what she was trying to say: "Ghosts don't go to the other side like in the movies. They never leave the place they haunt. They're forever attached to that place. Everything in our world has a spiritual dimension. Just as you and I, and Samuel have a spiritual dimension, a house also has a spiritual dimension. Even this coffee table has a spiritual side to it. In fact, some say the physical world is only a representation of the spiritual reality that lies beneath it."

Jennifer looked at her as if she were suffering through the second hour of a church sermon. She almost glanced at her watch.

"What I mean," Susan continued, "is that 'Whitney' is as much a part of the house as the bricks and wood are. She's part of the spiritual definition of the house. She can't leave the house any more than the stone foundation can. Her destiny is with that house.

"How does that happen?" Samuel asked. "How does a person end up a ghost?"

"Well, people have different ideas," Susan said. "All I can do is tell you the one I think makes the most sense to me." She leaned forward and continued. "I think a person has such an attachment to a place while they're alive that when they die their spirit becomes one with it. They form into the spirit of the place. Like wood becomes rock when it petrifies, I think a spirit can petrify into a place."

Susan turned to Jennifer. "You said this girl killed herself, right?"

Jennifer nodded.

"Well, sometimes a haunting centers on that kind of tragedy. But what's interesting is that her mother isn't haunting the place, and suicide alone usually isn't enough to cause a haunting. I suspect there's more to this girl and Eternity Vineyards than we know, maybe some family secrets that never saw the light of day."

Jennifer fidgeted in her seat and felt tempted to spill what she knew, but how would she explain bricking up the place so Mike and her could get a bigger profit? She began to feel connected to the events in the cellar, complicit like a co-conspirator. She kept silent as Susan continued.

"Jennifer, the bottom line is this: we can do a séance, and I hope you will let me do that, but all we're going to accomplish with a séance is maybe finding out what happened to Whitney. We can establish it's a true haunting; we can make contact; maybe we can find out why she's scaring away your clients, but we can't *bust* this ghost, because she can't leave, even if she wants to. Whitney will continue for as long as Eternity Vineyards continues."

"So, what am I supposed to do?" Jennifer found it hard to hide her frustration. She crossed her arms and spoke with exaggeration bordering on sarcasm. "Burn the place to the ground to get rid of her?"

"Even if you did," Susan responded, "she'd probably still haunt the vineyard, just like when Samuel saw her twenty-some years ago."

Jennifer dropped her head. "This deal is dead. It's as dead as the Maddock family. My partner and I were going to sell the estate and be set. We got it cheap, and it's worth so much. I thought in the beginning that even if it had a ghost that would just add to its charm, but it's nothing like that. This thing is horrible."

Everyone was silent for a moment. Then Susan spoke, "People like the idea of a ghost, but that's because they've never really seen one. The truth is apparitions are terrifying. They disrupt our physical world in a way most people can't understand. To be in an environment like that just makes a person feel confused and threatened. Just like your client was."

"Mike's gone," Jennifer said. "I don't know where he is. This problem with Eternity Vineyards is something he and I have to solve, whatever the outcome, especially since the outcome looks like we're out of business. We put everything we had into that house. I don't know what we're going to do." Jennifer looked to Susan: "You haven't seen or heard from Mike have you?"

"No; I didn't know he was missing."

"He's been gone for a few days now," Samuel added. "She's even filed a missing person's report, but there's nothing."

"That doesn't sound good," Susan said. "I've known Mike for a few years now; he's one of my regulars." She got up and went to her desk, and from a side drawer retrieved a large deck of ornate tarot cards. "I can do a location reading for him, maybe we can find him."

Jennifer stood up and grabbed her purse from the couch. "I'm sorry, Susan. I don't mean any disrespect, but I can't make decisions based on this stuff." She motioned to the tarot cards Susan had already begun laying out on the coffee table. "I just don't work this way."

Susan didn't look offended; rather, Jennifer noticed a look of concern. "I understand," she said and gathered the cards back into the deck.

"No, wait," Samuel interrupted. "I want to know. I *have* made some decisions this way."

Susan looked back and forth from Samuel to Jennifer waiting for a cue.

"Fine," Jennifer said incredulously, "whatever you think will work, go ahead." She sat back down, but kept hold of her purse like a shield. "I just hope my lack of faith doesn't spoil things. I mean, I believe in what I see. I've seen this Whitney as you have, Samuel, and just like Melissa did. So, I believe in that, even if I don't know what it is. But I'm not ready to start burning incense and looking into crystal balls. I'm a realist."

"So am I," Susan said, looking up indignantly from her cards. "I only believe in what *I* see, but I see things differently, that's all." She continued to flip cards, and a distressed look came across her face.

"What?" Jennifer asked, realizing with some shame that she was surrendering the point she just tried to make.

"I'm inquiring about his existence," Susan said. "It's a test I do to make sure I'm in tune. It's an easy question; if I don't get anything here. I give up until another day, because I know that he exists. But the cards say he doesn't."

"Oh my God," Jennifer said. She put her hand to her mouth. "Please don't tell me that."

Susan continued to look at the cards as if she didn't hear her. "Jennifer," Susan asked, "when was the last time you saw him?"

Jennifer reflexively gripped Samuel's hand, "Last Saturday night, early in the evening, when I dropped him off at his apartment."

"Because the reading I'm getting is that he hasn't existed since that morning."

"Are you telling me that he's dead?"

Susan looked genuinely puzzled as she examined the cards laid out before her. "No, not really. It's not like he's dead, it's like he doesn't exist anymore."

"I don't get it," Jennifer said.

"I don't either," Susan replied. "I really don't understand at all what the cards are saying. I'm sorry...I hope he turns up. I hope everything is alright with him." Disturbed by her results, she gathered her cards back into the deck.

Jennifer looked at Susan for a moment, then to Samuel, then back to Susan: "What kind of shit is that?" Jennifer said.

Susan looked stunned.

"Jennifer, please—" Samuel said.

"No, Samuel, this is bullshit. I thought psychics were supposed to tell you good things. I thought you were supposed to tell people what they wanted to hear, to make them feel better." Jennifer stood up and walked to the office door.

"Jennifer," Susan said, "the reason I'm always booked is because I don't do what you think I should be doing right now."

Jennifer tried to think of something to say, some way to justifiably extricate herself from the situation, but she hadn't told Susan everything; she couldn't, so she turned and walked out.

Behind her, Samuel was apologizing, and when she got to the car, she heard Samuel calling out: "Jennifer, wait a minute." He ran up to her.

"Samuel, I'm sorry. I know she's your friend, and she's a nice person but—"

"No, don't worry about that," Samuel said. "People walk out on her all the time. It comes with telling the truth, I think."

"Samuel, the truth is my life is falling apart."

"So, I'll help you pick up the pieces."

"You don't understand; I haven't told you or her everything there is to know."

Samuel's expression begged her to be reasonable. "So, tell me, for God's sake."

She paused. "Do you still want to see the ghost? And can you keep a secret?

"Yeah, of course."

Jennifer considered what she was about to say, and would have said nothing at all, but she had no ally without Mike. If Mike were around, they could solve this together, but there was no way she could handle what was happening to her alone. "Okay," Jennifer said cautiously, "I'll tell you on the way. But you can't say anything to anyone."

TWENTY-FIVE

W hitney went to the study. She drifted there on the ether after Jennifer had left, after she closed the bedroom door and drove away. Once there, she never moved or averted her gaze. She held her stare from the vantage point of the desk, watching as the light grew in the library in the morning and faded at night. With the increase and diminishment of the light, the shadows in the room changed their shape, and she felt the possibility of unity with them—if only they were constant, just as she was constant. If the physical world would stop moving in front of her, she could sit and stare at it forever and feel at peace. But the world continued to change, and she remained its unchanging witness.

She was sorry for the Melissa-thing. She should have behaved better, but even the horrors of being alone were better than Eternity Vineyards ending up in the wrong hands. Robert proved that to her with the whole of his life.

She watched the study fill with the light of another morning, and then she heard the sound of crunching gravel. A car was approaching out front—it had to be Jennifer. She was back!

Whitney shot her consciousness through the roof of the house and viewed the estate from above. But it wasn't Jennifer at all; it was the gray car again. It stopped by the front door, and the same bald man as before step out. From the other side, Mike got out, and then all her hope crashed before her, because she saw the object in his hand.

Mike carried a black bottle, the same kind her father stored in the cellar. He took sips from it as he walked to the front door. Then he set the bottle down and produced a ring of keys from his jacket pocket. The bald man came up behind him, and like before, he looked around as if someone could be watching. She knew what the wine could do. She knew how it ended her father and began a monstrous version of him. If Mike was drinking it, then he was a monster, and if the bald man was drinking it, then he was a monster, too. There were no exceptions. The wine made monsters out of men. She knew it.

She wanted to run, but there was no getting away. She'd tried it before, when her father was alive and working in his room. She could only go up in the air to the point where the vineyard disappeared. From the height where the last view was possible, her upward travel ended, and she could only go to the edge of the property in any direction, and when she got to the property lines, her travel ended. There was no way for her to leave.

And if she didn't consciously try to stay at the extremes of Eternity, she gravitated back to the house. Once back at the house, if she didn't put forward at least a little effort, she ended up in the corner of her room where she had huddled for safety as her father took Kerrie to the basement. Somehow, she was attached to that corner by an invisible tether that she could neither see nor understand. If she allowed herself to float on the ether of Eternity long enough, it always deposited her there.

Mike let himself in, and the bald man followed close behind. She stopped her psychic effort, and like a diver, she gracefully accelerated in a fall that took her all the way to the foyer. There she put herself in a corner of the ceiling and watched.

"*Wunderbar* (wonderful)," the bald man said quietly to himself as he looked around the foyer.

"I told you you'd like it." Mike said, trying to over-please. Then he consoled himself with another sip from his bottle.

Wolfgang put up his hand to silence him and walked slowly into the office. Whitney followed invisibly along the edge of the ceiling. He ran his fingers over the books in the bookcase, and then along the dark wood paneling of the wall. "*Das ist ein schönes Haus* (This is a beautiful house)," he said, "*Das ist vollkommen* (This is perfect)!"

He walked to the desk and sat in the leather chair. He straightened his sport coat and stretched his neck from side to side. Then he ran his hands over the desktop, taking in the polished wooden surface.

Whitney saw the similarity at once: behind the desk, in the leather chair, in front of the window, he was her father all over again, but maybe even worse. He didn't drink the wine like Mike did. Mike drank the wine like her father, constantly sipping. Wolfgang didn't seem to want it at all. As bad as the wine was, the ability to resist it and yet be associated with it suggested an even darker character.

Mike walked into the office. "What do you think?"

"We must acquire this property for ourselves," Wolfgang said. His image was framed by the stained glass edges of the window giving it an almost immortal religious quality.

"Jennifer wants to sell it."

"*Quatsch* (Nonsense)," Wolfgang spoke arrogantly. "Maddock would never have given it to her if she was selling it."

"It's true. Maddock made her promise not to sell, and then he took her word for it. It was just a verbal agreement. It means nothing." Mike quickly wet his lips with more wine.

Wolfgang looked down at the desk considering the actions of Robert Maddock, then he smiled slightly: "Maddock *ist ein Idiot* (Maddock is an idiot). What was he thinking? Silly prophecies, no doubt."

"That's right," Mike said. "He had a dream that Jennifer was the new caretaker. She went along with him just to get the place. After the sale, he wouldn't have a leg to stand on. Him dying just made everything easier."

"This property," Wolfgang said, "*das ist* yours as well, *ja?*"

Mike looked suddenly ashamed. "Well, technically, the title is only in Jennifer's name. Maddock would only sell it to her, no one else. But I invested thirty thousand of my own money; that's one-third, and I have a promissory note. I get thirty percent of the profit when it sells."

"*Und wo ist dieser Vertrag* (And where is this contract)?"

"What?"

"The note, where is it?" Wolfgang prodded impatiently.

Mike went quiet and looked down. "I think Jennifer has it." He sipped his wine again.

Wolfgang shook his head slowly. "*Scheissidiot* (fucking idiot)," he said softly. "This Realtor screws over an old man, but she's going to keep her word to you, *ja?*" Wolfgang stood up from behind the desk. "I will have to acquire the property from her myself. When she pays you your share, you will give it back to me."

Mike looked hurt. "Give it to you?"

"*Ja*, Michael," Wolfgang said calmly and offhandedly. "You don't think you can buy that varietal in the market do you?" He pointed at the bottle in Mike's hand and chortled: "*In*

Ihrem Safeway; in Ihrem Walmart (In your Safeway, in your Walmart)?"

As if Wolfgang might take it from him, Mike gripped the bottle tighter and held it close to his chest.

"Don't worry, Michael, soon we will be making kegs of it, and you will help me, *ja?*"

"Mike looked at his bottle: "I will."

"You are positive the candelabra, the pentagram, the book—these things are still in *das* room?"

"Yes, absolutely. Everything is exactly as I described it to you, and no one has been in there since I bricked it up."

"*Das ist gut* (That's good)." Wolfgang said.

Whitney panicked. It was going to start again. She'd have to watch it all over, just like when her father did it. The screams, the children, she couldn't go through it again. She couldn't be responsible again. Doing nothing was the same as doing everything. She had to try.

She lowered her consciousness to the middle of the doorway. When they turned to leave, they were facing her; so she willed herself into stillness, and when Mike started screaming, she knew they could see her.

"That's her, Wolfgang! That's the thing from the cellar! How did she get out?"

Whitney summoned all her mental strength and let out a curdling screech. Mike tried to cover his ears while still trying to hold the bottle. It sounded like a child burning in a tub of scalding water. He stumbled backward toward the desk and fell on the Islamic rug in front of it. He curled his knees to his chest in a feeble attempt to protect himself.

Wolfgang looked down at him and snapped loudly: "No wine on my rug!"

Then he turned to Whitney and smiled. Whitney stopped screeching: "*Dummes kleines Mädchen* (silly little girl)—don't you know that hell is waiting for you? When you get there, say hello to Kerrie for me." Wolfgang let out a laugh and didn't stop laughing as he walked through the office door and through her apparition as if she were only smoke.

She felt him pass through her, and for the first time since the instant before her suicide, she felt pain—a searing pain. She shrieked loudly enough to fill the house; Mike shrieked in response to her shrieking and for the moment they sounded like a tortured choir.

In the foyer, Wolfgang felt for his car keys and smiled at the satisfactory sound behind him. He walked to his car, and within seconds Mike came running out, stumbling behind him.

"Wait, Wolfgang!" Mike yelled. He slipped on the gravel as he ran after him and dropped the black bottle. Wine spilled like a natural disaster. "Oh God," Mike shouted. He quickly picked up the bottle without considering his scraped palms.

"Come, Michael. *Das Haus ist vollkommen* (The house is perfect). Let's go call your friend." Wolfgang began to whistle a tune as he climbed behind the wheel of his Mercedes.

TWENTY-SIX

T hey took Samuel's Crown Vic. Jennifer wished she could relax as they made their way south on the I-10, but she wasn't sure how Samuel was going to take the truth. She hoped he didn't just pull over and tell her to get out. She could see him speeding away in moral outrage.

"There's more to this vineyard and this ghost than I've told you," Jennifer said.

"So I gathered. Is it something illegal?"

"I don't think so, not on our part. But that doesn't mean we've done the right thing. When we went out to take possession of the property, as you know, we found Robert Maddock dead. When we found him, he had an old piece of paper in his hand; I think it was Whitney's suicide note."

Samuel glanced at Jennifer and then looked back to the road.

"It said, 'I gave her to him, Whitney 1957.' We never showed that to the police, and it probably didn't matter. The old guy looked like he had a heart attack, or a stroke, or something, you know? Totally natural."

Samuel looked at her again, and she felt a need for correction: "Well, as natural as anything is out there, anyway."

"Why didn't you show it to the police?" Samuel asked.

Jennifer sighed. "Because we didn't want anyone looking around. We found something else in the basement that Maddock never told me about, and needless to say, failed to include in his disclosure statement. In the basement is the wine cellar, but behind one of the wine racks, is a room, and in that room..." Jennifer had difficulty bringing herself to say it.

"In that room..." Samuel led.

"In that room is a kind of religious set up, I think some kind of witchcraft or satanic thing."

"You're kidding?"

"I wish I were."

"Maddock was a Satanist?"

"I don't think so. I mean, I don't know, but I think he wanted me to see it. To know what I was buying in to, so to speak."

"He could have just told you, for God's sake."

"That's just it; he really didn't have to. I promised him before he died that I'd never resell the place. He thought I was some kind of chosen one to take over as the caretaker. Truth is I was lying to him all along. We were working a scam on him. I was going to dump the place as soon as he moved out. He thought I was a good person...big idiot."

Samuel didn't comment.

"But that's not the worst of it," Jennifer said, acutely aware that Samuel hadn't yet corrected her ...*big idiot* statement. "In the room, I think—no that's not true—I *know* that children were sacrificed in there."

"What?"

"There was some kind of old book, a handmade book with drawings that described the exact intricacies of, I guess, the ceremony." Jennifer's spoke faster, trying to hurry through the unspeakable. "Samuel, they made wine and mixed in the children's blood."

"Oh good Lord, tell me you're joking," Samuel said. He looked much older and more serious than she had ever seen him.

"No, I'm not joking. I don't think the room has been used in a long time. The dust was so thick; I don't think it could have been used in a very long time. Maybe decades. That's why I don't think Maddock used it."

"It must have been his brother's," Samuel said.

"That could be. I mean maybe that would explain the suicide of his daughter and his wife." Jennifer looked out her side window. "When I think back on it, Robert Maddock was certain I'd never sell the place. I think he knew what Whitney would do whenever I brought someone around to look at it. But here's the thing: Mike and I bricked up the entrance to that room. We never told the police about it. We never told anyone. There were bottles of wine inside the room. We know children were killed there, but we bricked it up so we could sell it."

Jennifer grew more desperate in her speech. "We got the place for a hundred thousand in cash; we were going to sell it for two-and-a-half million. Robert Maddock believed I would live in the place. He had some dream that led him to Call-It-Home Realty. I just can't believe what I've become involved in—what I've done."

They sat in silence for a mile. "Like a babysitter," Samuel eventually said.

Jennifer looked at him quizzically.

"Like someone who would never use the room," he continued, "who would just watch over it. If you sold it, if anyone else got it, Maddock must have worried they'd use it."

"I think there's a power in the wine," Jennifer added. "I think it makes a person act like a kind of follower, a disciple maybe. One of the illustrations in the book seemed to suggest that."

"Sounds like the Maddock's were hiding quite the family secret."

"And I'm part of it," Jennifer said despondently. There was another pause with another non-correcting by Samuel. Jennifer knew he was passing judgment on her. Now she'd lose him, too.

"Well, I don't know about that," Samuel said. "It's still your place, right?"

"I didn't tell the police," Jennifer said. "Mike and I just bricked over the secret; we're supposed to sell it."

"It's probably just as well," Samuel said.

Jennifer looked surprised. "You think it's right to hide what happened in there?"

"Yes."

Jennifer began to wonder if she were the only one who thought what they did was wrong. "What about the children?" Jennifer said with growing irritation.

"What children? Did you see any dead children? And even if there were children killed, from when, the nineteen-fifties? There's nothing you can do about the past. It's not even your past. The past is as dead as Robert Maddock; it doesn't even exist anymore. All any of us have is here and now, and what we try with our best intentions to make of the present moment."

"So, you think I should sell the place?"

"I didn't say that. Personally, I think you should keep it."

Jennifer sank back in her seat. "I can't afford to. I can't afford to hold on to that kind of property. I have nothing coming in. I'd have to go back to slogging my guts out at McWilliam's."

"And yet, if you sell it," Samuel countered, "you know what might happen. You're not guilty for the past or what other people did. It seems to me, you haven't broken your word yet. It seems to me you're at a crossroad: go one way, and you give up control of the place, and for all you know, children might die again. Robert Maddock thought so anyway. Go the other way, and you're the saintly caretaker."

"I can't afford to be a saint," Jennifer said.

They were on the I-10 out of Phoenix, but traffic on the way to Tucson remained heavy. From the passenger window, she watched the desert go by. A hundred miles to go, and Samuel wasn't breaking the new silence that formed around them. He just drove.

So as he drove, she thought. And as she thought, she came to realize that every time she had an ethical decision to make, she used the same words. Eight years ago, Tammy begged her to stay with Dan. She begged like she was pleading for her life, even though it was only her crumbling security along with the solidarity of the Dickerman family that she begged for. But what could a twelve-year-old know about the irreconcilable differences of adults?

"I can't afford to be a saint, Tammy."

"Why can't you just give it another chance?" she had said.

It hadn't been violence or infidelity that made her want to file for divorce. Much worse was the conflict between her real estate career and the demands he put on her as a wife and mother.

Work was her necessity, even if they didn't need the money. She had to work to be free from him in her mind. Dan was going to take care of her completely, if she would take care of them completely. But the standard family roles were a prison for a salesgirl like her. She'd rather he beat her with a mistress tag-teaming in to help.

Tammy pointed out that he was offering a fair trade. She listened to their arguing, and knew her mother was the selfish one. The day she and Dan separated, she cried behind the closed door of her office at McWilliam's. Mike was with her, and she said the same thing to him, "I can't afford to be a saint, Mike." He agreed with her completely; he always did.

* * *

"I never thought I'd see it again," Samuel said when Eternity Vineyards came into view. "My God, it hasn't changed at all. Up on the hill like that, it looks out over everything, doesn't it? Just like a Spanish mission."

"When I first saw it," Jennifer replied, "when I first came out here to see Robert Maddock, I couldn't believe my eyes." Jennifer seemed distant. "Just park in the front by that Range Rover."

"Whose is that?"

"It was Robert's. I guess it's mine now."

Jennifer and Samuel went to the front door and Jennifer unlocked it. Samuel looked off toward the fields and pointed. "It was right out there, about halfway into that vineyard where I saw her."

"The first place I saw her," Jennifer added, "was in an upstairs bedroom. I've seen her every time I've been out here since." They entered the foyer.

"This is fantastic. It's almost identical to how I remember it."

"I never got the impression he messed with the place very much," Jennifer said. "It wasn't like he bragged to me about anything in here, except once he changed out the old boiler for a propane one. He never told me about any interior improvements, or projects, or even a garden. I think he simply lived here."

Jennifer pointed to the back of the house that existed beyond the staircase. "Just in those back rooms. Every other room, except maybe the study, is covered in dust and cobwebs, and the study's pretty dusty, too. We were going to get it cleaned before we started showing it."

"Hello, Whitney," Samuel said jokingly, his voice echoing off the walls.

"Shush!" Jennifer said. "Let the little bitch sleep, or whatever she does when she isn't costing me money, or ruining my life, or driving me crazy..." Jennifer let the words trail off as she walked into the study and flopped her keys and purse down on the desk. "Take a look around, if you like. If you see the little tart, tell her she's pissing me off." She put her head in her hands and rested her elbows on the desk.

"You look like a painting," Samuel said pointing behind her at the frame created around Jennifer by the stained glass margins of the window.

"It's nice isn't it?" she said? "I wonder what ego created it?"

"I should take your picture."

"I should show you the wine cellar," Jennifer stood up and came around and took Samuel's arm. "I'll give you my best sales pitch. I'll give you the million-dollar tour." Jennifer chuckled at her own gallows humor.

She took him to the entrance behind the stairs. The door opened without a creek, and she reached above the descending stairs to pull a string that attached to a light socket above. "After you." She motioned with her hand.

In the cellar they walked between the rows of towering wine barrels. Eventually, they made it to the concrete ramp, and Samuel looked up at the large double doors. "Wow."

"They're the same as the front doors," Jennifer said, "only bigger. Notice how it stays cool down here? It's almost a constant fifty-eight degrees."

Samuel turned around to a massive and ancient china hutch that sat opposite the ramp. In it were several types of wineglasses of different shapes. He opened a wire-mesh door and picked one out. "I think these wineglasses are real crystal." He flicked the delicate rim producing a steady tone. "Jennifer," Samuel said, marveling at the overall impression of the cellar, "I was looking at the equipment outside as we drove up, and now down here; this place is practically a turnkey operation. If you wanted to keep the place, it might be possible to make some serious wine here. I think these barrels are full, so there's already stock. These barrels might have some good wine in them."

"What if it's all bad?" Jennifer said.

Samuel realized her irony. "Then we destroy it all and start over...I mean *you* destroy it and start over."

Jennifer looked up at him and smiled, not minding at all his pronominal slip.

They went to the wine rack that covered the back wall. "All these bottles look like they're from other vineyards," Jennifer said. "There's all different kinds." She pulled at the wine rack at a seemingly arbitrary point. It opened smoothly to reveal a solid brick wall behind it. "Beyond those bricks is the room."

Samuel reached out and ran his fingers over the brickwork. "You did a nice job."

"Mike did it. He was a contractor and inspector for McWilliam's before we went into business together. He knows construction."

"It's strange that he just disappeared," Samuel said.

"Right after we left here, he seemed upset. By the time we got back to Phoenix, he was like a different person altogether. I thought he was feeling guilty or something for what we did. But, I hate to say it; guilt isn't something that bother's Mike a lot. Actually, it was his idea. I was going to call the police right away."

Jennifer realized she was sounding childish and corrected herself. "It was *our* idea. But by the time we got back, it's like he was completely blaming me, or at least I think he was. He just wasn't himself."

"Susan said it was in the morning when he stopped existing," Samuel recalled, "but not like he was dead."

For Jennifer, the connections began to form. "That's right. She did say that, didn't she? I wasn't down here with him when he was working. I was trying to inventory the contents of the house. I wonder if something happened. What if there's a kind of poison in the air, an environmental hazard in there or something worse?"

Samuel interrupted, "But you were in the room, too, right? At one point, you were in there, too, and you're fine. If all he did was brick up the entrance, then it can't be environmental."

"He said I was killing him. I thought he was just pissed off at me. Maybe it's more than that. Maybe he just wishes he'd never met me."

"Well, I'm glad I met you," Samuel said.

Jennifer looked up into his eyes again, and he pulled her in close. She leaned into his embrace and felt his acceptance that she was sure she'd lost after admitting the truth. But it was still alive and well in his touch, and she liked it. When they parted, she closed the wine rack door.

"I don't think it's a good idea to keep it bricked up." Samuel said.

"What do you mean? I know you probably want to see inside, but—"

"No, I don't want to see it at all, but there's only one way I know that really defeats something evil, entirely and finally, and that's to expose it for what it is. If it can't be hidden, it can't survive. I think Susan told me that, once."

Jennifer looked at the wine rack. "I just want to get rid of this place."

"What if it's true that you're the new caretaker of Eternity—"

"Oh my God," Jennifer cut him off. Her voice changed to a shouting whisper as she pointed down the aisle in-between the barrels. "Look, Samuel."

Samuel followed her gaze and in the aisle stood a pale young girl in a thin blue nightgown. Her black hair hung straight down on her shoulders and her eyes and mouth were pure black voids.

"What the..." Samuel gasped. He backed up reflexively until he pinned himself against the wine rack. As they watched, her blue eyes came into focus, her mouth formed, and she seemed to solidify from a vapor into a solid body. She stretched out her arm toward them, as if beckoning them.

Jennifer stepped forward, and Samuel tried to grab her back, but he was unwilling to move from the wine rack far enough to reach her. "Jennifer, no!" Samuel said.

"Why don't you just leave?" Jennifer shouted at the specter. She walked closer to it and made shooing motions with her arms and hands. "Go, there's nothing here for you. Just leave. This is my place, and I'll do what I want with it."

As Jennifer approached, Whitney spoke to her. Later, Samuel would say that he never heard anything from the ghost, that he'd only seen her and the ghost, and heard Jennifer talking to it. But Jennifer heard Whitney say four words before she faded from sight: "You promised. You promised." The words sounded in Jennifer's head like soft plaintive whines of a child just coming to the knowledge of injustice and wrongdoing and the meaning of fair play.

"He's dead!" Jennifer shouted to what was now an empty cellar.

Samuel managed to take a step toward her. Her voice echoed off the concrete floor and brick-lined walls "He's dead, Whitney, and I can do whatever I want. Do you hear me? I can do whatever I want!"

Jennifer turned to Samuel behind her. He was too stunned to speak. "I can do whatever I want." She said to him, but Samuel seemed to miss it.

"That's the girl! Oh my God, that's what I saw in the vineyard. I never forgot it, not ever." Samuel spoke quickly, adrenaline moving his words. "I can't believe it; she looks exactly the same."

Jennifer walked past Samuel more frustrated than angry. She started up the stairs that led back to the foyer. "Well, now she's here all the goddamned time."

TWENTY-SEVEN

———— • ————

ou were yelling at it," Samuel said as they drove away from the vineyard. "Did it speak to you?"

"Didn't you hear her?"

"No. I just saw it, and then I heard you yelling at it.

"I'm sorry," Jennifer said, "I know you wanted to hang out awhile and see some more, but I'm sick of that place. I don't want to come out here anymore. All it means to me is the loss of my fortune. Everyone gets one shot in this life, and I've just lost mine. I'm never going to be able sell it with her floating around."

The absurdity of Whitney's only words to her made Jennifer want to laugh out loud. The absurdity of someone saying to a person like her, *you promised,* was naiveté beyond imagination. She'd built her life on the broken promises she sold.

But she didn't laugh. She wondered how she was going to pay her rent two months from now, or when the money for groceries would run out, or what they would say at McWilliam's behind her back as she walked in with her plastic smile ready to get back to work. How satisfied Joel-the-Fuck would be when she had to ask for an advance against future commissions just to get by. He'd love to give it to her; he wouldn't even want it repaid. He'd just peel off a few hundreds from the wad in his pocket and pontificate some life lesson before letting go of them.

"You don't need me in your life right now," Jennifer said flatly, "I have some tough times to go through, and I really don't think I'd make you very happy."

Samuel ignored her. She saw in his face a slight contortion of pain and pride. "You promised there'd be a next time for us." He looked at her.

Jennifer began to cry. She pulled a tissue out of her purse and dabbed carefully at the tears that leaked out against her will. "I don't keep promises, Samuel. I'm a liar. I've always been."

Samuel chuckled absently.

"This is funny to you?" she snapped.

"No—not at all. I was just thinking that you said the Liar's Paradox. You said: 'I'm a liar.'"

"What's that supposed to mean?"

"A liar can't say that." Samuel said. "So you're not a liar, but maybe you were lying to me about us?"

"I wasn't lying. I'm thinking of you. I'm thinking about what's good for you."

"I'm doing just fine," Samuel said quietly, indignantly.

"It's ironic, you know?"

"What?" he asked.

"The ghost spoke to me this time. She's never done that before."

"What did she say?"

"She said, 'You promised,' and I know she's talking about the promise I made to Robert Maddock."

"That you wouldn't sell the place?"

"Yes."

"So don't," Samuel said.

Jennifer looked at him, his lack of comprehension astounding her. "Samuel, I'm broke. I put it all into this place. It was a guaranteed sale. Not to mention I owe Mike thirty-thousand on a promissory note."

"If you want to keep your word," Samuel said, "and you want to make a living, it seems to me you only have two recourses. And, it looks like that ghost is going to keep scaring away your potential buyers, so keeping your word to Maddock may not take a lot of willpower."

Samuel playing the devil's advocate irritated her. But Jennifer sensed he was trying to save more than her financial future or moral character. He was fighting for them as a couple, and she knew it, and she needed him to win.

"Two recourses?" she asked.

"Yes, rent the place out, or live there and make wine."

Jennifer laughed. "I'm sorry—what?"

"If you rent the place," Samuel explained deliberately slow, "then you're still in complete control of it, and you already own it outright, so you don't have to pay a mortgage. Or you could get into the wine business. Maybe we could be partners." Samuel said modestly.

"I don't know anything about wine, and I don't know anyone who would rent a place out in the middle of nowhere."

"When we get back," Samuel said, "I know three different people, who if they knew about the complete turnkey aspect of that winery, they'd be willing to lease it. They'd probably want to buy it, but they might well lease it just to try it out. I know an agriculture professor from ASU who might even get the university to lease it and use it for vocational training or internships."

Jennifer considered what Samuel was saying, "So much for getting rich, though, huh?"

"Probably. I don't know. Maybe it depends on the definition of rich."

* * *

Evening was just taking hold as Samuel pulled into the entrance of Jennifer's apartment complex. The Phoenix winter felt cold to her. She was used to the heat, and any cooling off made her shiver.

"I have to think about things, Samuel. I'm so confused and disjointed right now."

"Are we going to see each other again?" Samuel asked.

"If I were your relationship real estate agent, I'd advise against it, for your own sake." Jennifer paused, "But as your girlfriend, I don't want to walk away. I can't walk away."

They looked at each other and that look held them together in the moment. "If you want to come up," Jennifer said, "I want you to."

From the sidewalk, Samuel pressed the lock button on his key chain remote. The parking lights on the Crown Vic flashed once and the horn chirped as Jennifer held his hand, and they walked together to her front door. She was warm again, and rode the roller coaster of happiness and tragedy that she couldn't get off of. But tonight she was happy, and that's all that mattered. She felt the vibration of her cell phone in her jacket pocket, but she let it go to voicemail. Tonight, she would be one with Samuel, and nothing else mattered.

* * *

They slept in late, but Jennifer rose before Samuel. She looked at herself in the bathroom mirror, and giggled. She wanted them to go forward, and now it seemed like they just might. In the past, she'd always shared this kind of good news with Mike, or with Tammy, if they were on speaking terms, but they weren't on speaking terms, and Mike was AWOL.

As she brushed her teeth, it hit her: the memory of the call came to her like a nearly imperceptible noise. *There's a message on your phone.* "Oh my God," she said into the sink after she spit, "Mike."

She pulled a towel off the rack and wrapped it around herself. She moved stealthily through her bedroom where Samuel was still asleep in her queen bed and made her way passed the fallen clothes on the floor to the living room where she had flung her coat. She reached in the pocket of it and retrieved her cell. The screen showed 1 NEW MESSAGE.

She hit voicemail and tapped in her birth date as a password.

"*Frau Dickerman*, my name is Wolfgang Shlegel," Jennifer could barely understand the caller through his thick European accent, yet each English word was spoken with precision.

"I received your name from the Santa Cruz County tax office. I am a winemaker, and I understand you are the owner of *die* winery off of Highway 83. I believe it is known as Eternity Vineyards. I am interested in acquiring das property, *Frau Dickerman*, and I would greatly appreciate it if you would call me back any time of the day or the night, so we might discuss the subject further. My number is, 229-185-1212. *Danke, Frau Dickerman; auf Wiedersehen.*"

TWENTY-EIGHT

E xcitement temporarily blocked out the disappointment she felt that it wasn't Mike. She quickly grabbed a Post-It pad and pen off the kitchen counter and wrote down the name and number. Glancing at the clock above the sink, she realized it was nine-thirty.

She went back to the bedroom finding Samuel awake.

"Hey, you," Jennifer said.

Samuel smiled at her, and she sat down beside him. He was covered with only her quilted blanket for modesty. "What do they say? Today's the first day of the rest of your life?"

"Miracles do happen." Jennifer continued the clichés, "Lightning strikes twice."

"Is that what we are? Miraculous lightning?"

She kissed him. "That's what you are."

Jennifer opened her phone. "Listen to this." She played the message on speakerphone, and Samuel listened with interest.

"So what are you going to do?" he asked.

"You don't think I should sell it, do you?" Jennifer said.

"I don't think you can."

"But you don't think I should even try."

"Jennifer," Samuel became serious, "normally I wouldn't bring this up, especially now after we've...been together, but a long time ago, as you know, I was married, and she died."

Jennifer nodded. Inside she worried he would compare her.

"She left a party where she'd been drinking. She was a passenger in a car driven by someone who'd also been drinking. Someone who was drunk drove the car that hit them. What always seemed wrong to me is what her friend told me at the funeral.

"We're standing there at the open grave after the minister finished speaking; I'd thrown in my handful of dirt, and she says to me, 'I knew they were all drunk. I'm pregnant, so I wasn't drinking at all. I should have stopped them.'

"Of course I told her it wasn't her fault. But later I got to thinking about it: She didn't stop them. It was her car; she let them have her keys. They were on their way to the store to get more beer for the party, and she knew they were drunk. I mean, you can blame drunks all you want, but in the end—they're drunk. The one who wasn't drunk let it happen. The only one with the ability to stop that accident didn't do it. Later on, honestly, I saw no difference between what she allowed to happen and if she had just taken a gun and shot all three of them."

Jennifer said nothing.

Samuel finally said what was on both their minds: "What if someone got hold of that room? What if someone fired it back up and started to use it?"

"That would be horrible," Jennifer said. "That would be truly horrible."

"So long as you own the house, you're in control of the house. Once it's sold, you have no control anymore."

"But I would still be to blame," Jennifer added.

"I'm not saying—"

"That wasn't a question; that's just a fact." Then she laughed resignedly.

"What's so funny?"

"The irony," Jennifer said. "I have a four-million-dollar estate that will grow in value every year that it exists, and yet it's worthless."

"So rent it out," Samuel said. "Lease it. This guy's a wine-maker, a businessman; he may not even want to buy it. He might want to keep his liability down. Why not see if he'll rent. He's just taking a shot in the dark. He has no idea if you're even on the market."

"I'd still own it," Jennifer acknowledged. "I'd still have control of it. I could still enter the property on occasion to inspect it. But I wonder what he'll do when he sees Whitney?"

"If you're not selling the place, maybe he won't. You're agreement with Maddock was that you wouldn't sell it, and you're not. But there's no way to know until we try."

"We?" Jennifer asked. "Are we partners now?" She smiled coyly and scooted in closer to him.

"If you'll have me," he said.

"I'll take you head over heels." Jennifer replied.

* * *

Mike curled in the corner of Wolfgang's apartment and cried out as Wolfgang stood above him slapping at his head. Wolfgang drew back his hand, and each time before he launched it, he considered his aim with cool concentration. He wore black leather fingerless gloves to protect his hands as he went at him.

"What did I do?" Mike pleaded.

"You did nothing," Wolfgang said calmly, almost compassionately, as he slapped him again. "*Das ist die* problem; you have not finished *die* letter." He wore the slacks he would wear with his suit that day and a clean tank-top undershirt tucked in and tight-fitting. Mike kept his head down and reached up blindly trying in vain to stop Wolfgang's violent onslaught. His hand touched Wolfgang's abdomen. Wolfgang grabbed his wrist and bent it backwards until Mike screamed. "Shut up!" Wolfgang demanded. "You'll disturb our neighbors."

"Please! I'll do anything you want."

"Then I want to you to feel pain," Wolfgang said and slapped him with all his strength.

"Why!"

"Because it gives me pleasure, Michael." Wolfgang kicked at Mike's body arbitrarily. "Don't you want to give me pleasure?" Wolfgang raised his fist to slam down on Mike's head, but stopped short when he heard *Beethoven's Fifth* as a ringtone on his cell. "*Warten Sie hier*. I'll be right back."

Wolfgang reached for a towel that hung over a chair by the kitchen table and wiped the sweat from his face and neck. He went to the counter and picked up his phone.

"*Hallo, das ist* Wolfgang Shlegel."

"Mr. Shlegel? This is Jen Dickerman."

"*Guten Morgen, Frau* Dickerman! *Gut von Ihnen zu hören*! Excuse me, I mean, good morning, Ms. Dickerman; good to hear from you!" Wolfgang heard Mike whimpering in the corner and became annoyed. He turned to him quickly and covered the mouthpiece, "Silence!"

"I'm returning your call about Eternity Vineyards," Jennifer said.

"*Ja, Danke shön!* I was wondering if you were by any chance perhaps attempting to sell *die* winery. You see, I am a winemaker, and I have come here from Austria to live, but also perhaps to make wine for a business, just as I did in my homeland."

"You're from Austria?" Jennifer asked with pseudo-enthusiasm while drying her hair with a towel.

"*Ja, das ist* correct, but I have been in America now for several years, and Arizona for some of those years."

"Well, Mr. Schlegel, the truth is I'm not looking to sell the vineyard, but my partner, Mr. Ansell, and I are attempting to lease the property for commercial purposes."

Wolfgang put his hand over the microphone of his cell and snickered. Then he looked to Mike who cowered in the corner waiting for his next beating: "*Sie hat einen neuen Partner—ein Jude.* (She has a new partner—a Jew.) So much for your promissory note, *Dummkopf.*"

Michael didn't understand his broken English.

"Please excuse me, Ms. Dickerman, I was just telling my dog to behave."

"Oh, how cute," Jennifer said.

"*Ja.* Now, tell me, what would be the terms of such a lease?"

There was a pause.

"Well, we honestly couldn't let it for less than forty-eight a year, but that could be made in monthly payments, of course, and I think if you let me show you around this winery, which is a turnkey operation, you'll see that's a very reasonable price for the commercial potential. We're even willing to take just fifteen percent of the gross selling price of the present stock, which is appreciable—"

Wolfgang interrupted: "*Das ist* not too bad. I mean that is a good price for me. But if I am taking all the risk on the harvests, I would have to insist the profits from the future wine I make be one hundred percent mine."

"Oh, of course, Mr. Shlegel, we're only interested in the real estate aspect. What you do with the wine is all up to you."

"*Das ist gut Sie sagen das*...What I mean to say is that I am glad to hear you say that. I think we might be able to work something out, Ms. Dickerman. We should meet at the property and discuss this further, *ja*?"

"Absolutely," Jennifer said. "When is a good time for you?"

"*Das ist* still early, perhaps we could meet today?"

"Certainly, I'm in Phoenix, so it will take me a few hours to get there, but that's fine if it's fine with you, what about two o'clock?"

"*Sehr gut.* (very good) I will see you then, *Frau* Dickerman; *auf Wiedersehen*, for now. I have a pressing matter I must attend to at this moment." Wolfgang glared at Mike who was attempting to stand up in the corner."

"Certainly, Mr. Shlegel. I'll see you then."

Wolfgang tapped off the phone and returned to Mike. He put a foot on one of his shoulders as he tried to stand causing him to fall back into the corner. From the kitchen table he retrieved the open black wine bottle and shook it noticing it was only a quarter full. He shook it again in front of Mike's face. Mike reached up for it with both hands, but Wolfgang pulled it back.

"I have only two more of these, Michael. What will you do when there are no more?"

"We have to get more," Mike whined.

Wolfgang raised his hand and struck Mike across his head. The hit made a slapping thud. "Maybe we can get it at the store, *ja*?"

"We have to make more," Mike said desperately.

"Then we need ingredients, *ja?*"

Mike looked up; clearly he understood what Wolfgang was saying to him. "No, we can't—" Mike began instinctively.

"We have many kegs of wine, Michael. If they are not yet finished, one or two children would complete them. Then you would have enough for your..." Wolfgang smiled, "...entire life. You will help me with this, *ja*?"

Mike looked down. "I don't want to, Wolfgang."

Wolfgang smacked Mike's head again. "Then you will die! If I did not provide you with this wine, you would die! You know this, *ja*?" Wolfgang suddenly softened his tone and stroked Mike's hair as if he cared for him: "Surely even a *dummes arschloch* like you can feel this inside your body.

"You will bring the children to me, Michael, and then you will feel how good it is to have all the wine you will ever need. You will be set for life."

Wolfgang handed him the bottle, and Mike immediately sucked from it as if nothing else in the world mattered. He nursed it like an infant sealed on a breast, then groaned with pleasure.

"It's either that, Michael," Wolfgang continued in the manner of a caring therapist, "or in a month, after I have driven away, the cells of your body will begin to rupture and you will die; you will die slowly and in pain, and no one will be able to help you. I have seen this many times. And if you leave my apartment while I am gone, you will never see another drop of this wine. Do you understand this?

"Yes," Mike said.

"And you will have the letter finished, *ja*?

"Yes."

"*Gut*, Michael. *Das ist gut.*"

TWENTY-NINE

W hitney howled in the empty house. Howling filled the hallways, the staircase, and sounded throughout the bedrooms. But howling in an empty house was useless, and she knew it. So eventually, as always, she fell silently upon Eternity's ethereal tide, and it carried her to her room. But instead of letting it put her naturally in the corner, she moved to the window and watched as dark clouds formed over the landscape of Southern Arizona. They hung low and covered the tops of the distant mountains in fog, and the gray that overtook the cold winter sunshine muted the colors of the vineyards and the grasslands.

She wanted Jennifer to come back. There shouldn't be tension between them, but if her father was bad—Wolfgang was even worse. She would have to find a way to warn her, a way to tell her without making her fly off the handle or storm out again. Listening to the first drops of rain hitting her window like small fingers tapping on the glass, she sensed the storms growing darkness within her room, then a faint clap of thunder rolled though the atmosphere. How strong would the storm would be?

She could move to another part of the house, but in front of her window was as good as any place to be. A minute spent staring, a year, a decade, if she was alone, it didn't count for much. Then, off in the distance, coming up the highway, a blue Durango came into view making its way toward the vineyard. Its windshield wipers moved in a steady rhythm, and its headlights cut through the gray weather.

When she saw it, she shot through the ceiling and into the rain that fell steadily on the gravel and streamed off the clay tile roof of the Spanish mansion. In death, she couldn't feel the water, but even if she could it wouldn't matter. Jennifer was back! Maybe this time she was home to stay.

From above, she watched her pull up close to the front door, but when she stepped from her car, she wasn't in blue jeans and sneakers, and she didn't carry suitcases or blankets. She wasn't moving in. She was in her business clothes; this time a gray suit, blue ruffled blouse, and black pumps. She carried her briefcase over her perfectly formed hair to protect it from the heavy drops as she quickly stepped to the covered walkway by the front door. Dressed in those clothes, it could only mean she'd be showing the vineyard again.

Whitney fell from the sky to the roof and descended through the floors into the foyer, moaning, as what should have been joy morphed into pain.

Jennifer walked into the office and glanced around, looking for the source of the noise. She sat her briefcase on the desk as she turned to the empty room, and with her hands on her hips, she yelled into the grand emptiness, "You win, Whitney! I'm not selling the place. I'm keeping my word, just like I gave it to Robert. But I *am* going to rent it out. I can do that. He never said I couldn't. A very nice man is coming here today, a wine-maker, and he wants to rent the place. So back off. I'll still be in control, but I can't live here, and I don't have to. I have a life, you know."

After she said this, Whitney stopped moaning, and Jennifer smiled with self-satisfaction. "That's better," Jennifer said and walked back into the foyer.

Maybe Wolfgang wasn't getting the place after all, Whitney thought. Maybe he was too late or maybe Mike warned her. She followed Jennifer from room to room remaining hidden in the corners of the ceiling as Jennifer first opened all the downstairs drapes. Even with the gray rain outside and dust and cobwebs within, the sheer increase in light changed the mood of the place entirely. It gave the ground floor a cheerful appearance that Robert never allowed.

Jennifer walked up the staircase and starting in the bedroom opposite Whitney's, she opened each room's curtains and left each door open. When she made her way to Whitney's room, Whitney raced ahead of her and sat on the bed. She stilled herself and concentrated on her eyes and mouth. She wanted Jennifer to see her in the best light.

When Jennifer opened the door, she saw the apparition and instinctively startled, but this time she didn't run away or get angry; she only looked at Whitney, and for a long moment they stared at one another.

"Seeing what so many people have never seen," Jennifer said, "it's very special."

Whitney sat motionless, listening, concentrating on her complete appearance, and enjoying the calm warm tones of Jennifer's voice talking to her just like she was a real person. The drapes were already opened, but Jennifer went to the window and tied them back with the satin ropes that hung at either side.

"There has to be some peace for you," Jennifer said. "When this man comes, you have to stay hidden." Jennifer walked back toward the bedroom door. "He's a real winemaker, a farmer. I'm sure he's great. He sounds great. He's going to be here in about fifteen minutes." She paused near the bed where Whitney sat and cautiously reached out toward her until her hand passed through her. To Whitney, Jennifer's hand passing through felt like it did when her mother held her. It felt like safety and love.

"It's truly amazing to see you," Jennifer said as she pulled back her hand and continued to the door. "I don't know what horrible things happened in your life. I don't know what you've seen here. It couldn't have been very good, but it was fifty-one years ago. I'd try to forget about it if I were you. Things work themselves out; every bad thing eventually works itself out."

Whitney wanted to talk to Jennifer again, like she did in the cellar. She wanted to tell her about her life and tell her about Wolfgang and Mike and what they were planning, but communicating in that way required too much energy, too much concentration, and Jennifer was moving too fast around the house. It was all she could do to maintain the appearance of her eyes, mouth, and hair, but maybe now it didn't matter.

Maybe Jennifer was right. Perhaps it could work out—a simple winemaker, a farmer, just like her Uncle Robert. She wanted Jennifer to stay and keep talking to her, to reach out again and pass through her, but Jennifer closed the bedroom door. And when she was gone, Whitney let her mouth and eyes go black along with her hair. Then her phantasm faded altogether.

She moved from the bed through the bedroom wall and followed Jennifer as she went through the house checking the water taps in the bathrooms and making sure the washing machine and dryer worked. She went into the kitchen and made sure the stove worked and that the refrigerator was running. Then she looked out the kitchen window and nearly shouted, "Oh, shit, he's here already."

Excited, Whitney shot up through the ceiling into the bedroom next to hers, through the ceiling of that room into the attic, past the white-sheeted furniture and boxes therein, and out through the roof to a point overlooking the estate from above. But the gray rainy day only matched the familiar gray car as it pulled into the long gravel driveway.

She screamed, and her scream sounded like the shrill of a hawk echoing over the Arizona outback, protesting the constancy of nature.

THIRTY

————— •◗ ◖—————

ennifer couldn't wait to meet the man who sounded so foreign yet so dignified on the phone. The chrome four-slot toaster provided a quick quality check of herself: hair-check, clothes-check, no-lipstick-on-the-teeth-check. Then she went to the front door and stepped out onto the covered walkway as the S600 pulled in next to her Dodge. "Jesus," Jennifer said quietly; the contrast in class was startling if not a little depressing.

She smiled as Wolfgang climbed out and quickly made his way to the covered walkway. He wore a tailored black suit, white shirt and a blue silk tie. Jennifer noticed his smile was large and his teeth nearly perfect, just like hers, only real. And he was bald, completely so, and not at all an old man like she expected. He had to be close to her age, attractive to say the least, even if his black goatee was somewhat sinister.

He approached her with his hand extended. "*Frau* Dickerman, how good to meet you. Thank you for see-ing me today."

"Mr. Shlegel, good to meet you, too." Jennifer took his hand. "But please, call me, Jen."

"Jen, it is."

"Not the best weather to see the place in, I'm afraid," Jennifer said.

Wolfgang looked far out across the estate. "*Ja*, but *das ist gut for die* water tables. *Das ist gut* for irrigation later on."

Jennifer nodded as if learning something new. "Good point."

"And to be honest, Jen, I have been out here before, and I have seen the exterior. I confess I have even walked in the vineyards. I hope you will not consider me a trespasser."

"Oh, not at all," Jennifer said with a wave of her hand. "I'm glad you had a chance to see it in a better light." Jennifer hid her absolute certainty that he broke the lock off the cellar door. But how could a person so obviously polite and dignified—and rich—so brazenly break-and-enter her property? Jennifer tried to banish the thought. Who cared anyway? It didn't matter; nothing was stolen. She pushed the thought aside.

"Mr. Shlegel, let's go in and look at the interior. I think you're going to like it."

They went through the double doors, and as they did Wolfgang said, "*Diese Tür ist schön.*"

Jennifer looked confused.

"I apologize," Wolfgang said. "I still mix my native tongue with my English. Bad habit I'm afraid. I was just saying this door is beautiful."

Jennifer smiled, relieved by the outcome of the translation. "No, please; I love your accent. And, yes, the entire place is decorated in this same Spanish colonial styling. In fact, it really is Spanish colonial. Eternity Vineyards is over three hundred years old. I suppose when it was originally decorated, it would have been considered modern. But look," Jennifer said as they entered the foyer, "everything is like new. Like it just sat here unused all that time. It's incredible, but this place was here long before Arizona was even part of the United States."

Jennifer noticed Wolfgang slowly looking around in all directions. "*Das ist wunderbar,*" Wolfgang said as if speaking to himself. Then he turned to Jennifer, "That means it is wonderful in here."

"It is wonderful," Jennifer said excitedly. "I really wish I'd cleaned it before showing it to you though. I apologize for all the dust, but I just acquired it, and I haven't had the time. Of course, we'd have it professionally cleaned before you moved in—if you decide to that is."

"This is not a problem for me," Wolfgang said. "I like it just the way it is."

As Wolfgang pretended to take in the house from the vantage of the foyer, Jennifer looked to the top of the stairs and saw Whitney standing there. Her mouth was a jagged black opening and her eyes were completely gone. Jennifer gave her a dirty look and made a quick shooing motion with her hand while Wolfgang was turned toward the dining room. But Whitney began to moan like a person dying in chronic pain, and the moaning echoed pathetically in the foyer. Jennifer looked at her with fury and mouthed, *Fuck off!* the best she could.

Suddenly, Wolfgang spun around, and Jennifer returned to instant smiling.

Game over, she thought and waited for Wolfgang to run in panic, tripping in the wet gravel, ripping the pocket of his slacks as he fished for his magnificent car keys.

"Is that the original dining furniture in there?" He asked, pointing at the massive oak table.

Jennifer failed to comprehend his reaction. It was impossible to miss the wailing from the little bitch at the top of the stairs. Struggling to keep a cool façade, she answered the best she could: "Yes...uh, absolutely...as far as I know, those are real antiques not reproductions."

"And *das ist die* office in there?" Wolfgang looked in the opposite direction from the dining room.

"Yes, it is." Jennifer felt herself sweating. She noticed Whitney descending the staircase. "Maybe we should take a look; come with me." Jennifer tried not to raise her own voice over the racket Whitney had launched into. Wolfgang still didn't seem to hear it. He wasn't hard of hearing. How could he miss it? But she had no more time to question it. She was on stage in the middle of her play. Together they walked into the study.

"*Wunderbar!*" Wolfgang said again. *Das ist absolut wunderbar*. He looked around the office and moved to the chair behind the desk. Jennifer remembered the first time she'd come into the fine colonial study and felt just as awestricken.

Whitney was getting louder.

Not sure what difference it would make, but hoping for the best, she closed the door behind them. Maybe Whitney would get the point and stay out. Wolfgang remained entirely deaf to the haunting racket. He opened and closed the various drawers of the large desk.

"I am a very private person, Jen. I must see the rest of the interior of the estate, of course, but I am more than willing to meet your price for leasing a place such as this." Wolfgang looked about him as if he had come home. "I must pay you in cash, unfortunately, and I can only pay six months in advance and *und* extra month *für die* security deposit. I have no children, no wife." Wolfgang smiled. "I do not have any loud parties, and my company is usually only other winemakers from

California or perhaps *von Österreich*, what you would call Austria.

Jennifer tried to keep her jaw from dropping and calculated—through Whitney's incessant crying—that he was about to give her twenty-eight thousand in cash. "I think we could work with that," Jennifer said trying not to sound like she was closing her first childhood lemonade sale.

Then it struck her as he looked at her. The stained glass window that framed all who sat at the desk framed him in natural majesty, as if power was something he never had to strive for. He looked comfortable with it. Surely Austrian aristocrats don't move to Arizona. Still, he looked bred for Eternity Vineyards, groomed to rule over the Indian populations of Mexico hundreds of years prior.

And neither could she deny his good looks, nor his bright eyes. And being bald made him look clean and potent. She was about to scream at Whitney to shut up, but he still made no indication he could hear her, and she feared the ugly appearance of instability should she suddenly holler into the air for no reason. Her head was spinning but she tried to hang on.

She noticed the thought of Samuel rising from her superego like a shame as she allowed herself another eyeful of Wolfgang, and at the same time, the phantom of Whitney arose from the floor in front of the desk, her back was to Jennifer, and thus she faced Wolfgang directly.

Jennifer watched through the horror of a ruined deal as the ghost-girl raised her arms from her sides and began to scream at such a pitch that it should have broken the window glass. It was a sound Jennifer never heard before, an adult screaming like a newborn infant. The sound continued and Jennifer covered her ears, winced, and ducked down as if avoiding something thrown at her. Wolfgang never flinched.

Suddenly his look became one of concern, and his eyes widened as he looked at her through the apparition of the screeching girl. "*Oh Gott Frau Dickerman*! What's the matter? Are you in pain?" He got up quickly from the desk, and walked past Whitney, who turned to watch him. He put his arms on Jennifer's shoulders and helped her to stand. "Is it your head? *Ist es Ihr Herz*?" (Is it your heart)

In the split second that she regained herself, Jennifer noticed that his words seemed perfunctory, as if faking concern, as if he already knew she was all right; he wore a salesman's concern; she recognized it all too well. But more importantly, he didn't seem to notice Whitney at all.

Jennifer stood up straight and adjusted herself, thinking quickly even as the phantom screeching continued in her ears and surely throughout the room. She immediately pretended nothing was wrong. "Oh I am soooo sorry, for that. I just got a little dizzy for a moment. I'm fine." Jennifer could barely hear her own words, but Wolfgang responded to them normally.

"*Kommen Sie, setzen*." (Come, sit down) Wolfgang motioned to one of the chairs by the desk.

"No, I'm fine, thank you—perhaps you'd like to see another part of the house?" Jennifer tried not to sound too anxious to leave the room.

"Of course," Wolfgang said, "but only if you are sure you are alright. Perhaps you need—how do you say—a physician?"

Jennifer thought she might have seen a slight smile as he suggested the doctor, but she couldn't be sure, and she stopped herself. It was surely just a language thing; it didn't matter. All that mattered was closing the deal.

She showed him the bedrooms, the kitchen, the bathrooms. They looked through the windows at the rainy back veranda and at the fountain.

Whitney followed and howled along the way.

"*Das ist sehr schön,*" (It is very beautiful) Wolfgang said as he looked to the fountain that overflowed with rainwater. He turned to Jennifer, "You have here a wonderful house. It is like a museum, *ja?*"

"Now that you mention it," Jennifer said, "I suppose it is. But the man who lived here before was here for three decades. So, it's livable as well. Let me show you the cellar."

"*Ja*, please," Wolfgang said.

In the cellar, Whitney appeared again. She stood at the wine rack, where the secret remained bricked up. She moaned and repeated over and over from her own mind to Jennifer's, *Not him, Jennifer—not him!*

Jennifer could barely ignore her, but she persisted and pretended normality, and Wolfgang never reacted to the specter or the sounds she made.

"I must sample this wine," Wolfgang said as he ran his hand over one of the oak barrels.

"Of course, absolutely," Jennifer said through Whitney's carrying on. "But I'm not sure how to get into them."

"*Sieh hier* (See here)," Wolfgang said and pointed at a large wooden bung on top of one of the lower barrels. "We remove this and use a siphon to pour a glass, or perhaps..." Wolfgang corrected himself and smiled, "...two glasses. Surely these things must be down here somewhere." He looked around the immediate area. "This must be done regularly when der wine is stored in oak barrels."

Jennifer noticed the way he said wine sounded like vine. "I think those things are over here," she said and led him to the china hutch near the loading ramp.

Wolfgang walked over with her and opened the large top drawer.

Not him, Jennifer! He's evil! The room! Whitney faded from view completely as she forced her communications into Jennifer's consciousness. It was still too much for her to talk and appear at the same time.

"*Ja, sieh hier,*" Wolfgang pointed to the interior of the drawer. He lifted out a large glass tube. "*Das ist* called *und* wine thief. We can draw up *der* wine from the barrels with it for sampling. I saw a bung wrench hanging on the barrel rack just over there.

"Please *meine gute Dame* (My good lady), if you would bring us two glasses."

Jennifer puzzled over whether he had just swore at her, but given the context and tone, she decided not. Again, it didn't matter. She followed him with two of the crystal wine glasses.

Jennifer, no! Whitney moaned from somewhere unseen. *Jennifer, not the wine!* But she was getting quieter.

Whitney came partially into view, but remained nearly transparent, as if fighting to remain relevant. She stood at the end of the barrel rack where Wolfgang was wrenching off the bung. She looked monstrous with her black mouth and eye sockets and hung over Wolfgang like a living fog poised to attack him at any moment.

Wolfgang seemed to sense nothing of her presence, and then it dawned on her: Whitney was invisible to him because she wasn't selling the vineyard. Whitney had no power unless she was breaking her promise to Robert. That had to be it. Renting wasn't selling! Jennifer smiled, and felt some semblance of control; now she understood the rules.

Behind Wolfgang's back she pointed at Whitney and mocked a silent laugh.

Jennifer, not the wine, Whitney said again, but the volume was turned down. Her faded image disappeared altogether. She had exhausted her energy to continue. She could no longer howl, communicate, or appear. All she could do was watch the inevitable constancy of Eternity's nature.

Jennifer reveled in her defeat over Whitney, but what Whitney said to her stuck and made her cautious. Maybe the wine was bad.

"What if the wine isn't safe," Jennifer said to Wolfgang as he withdrew a sample using the wine thief.

Wolfgang didn't reply to her question but only said, "Please, may I have one of the glasses." Jennifer handed him a glass, and Wolfgang let the contents of the wine thief drain into it until the glass was a third full. "*Das ist nicht die richtige Farbe.*" (This is not the right color.) He mumbled as he held the glass up and looked through it.

"What if it's poisonous?" Jennifer asked.

Wolfgang continued to ignore her as if he couldn't hear. He put the glass to his nose and inhaled deeply while closing his eyes. "*Das ist nicht der richtige Geruch.*" (This is not the right smell.) He shook his head. "This wine is not poisonous. *Das ist* ordinary." He quickly drank back the entire contents of the glass. "It is fine, Jen. It is, as you would say, a good quality wine. I think it is more than ready for bottling, but perhaps I can make it even better."

Jennifer noticed he sounded exceptionally confident, maybe too much so, almost arrogant.

"Each bottle from these barrels," Wolfgang continued, "could bring a hundred dollars if marketed correctly." He handed his empty glass to Jennifer without a thought, as if she were a waitress.

She was stunned by his sudden expectation of her as his cupbearer. He seemed to forget completely that she had a glass, too. So much for toasting the occasion, she thought and saw herself handing the glass back to him with a hearty *fuck you*, but she controlled her impulse.

"Did you bring the paperwork with you, *Frau Dickerman?*"

"I did." Jennifer said with a fake smile.

"If it is acceptable to you, I would very much like to lease this winery today."

"I can't imagine there could be a better time or tenant, Mr. Shlegel."

Not him! Whitney screeched one last time, but it seemed like she was miles away. Jennifer couldn't tell if it was a silent thought this time or a sound in the cellar, but she had grown used to ignoring her, and Wolfgang apparently couldn't hear it—and that was a fine combination.

Jennifer walked with Wolfgang to the stairs that led up from the cellar. She climbed them first and heard Wolfgang say behind her with a chuckle in his voice, "*Dummer Geist.*" (Silly ghost)

She responded to what she thought he said, "Yes, it is very nice, isn't it?"

Wolfgang smiled. "*Das ist* perfect."

THIRTY-ONE

ello?" The young woman's voice sounded positive on
the phone.

"Hi, honey, it's your mom, I just wanted to call and see
how you're doing, see if we could touch bases." Jennifer
listened to the pregnant pause on the other end of the line and
fought an overwhelming impulse to scream *Answer your mother!* But she kept her passions restrained, and waited.

"Hello, Jennifer." Tammy said.

"*Jennifer*? You call your mother, Jennifer?"

"I don't want to fight with you, Mom."

"Who's fighting? I'm just wondering why you don't go
ahead and call me, Jen? My clients call me, Jen."

"But I'm not one of your customers, so I guess I'll just have
to wait in line, won't I?"

"I'm not going to fight with you either," Jennifer said with
false stalwart determination. "I just want to know if you're still
interested in coming to Phoenix for a bit. Things are looking up,
and I want you to meet someone special. His name is Samuel."

Another slow-motion pause grated on Jennifer's patience. "Are you getting married again?" Tammy asked, as if it were an annual event.

"I don't know," Jennifer said.

"I only have one dad, Mom."

"When did I ever say anything different? Your dad is your dad; I know that. But maybe you could make room in your life for a friend. That's what he'd be—a friend."

"I don't need a stepfather," Tammy said with disdain. "I don't want lots and lots of parents."

"I wonder what happened to you and me." Jennifer asked, "When you were a little girl?"

"What! When I was a what?"

"I'm just saying that when you were young, we were closer; me and you were a pair." Jennifer sat at her small kitchenette table and wiped a silent tear from the corner of her left eye but she spoke to her daughter as if she weren't moved. "Now it's just a war between us."

"Well, mom, if you cared about me so much, maybe you should have tried harder. Dad still talks about you even now, you know?"

"Tammy, that part of my life—that part of *your* life—is over. It's been over for years."

"Yeah, it has been years..."

"I know you think you can walk away from me, but you're going to find out that you can't. I won't let you."

Another silence.

"I have to go, Mom."

"Why don't you give it another chance?" Jennifer said quick and direct, trying hard not to sound like she wanted it and hating herself as soon as the desperate words passed through her lips. She held the phone away from her while she sniffed back her running nose. Pride was her impenetrable fortress, and Tammy was just like her in that regard. But Jennifer knew her own fortress was starting to crumble with time and age while Tammy still had the confidence of youth.

"I just have to concentrate on classes right now," Tammy said, "or I'd come, okay? Maybe we can get together next semester break."

"Sure, I'd like that."

Silence fell over the phone call.

"I love you, Tammy," Jennifer finally said.

"I have to go."

"Should I call you again? Should we talk in a couple of weeks?"

"Sure," Tammy said, as if granting reluctant permission, "but I have to go now, okay?"

"Look Tammy, I'm sorry we got off on the wrong foot just now; maybe if you have some time I could even come up there."

There was nothing, and Jennifer looked at the screen of her phone. "Hello?" Jennifer spoke into the microphone end, vainly hoping to retrieve the lost connection, but she knew it wasn't a dropped call. She set her phone down with resignation.

In the sink, she washed her cereal bowl and began to cry again as the hot water rinsed the dish. The sun coming through her kitchen window promised a warmer day, but the February morning seemed to grow even colder. There was no repair for them. There was nothing anymore. Their relationship was totaled years ago, and when she was working, she could ignore it, but now there was no work and nothing to keep her mind off her domestic situation.

No one knew Call-It-Home Realty; she had no listings, no customers, and no money to acquire any properties to flip. The income from the lease on Eternity Vineyards covered her living expenses, but she would have to close the office.

She walked into her living room and sat on the sofa. She powered on the television to the morning news and blankly watched a report about the Border Patrol. Once again, they were too undermanned to stop the flood of illegal immigrants streaming into Southern Arizona. In order to increase their surveillance efficiency, they were encouraging all property owners between Nogales and Tucson to check their property for signs of trespassing; they wanted to put together a picture of new routes border crossers might be using. Jennifer picked up Mike's letter again from the coffee table and read it.

Dear Jennifer,

Please forgive my sudden departure. I had to get away, and I don't want anything to do with Eternity Vineyards. I'm not judging you in any way, nor am I suggesting you take any different course of action. I only hope the best for you and Call-It-Home Realty. When you sell the property, please set aside my share, and I will collect it at a later date. Right now, I just need time to myself, and I can't fully tell you why, because it's just too personal. You might remember Stephen. You met him at Fifty-Five Degrees that one night. I have taken up his offer to stay with him in Santa Barbara where he recently transferred, and that's where I am now. Take care, Jennifer. I know you will never forgive me for running out on you, but I have to do what I have to do.

Your Friend and Former Partner,
Mike

When she first got the letter, she took it to the Phoenix police. They made a copy of it to close out the missing persons report. Now, she folded the letter, keeping it in her hand and staring off into space.

She didn't know who she was anymore, and she worried every day that Samuel would grow cold on her. She used to get ready for work in the mornings, but now waiting for the time when she could see Samuel again was her only agenda. What if he tired of her? What if he met someone else in the restaurant? He hadn't grown cold yet, but if it weren't for him, there'd be no one. She loved him now, so the potential for loss had entered her world again, as if God were getting ready to take another swing at her after Mike and Tammy.

Her cell phone rang. Caller ID showed it was Samuel.

"Well, hello," Jennifer said. "I was just thinking about you."

"Me, too! Hey, Jennifer, I hate to ask you this, but Denise called off, are you doing anything over lunch?"

"I get the feeling you don't want to eat together."

"Actually, I was hoping you could work the bar."

"You're kidding?"

"It's not too hard at lunch and really easy to learn, and no one will say anything if you're slow—because you're my girl."

"Oh, that's a good one," Jennifer laughed. She might have laughed too hard. "I'm going to write a book someday on selling, and steal that line."

"Any more word from Mike?" Samuel asked.

"No, just the letter. Tammy's being a little bitch, too."

"You talked to her?"

"Sort of. We never seem to connect very well. I don't know. Look, I'm not opening the office this morning just to sit there searching the web again. I'd love to come out. What are you going to pay me?"

"Well, I won't insult you with what my staff gets, but I'll pay you a very nice dinner and wine. Serve at lunch; be served at dinner?"

"I think you just convinced me to work for food. All I need is a cardboard sign."

"See, I could be a salesman! I just closed, right? Isn't that what I just did?"

Jennifer laughed again. "I'll see you in a couple hours," she said, and then disconnected. At least his call lifted her spirits up somewhat, and the thought of tending bar sounded strangely cool, almost free. She could handle that for an afternoon. At least it would pass an afternoon.

Before she turned off the television she noticed the report on illegal aliens was still airing. There were images of Mexicans scaling a fence and groups of men and women with children running across a freeway. She stopped to watch and recognized one of the police cars parked next to a Border Patrol SUV. She'd seen it before. It was a Santa Cruz County Sheriff's car. She thought about Eternity Vineyards.

"Imagine that," she said out loud as she realized she was now one of the property owners they were appealing to. She'd have to give Wolfgang a call to give him a heads-up. She let the thought roll in her mind again like she did the first time she was alone in the house. It felt strange like a distant déjà vu: I am the owner of Eternity Vineyards—eternity's vineyard—Eternity Vineyards. It rolled in her mind as she prepared for the day.

THIRTY-TWO

For weeks, Whitney sat in her room and watched through the window as the days gave way to the darkness of night. Whatever Wolfgang was, she didn't want any part of him. She only wanted to hide. Then, somewhere off in the dark grasslands that surrounded the house, a pack of coyotes wailed.

Maybe she was in hell, she thought, and then suddenly became sure of that idea. Maybe they were wrong when they said hell had a lake of fire and demons with red skins and horns. Maybe hell looked just like the world. Maybe hell was the inability to stop evil and the inescapable chore of watching it unfold. Or maybe God had simply made this her hell for what she had done.

When the pounding from the cellar began, so did Whitney's prayer: "I'm sorry for what I did to Kerrie," she spoke quietly into the atmosphere of the room. "Why can't you give me another chance? I'd give you another chance if you did wrong.

So, if I would, shouldn't you?" But Whitney heard nothing back, only the pounding from downstairs.

"God doesn't hear ghosts," Wolfgang said from behind her.

She didn't turn around.

"God has abandoned you. Between you and Him is the Grand Canyon. Don't you know He created little girls for hell? Why don't you come down and see what we're doing. Why don't you, how do they say, 'hang out with us'? *Wie kann es jemals gut sein, allein zu sein?*" (How can it ever be good to be alone?)

Whitney began to howl, and her howling did not stop even after she heard Wolfgang's laughter and his footfalls receding down the hallway.

*   *   *

It was a solemn night, even historical, he thought. On such an occasion as this, it seemed wrong to use electric lights. Instead, Wolfgang lit candles in whatever room he was in at the time. The sounds of Whitney's howling from the darkened house made him smile as he sat at the head of the table in the dining room sipping whiskey. The candelabra in the center of the table illuminated his features in an orange-red glow, and he didn't move except to bring his glass to his lips. When the pounding from the basement stopped, he frowned. He rose and blew out the candles and made his way down the stairs to where Mike was working.

Mike was covered in concrete dust. The wine rack was open and the doorway of the anteroom was busted open a third of the way down from the top.

"*Warum haben Sie angehalten?*" Wolfgang said, but Mike looked confused. "Why have you stopped?" He repeated impatiently.

"I heard that thing. She's moaning. I don't like being here."

"Don't you find her song beautiful?" Wolfgang toyed.

"I don't like it at all."

"Your last two bottles are in *das* room. I suggest you pick up *der* sledge and persist, and don't worry about *dieser kleine Geist.* (that little ghost) She is under control. She is just noise." He ruffled Mike's hair as if he were his son. "When you have finished and completely cleaned the room, come and see me in the study. Bring me the bottles you find. Don't open them. If you open one, it will be your last. Only I open the bottles from here on out. Do you understand?"

"Yes," Mike said.

When Wolfgang left, Mike picked up the sledgehammer and continued to bang against the brick wall he had built. Whitney continued to howl as he worked, and every third or fourth swing he would stop to look around, worried she might appear. The bricks fell mostly inward into the room, and after another half hour, all the bricks were dislodged and lying loose on the floor. The meager light in the cellar provided by a dozen candles provided a dim view, but Mike used a flashlight and shined it in the room. He looked cautiously in as if expecting to see the ghost of the girl lying on the table as he had left her, but the room was empty. Only the fixtures and fittings of the satanic practice remained.

The bottle he had opened before and the goblet were still on the table where he'd left them. He stumbled past the fallen bricks and grabbed the bottle off the table and took a drink from it immediately. He swallowed a mouthful of the coppery wine-blood mixture and sighed with relief. After that, Whitney's moaning bothered him less.

He whistled as he went to the loading ramp doors and opened them up. The wine circulated in his veins, and he felt the tickling of its mysterious fingers giving him hope and power. He went out and came back with a wheelbarrow and began loading bricks and taking them outside where they formed a pile of discarded protection from the evil of the estate. When he drank the wine, he didn't mind doing what Wolfgang told him to do. In fact, he was happy to serve him in whatever capacity.

After sweeping up the brick dust and concrete, Mike retrieved the one remaining black bottle from the wine rack under the bookshelf and the open bottle he had left on the table in the past. He was excited for Wolfgang to see his good work. He turned and bounded up the stairs of the cellar.

Because the lights were off, the entire first floor was in darkness. Mike could hear the constant moaning of Whitney from somewhere in the house, but an orange glow from the study provided a beacon of hope and safety. He made his way to it.

Wolfgang sat reading a book, supporting his temple with two fingers as he rested his elbow on top of the desk; the fire blazing in the fireplace glowed on his face.

"I've finished," Mike said with enthusiasm. "And I've brought the last of the wine."

Wolfgang held up a finger silencing Mike as he finished the passage he was reading. "*Das ist ein Geschichtsbuch.* (This is a history book.) It is of this Eternity Vineyards. It confirms that a wealthy Conquistador built it centuries ago. It was even further away from civilization at that time than it is now. *Das ist wunderbar.* (This is wonderful.)

There was no reason for a house out here," Wolfgang said with excitement. "It was always for the purpose we are using it now. I had to wait many years for Maddock to die, but now it's mine."

Without looking up from the book, Wolfgang took a deep sniff of the air and said: "Why did you open one of the bottles?"

"Oh no, Wolfgang; this bottle was already open from be-fore."

Wolfgang looked up and gracefully closed the book. "I told you, I open all the bottles that you drink from. *Verstanden Sie nicht*? Didn't you understand me?

"Yes, I understood, but—"

"Pour that bottle into the fire," Wolfgang said calmly. He nodded at the open bottle in Mike's grip and folded his hands on the desk. Contrasted against his navy blue turtleneck, his baldness and the flesh of his face looked completely red in the firelight."

"Wolfgang, please, I didn't—"

"Pour the wine in the fire, or I will beat you unconscious, and then I will put you in the fire, and you'll awaken in the flames before you die. *Glauben Sie das*?" (Do you believe this?)

One of the logs in the fire popped like a gunshot and startled Mike; he stumbled back and nearly fell. Wolfgang pounded on the desk with his fist: *"Giessen Sie Scheisswein!"* (Pour the fucking wine!)

Mike cried out as he moved to the fire. He didn't understand what Wolfgang said, but there was no mistaking his command. "No, please..." He began to blubber as he poured the wine onto the burning logs.

When he finished he fell to his knees in front of the fire. The fire quickly regained its fury after the dousing, and the empty bottle clinked on the stone hearth beside him. He put his face into his hands. Wolfgang smiled as he watched Mike's back heave and jerk with the sobs of loss.

"Michael...Michael," Wolfgang cooed compassionately. He held out his hand and flicked his fingers casually toward him-self. *"Bringen Sie mir andere Flasche."* (Bring me the other bottle.)

Mike didn't move. The shock of the wasted wine was too great for his brain to grapple with and move his muscles at the same time.

"Come," Wolfgang said. "Bring me the other bottle."

Mike gathered himself, stood, and brought the unopened bottle to Wolfgang, who produced a folding corkscrew from the top desk drawer.

"Silly," Wolfgang said softly, patronizing as he turned the corkscrew into the cork. He looked at Mike like a father about to hand his child an allowance, and pulled the cork free from the bottle. "There will be much more than this. *Sie werden alles haben, dass Sie wollen.*" (You will have all that you want.) He handed the bottle back to Mike who stopped crying long enough to take a reinforcing drink.

Wolfgang stood and turned to look out the window behind him. The dark of the night outside and the fire reflecting on the glass from inside made an exterior view impossible, but he looked into it anyway as if admiring a hellish vista. He crossed his hands behind him: "*Und die Welt wird die Ruhe verbrauchen,*" (And the world shall consume the rest.) Wolfgang said.

Wolfgang turned and looked at Mike who sat in one of the chairs by the desk staring blankly into the flames of the fireplace. "Now you only have one bottle left, Michael. We must make more, *Stimmen Sie?*" (Do you agree?)

Mike turned his blank stare to Wolfgang.

"Tomorrow a man is coming to pick you up, and you will go with him. You will follow his instructions completely. Do you understand this?"

Under the influence of the wine, Mike could not be sure if Whitney were still howling or if the wind outside was responsible for the sad moaning he heard. Under the influence of the wine, he didn't care. "Yes, I understand," Mike said.

"Now, it is time for you to retire," Wolfgang continued. He picked up a candlestick from the desk and lit it with a long match he gathered from the mantel. He ignited it in the flames of the fire and touched it to the wick. "*Kommen Sie*, I will lock you in your room."

THIRTY-THREE

sn't that Susan?" Jennifer asked looking toward the hostess podium.

Samuel wiped his mouth and turned in his chair to see a woman with long blonde hair and a tall man wearing a dark sport coat. "It is—and Jeff. I better say, 'hello.'"

"They should join us, if they want. I need to apologize to her, anyway. I haven't seen her since I stormed out of her store."

"Okay, sure." Samuel got up and went to the couple. Jennifer watched as he motioned to their table, and she felt some relief to see them smiling, even after she made eye contact with Susan.

As they approached, Jennifer stood, and they all shook hands.

"Susan," Jennifer said as she kept hold of her hand, "I'm sorry I was so rude the last time we were together. I just—"

"No, Jennifer, you were upset, rightly so, and things were very stressful for you; I can understand that. You didn't offend me.

My God," Susan laughed, "if I got fussy over that, I'd have no customers at all."

They sat down and a waitress immediately appeared to ask Susan and Jeff what they wanted to drink. Jeff looked at Samuel, "You're the expert. What do you suggest? I think we're probably having something vegetarian, right?" Jeff looked at Susan, who smiled and squeezed his hand.

"Well then," Samuel said with a pause as if studying the circumstances, "I'd go with a basic California white. We have a sautéed vegetable dish with Indian curry rice. If you're having that, which you'd be crazy not to, I'd go with something dry and medium-bodied. Give the BV Sauvignon Blanc a shot. We have a decent 2002 vintage.

Jeff looked to the waitress and handed back the wine menu unopened, "Who am I to argue?"

"Certainly," she said. "I'll be right back with your wine."

"Any luck finding Mike?" Susan asked.

"Actually, I got a letter from him the other day."

"He bolted to California," Samuel added.

Jennifer nodded in agreement, then noticed Susan smiling as she looked from Samuel to her. "What?" Jennifer asked.

"Nothing. Just that he finished your sentence, which he never does with anyone, and you let him do it without a second thought. The two of you seem to be quite the couple these days."

Jennifer looked to Samuel, "I hope so."

Samuel raised his glass to her and they toasted to themselves.

"It's funny you say that about California," Susan said. Her brow crinkled. "After you left, I tried to do another location reading on Mike, and I kept getting the same thing. You dropped him off that night at his apartment complex, but that morning you were at Eternity Vineyards, and I didn't see him existing after the morning, which if I were pressed to say, I'd guess he's at Eternity Vineyards—never left." Susan took a drink of her wine. "But, of course, I'm still off," she said matter -of-factly, "because he's in California."

"Yeah, well, that's what he tells me anyway." Jennifer said. "Really, I don't know. All I have is his letter, and you know, now that I know he's alive, I almost don't give a damn anymore where he is. All I know," Jennifer said to Samuel, "is if he wants his share, he's going to have to wait for it."

"Oh? Did you finally sell the place?" Jeff asked.

"No, I leased it to this winemaker, Wolfgang Shlegel. He says he's working on a special wine that he used to grow in Austria, or some place. He's a great tenant so far. I haven't heard as single complaint from him—about anything, and he pays six months in advance."

"What about the ghost?" Jeff asked abruptly.

There was a pause at the table, and Jeff turned to Susan who was scolding him with a look, "What?" Jeff asked indignantly.

"I'm sorry, Jennifer," Susan offered. "It's just such an inter- esting bit; I told my husband about it. I'm sorry."

"Oh, it doesn't matter at this point," Jennifer said, blowing it off completely. She answered Jeff, "Actually, when I was out there with Shlegel, showing him the place, I saw her several times. Heard her, too. But he didn't seem to see or hear a thing. You should come out and see the place, Susan—you, too, Jeff. It's beautiful, all ghosts aside. It's practically like a museum. I'm sure I could arrange it with Wolfgang, but I don't think we can do any ghost hunting. I mean if he doesn't know, I don't want him finding out."

"We're going out there tomorrow," Samuel added.

"That's right." Jennifer pointed to Susan and Jeff. "You two should come out with us. Get this: I have to check the property for signs of illegal alien traffic. Or at least that's what the Border

Patrol is asking the landowners in my county to do, and I'm now, officially, a landowner in Santa Cruz County. Besides, we've never taken a good look at the entire property line, have we?"

Samuel shook his head.

"I'd love to go," Jeff said, "but I have to meet with a new client tomorrow. You should go though," he said to Susan.

"Yes, absolutely," Jennifer said. "We can pick you up and all go out in one car."

"Well, it would make for some interesting research. I'd love to get a feel for the place."

"Then it's a date!" Jennifer said. "You're going to love it."

THIRTY-FOUR

———— • ————

A black pickup with a matching topper pulled up behind Wolfgang's Mercedes. It was a cold, overcast morning. Steam vented and condensation dripped from the large-bore tailpipe of the four-wheel drive. Santiago left the engine running when he exited the cab.

He was a small man with a nose that looked like it had been badly repaired after an accident of some sort. Running across his Adam's apple was a jagged scar that hinted at a life-or-death struggle in years past. He wore a straw cowboy hat, boots, a denim jacket, and sported a thick black mustache. When he looked at the estate he muttered to himself, *"¡Ijole!"* (Wow!)

Wolfgang opened the front door and stepped out to greet his guest. "Santiago! *Qué gusto verte.*" (Good to see you.)

"*¿Cómo esta, Señor Shlegel?*" (How are you, Mr. Shlegel?) Santiago looked towards the house. "*Esta muy bonita.*" (That's very nice.)

"*Gracias*," Wolfgang said.

Santiago nodded at the figure emerging from the front door. "*¿Es él?*" (Is that him?)

"*Sí*," Wolfgang replied.

"*¿Puedo confiar en él?*" (Can he be trusted?)

"*Sí, y no se preocupe el no a va dar ningún problema.*" (Yes, and don't worry, he won't give you any problems.) Wolfgang turned to Mike who was waiting on the covered walkway. "*Kommen Sie hier.*" (Come here.) He motioned for Mike to advance. "You have many hours ahead of you."

Mike did what he was told, and as he approached, Santiago looked him up and down. "*Pinche joto*," (Fucking fagot) he said disgustedly.

"*Él obedecerá completamente*," (He will obey completely) Wolfgang assured. Then he laughed, "*también cuando él grita.*" (even when he screams) They both laughed together. Mike, not understanding, laughed with them.

"*Le daré tres botellas para la niña. No necesito los demás. ¿Entiende?*" (I will give you three bottles for the little girl. I don't need the others. Do you understand this?) Wolfgang asked.

"*Sí, claro* (Of course)."

"*Muy bueno*," Wolfgang said. "*Recuerde qué usted tiene que volver antes de las nueve esta noche.*" (Remember, you must return before nine o'clock tonight.)

"*No problema*, Santiago said.

Wolfgang's expression grew perceptibly darker; the lines of his face became like cracks in a granite tombstone as he moved in close to Santiago. He towered over the Latino man, and looked down into his eyes: "*No chinges conmigo, y no fallar. ¿Entiende?*" (Don't fuck with me, and don't fail. Do you understand?)

"*Sí, entiendo,* (sure, I get it) Santiago said nervously as he stumbled backward into his previous personal space.

Regaining his former cordiality, Wolfgang said heartily, "*Entonces adiós y buena suerte,*" (Then goodbye and good luck)

Santiago nodded and quickly climbed into the driver's seat of the pickup.

As Wolfgang held open the passenger door, he motioned for Mike to get in as well. "Do what he tells you, and you get your bottle back, and many, many more. *Verstehen Sie* (Understand)?"

"I will, Wolfgang—but where are we going?"

"Don't worry about that; just bring the sacrifice back to me, *ja*?"

"I will," Mike said with depressive resignation.

"*Auf Wiedersehen,*" (Goodbye) Wolfgang said and closed the passenger door. He tapped twice on the side, and the pickup pulled away. Santiago waved from his open window, and Wolfgang waved back as if it were the end of a pleasant family reunion.

THIRTY-FIVE

ennifer noticed Susan became less talkative once Eternity Vineyards came into view. She spoke almost incessantly from the backseat the entire trip about the nature of ghosts and the various theories she'd read. She was obviously excited at the possibility of a real-life encounter, but upon arriving, Jennifer noticed her apprehension.

"I had no idea this place even existed," Susan said, "and yet you say it's over three hundred years old."

"I suppose no one really knows," Jennifer replied. "Its first title was generated in 1899 when the county was initially established. But the furniture and the Spanish Colonial design puts a much earlier date on it than that."

Jennifer turned off the highway into the gravel drive of the estate. By 11:00 a.m. the sun had broken through the scattered clouds increasing the temperature to the low fifties. They pulled up next to the Mercedes near the front door.

"What do you think of it?" Samuel asked.

"I think there's a lot of power here," Susan said.

"Is that good or bad?" Jennifer shifted into park.

Susan shrugged. "Neither—or both. It's just power. I suppose it all depends on who's got it."

"True," Jennifer said. "You guys wait here, I'm going to let Wolfgang know we're on the property, then we can take the perimeter road around the acreage and look at the fencing. He'll probably let us in after that."

Samuel and Susan watched her knock on the front door. It opened, and then she smiled and stepped inside.

"I think Jennifer might be a little sensitive to this," Susan said, "and I don't want to make her angry with me, but I should tell you, I think there's something wrong about this place. It doesn't surprise me that it's haunted. This place is definitely dark, and not just in the past; it's dark now."

Samuel had sworn to Jennifer never to tell anyone about the cellar room, and with Susan, the secret probably wouldn't keep, so Samuel carefully considered his response. "I hear you," he said. "I know what you're getting at, and you mean well. You're probably right, too—and I think Jennifer would agree. But I don't know if it would accomplish anything to hit her with your feelings about the place just now. I mean she's doing what she can. I think she's taking it bit by bit."

"I suppose I should mind my own business," Susan said.

"No, it's not like that," Samuel turned in his seat to face her, "but I think Jennifer will end up owning this place for a long time, and there are some things she has to work out at her own pace. She's always been a success-oriented person, you know." He turned back. "Always on top of a situation," he mused. "But I think this situation fell on top of her."

Just then the front door opened and Jennifer stepped out onto the walkway. Wolfgang stepped out with her, and when he did, Susan reflexively caught her breath. There was something wrong with him; she felt it immediately, but she said nothing, even when Wolfgang's eyes met hers, and they did so almost automatically, as if all along he'd expected her to be waiting in the car, and he never broke his gaze, even though Jennifer was clearly still talking to him. Susan couldn't tell if the snickering look he gave was meant for her or in response to something Jennifer had said. Then Jennifer looked to the car and pointed. Wolfgang raised his hand and waved casually. Samuel waved back and smiled, but Susan remained frozen.

"Who's that?" she asked.

"I suppose it's Wolfgang Shlegel. I've never met the man. God, I'll bet his head gets cold. He should cover that thing."

Susan said nothing as Jennifer walked to the car. She only watched Wolfgang, who continued looking at her until finally Susan turned away.

Jennifer climbed into the driver's seat. "Oh Jesus, it's cold out there. Okay, let's take a look at the perimeter." Jennifer put the Durango in reverse. "Wolfgang invited us in afterwards for lunch, which is fantastic, because Susan, you need to see this place from the inside—there's just no other way to fully appreciate it."

A worried look crossed Susan's face, "Are you sure we'll have time?" she asked.

"Sure," Jennifer said. "It's not even noon. We'll be back in Phoenix by four, no problem." Jennifer eased the Durango along the double-track dirt trail that ran the perimeter near the barbwire fence.

"It's so desolate out here," Susan said as they roved past the vineyard fields and into the grasslands. "Why would there be illegals around here?"

"What amazes me is that I've seen no evidence of illegals around here at all," Jennifer said. "I would have thought this would be a popular stop along the way up north into Tucson, especially during the years between William and Robert Maddock when it was empty, but there's nothing."

"Maybe they're afraid of it," Susan said.

"How would they know?" Samuel interjected. "I mean they'd have to trespass to know about the ghost."

"Maybe there's another reason for building such a magnificent place so far away from people," Susan said as she gazed out the backseat window. "Maybe they've always been afraid of it."

Jennifer glanced at Samuel, but Samuel slowly shook his head, almost imperceptibly yet telling Jennifer definitely that he hadn't said a thing to Susan about the anteroom.

As they drove along the south side of the perimeter, Jennifer looked toward the back of the house. "Those weren't there before," She said. "Look, Samuel." Jennifer pointed toward the house. "That pile of bricks; I never put those there."

"They must be Wolfgang's."

"I never gave my permission for him to alter—Oh no," Jennifer said. "Samuel, you don't think—"

"No way," Samuel interjected quickly.

"Think what?" Susan asked.

There was a pause, then Jennifer quickly lied, "Oh, I just hope he hasn't altered the house in anyway, that's all. It's a historical place, really, even if no one knows it's here. A person shouldn't mess with this place." Jennifer was nervous on the outside, and she hoped it didn't show, but inside she was beginning to panic. What if Wolfgang found out about the room? What if he's opened it? He'll think it's hers. What if that's why he invited them in for lunch—to confront her with it?

She had to consciously stop tapping the steering wheel with her fingernails, but she no longer looked at the perimeter for illegal alien trails or cuts in the wire fence. She looked only toward the pile of bricks as they continued their patrol. What was she going to say: *Wolfgang, you didn't bust down a brick wall and open a rather strange room did you?*

Susan bounced uncontrollably in the backseat, and Samuel held onto the overhead grip as Jennifer quickened her pace on the dirt trail.

"Whoa!" Samuel said to Susan as if having fun riding a mechanical bull. "Bumpy ride isn't it?"

Susan nodded worriedly in reply.

Eventually, Jennifer skidded to a stop beside Wolfgang's Mercedes. "Okay folks, we're here. Looks like no illegals." Then she jumped out and began walking toward the front door. Samuel unhooked his seatbelt, smiled at Susan, and clumsily leaned across the center console to pull the driver's door shut. "She's very protective of this place," he said.

Susan smiled out of politeness only.

By the time they were headed for the front door, Jennifer was already talking with Wolfgang, smiling and speaking sweetly like the marketer she was.

"Oh, *ja* Jen, I wanted to discuss that with you," Wolfgang said.

Jennifer felt it coming and knew there was no way to explain the room. She'd have to deny it and try to act as if it were a surprise to her as well. *Just keep smiling,* she told herself. *No one with a bright smile can be a suspect.*

"You see a friend of mine was going to throw these bricks away," Wolfgang continued, "and I said, *nein*, before you do let me have them."

Jennifer felt bewildered, but Samuel and Susan approached, so she forced herself to act normally.

"Wolfgang, these are my good friends Samuel Ansell and Susan Blake. Samuel and Susan, this is Wolfgang Shlegel."

Wolfgang put out his hand to Samuel. "*Guten Tag, Herr Ansell.*"

Samuel smiled broadly and returned his grasp. "Hello, Mr. Shlegel, it's good to finally meet you."

Wolfgang reached to take Susan's hand, "*Guten Tag, Frau Blake; wie geht es Ihnen?* I mean to say, how are you?" Wolfgang lowered his head slightly executing a fractional bow, but he cast his gaze upward resulting in a disquieting look, and he wore the same snicker she'd seen from the car.

"I'm fine, thank you." Susan said and took her hand back early.

Wolfgang turned to Jennifer. "As I was saying, my friend gave these to me, and I was going to call you and ask if I might construct a—how do you say it—barbeque?"

Samuel and Jennifer glanced at each other, relieved.

"Perhaps I did not speak that word correctly," Wolfgang said apologetically.

"Oh no, you said it right," Jennifer shot in quickly. "A barbeque, yes, sure, of course. That's fine with me, and thank you."

"*Ja*, I considered constructing it in the back, out of view, near the veranda."

"Absolutely. That would be perfect," Jennifer said. "Just take the cost out of your next lease payment."

"*Nein, Frau Dickerman.* It is my honor to be able to add to such a lovely place as this."

"Well then," Jennifer said, "*Danke shön, Herr Shlegel.*" (Thank you very much, Mr. Shlegel.) Then she laughed self-consciously. "I've been practicing that ever since our first meeting."

"*Ja, Ihr Deutsch ist sehr gut, Frau Dickerman*, Wolfgang said with enthusiasm, "*und Bitte shön!*"

"Okay, now I'm lost."

Wolfgang laughed. "I only said your German is good, and you are welcome." Then Wolfgang fixed on Susan. "Now, all of you, come in out of the cold. See the *mittagessen* (lunch) I have prepared. I apologize, though, because it is only a trifle." Wolfgang led the way, and the others followed him in.

THIRTY-SIX

Whitney watched from her usual corner of the ceiling as the four walked into the foyer. She wanted to warn them, to moan and scream and report what Wolfgang was doing—and what he intended to do—but she remained still and silent; she had to. She watched the new woman, Susan, obviously a friend of Jennifer's, looking all around the foyer, but she didn't have the same look of awe and wonder most newcomers invariably had when they first came inside the house. Most people loved the surface grandeur and opulence because they didn't understand its true purpose. But the new woman looked scared. Maybe she knew.

"Can I show Susan the study?" Jennifer asked eagerly.

"*Ja,ja*, for sure. Then come to *das* dining room I think you will find it appetizing. For now, I will take Samuel. Come Samuel; we'll eat like men before *die* women catch us." Samuel laughed and followed the bald man to dining room as Jennifer and Susan went to the study.

Whitney passed through the walls to follow Jennifer and Susan. She wanted to warn them secretly, but she remembered what Wolfgang had said to her earlier, and it worried her now.

He had come into her room while she was watching Jennifer's car roaming on the property. He came and stood beside her at her window. In his left hand he held a black automatic pistol. "You want to tell them, I know this," Wolfgang said. "But what I can't understand is why you would want to hurt Kerrie again."

Whitney could only bring herself to moan.

"*Ja, mein dummer kleiner Geist* (Yes, my stupid little ghost), Kerrie is under my control. *Glauben Sie das?*" (Do you believe this?) Wolfgang walked calmly back to the door to leave the room. "If you appear, if you make a sound, Kerrie will return to the table where you put her, and she will stay there forever, just like you are here forever. *Glauben Sie das?*"

Whitney turned and looked at Wolfgang, not giving him the courtesy of materializing her mouth or eyes. "And if they know," Wolfgang raised his Beretta. "Then I must kill them. *Ich hoffe dass Sie das verstehen.*" (I hope that you understand this.)

Then Wolfgang turned away and closed her door. Whitney returned to watch the blue Durango circling the property. Everything had become fear. Consciousness was nothing more than suffering. And Whitney *did* believe Wolfgang, and because of her belief in him, she knew she would do whatever he told her to do.

* * *

"Yes," Susan said anxiously without looking around the study at all, "it's very beautiful, and I'm really glad you brought me, but if it's all the same, I would like to leave." Susan held her handbag close to her chest. "Frankly, it scares me."

"I thought you were into haunted houses and all that?" Jennifer asked disappointedly. *Never bring a psychic to your place of satanic sacrifice.* The thought came to her like a new real estate rule.

"I am, but it's not ghosts that worry me. I think there's something else. This place has a negative energy. I don't know what it is."

"It is kind of a dreary place," Jennifer said. "I promise we'll leave real soon. Let's just do lunch, and then we'll go, okay?"

"Okay," Susan grudgingly agreed.

"And Susan," Jennifer said, "if you see anything strange, you know like the ghost, don't say anything to Wolfgang. He doesn't sense it at all, and I don't want him to. He's a really good tenant, and if he's comfortable, I want him to stay that way, you know? And don't say anything at lunch about negative energy or bad vibes or anything like that, okay?"

"Sure," Susan replied apologetically. "I know you've got a big stake in this place. I wouldn't do anything to screw that up. I just—"

"Frankly," Jennifer interrupted, "the place freaks me out, too. I thought the haunting would make it worth a lot more, but it's like it pollutes the place. I'm lucky to have Wolfgang here. I'm lucky he's so dull!"

Susan ran her hand over the spines of some of the books in the bookcase. "This place really is gorgeous, and yet it has dark secrets. It's like something's buried here." Susan said offhandedly as she scanned the titles.

"Well, it's very old." Jennifer said hoping to distract Susan from that particular train of thought. She didn't need Susan to start *feeling* things around the place.

"Doesn't that Wolfgang give you the creeps a little?" Susan said.

"Him? Oh no, he's sweet...Well, he can be a little arrogant, that's for sure. I think he must come from money."

"Hey you guys," Samuel's voice rang out. "You got to see this spread!"

When she heard the shout that interrupted Susan and Jennifer, Whitney passed through the structure of the house and up to the top of the staircase. She stood behind the balcony railing and watched.

Jennifer and Susan left the study and walked through the foyer, but Susan suddenly stopped and pointed to the second floor landing. "Jennifer, look."

Whitney stood barely visible in the sunlight that passed through the foyer windows—her blue eyes, brown hair, and pink lips materialized. Her thin blue nightgown swayed aqueous on an ethereal breeze.

"Hello, Whitney," Jennifer whispered.

"She's beautiful," Susan whispered back, as if commenting on a rare bird.

Realizing she had come into view, Whitney shot her consciousness into the dining room. There she hid in the corner of the ceiling. To Susan and Jennifer she simply vanished.

It was getting easier for her to form her features now, and it was taking less and less time, especially now that she was forcing her features to form more often. The appearance at the top of the stairs occurred by accident. She only meant to rest there and watch as they walked to the dining room. In the past, she wouldn't have formed so quickly.

"She's gone," Susan said disappointedly.

Jennifer looked at Susan and put a finger to her pursed lips, "Shhh. Besides, she's never gone." Jennifer whispered. "She's here every time I come out. I've never been here and not seen her."

"Hey you guys," Samuel said as he came out with a plate that held a gourmet-looking sandwich. He stopped and looked up the stairs, "What?"

"Whitney," Jennifer whispered matter-of-factly.

"Really?"

"Okay everyone, silence," Jennifer said. "We'll talk about it in the car. But right now—sandwiches, just sandwiches." Jennifer sounded like a mother scolding her children.

The three of them walked into the dining room. "Good Lord," Jennifer remarked as she looked at the table.

"I told you," Samuel said.

There was a breadbasket with sandwich rolls. There were silver trays with various deli meats, a tray with assorted cheeses, and silver platters that held lettuce and other vegetables. The mayonnaise and mustard, potato salad, and what looked to be sauerkraut, sat in their own silver serving bowls with individual ladles and serving spoons, and a crystal punch bowel held what looked to be a kind of sparkling fruit punch with orange slices floating in it.

"Mr. Shlegel," Jennifer said, "you shouldn't have gone to so much trouble. I thought we were having hoagies. And the dining room is so...clean, compared to the last time I saw it—I mean, wow!"

"*Es war nichts*," (It was nothing.) Wolfgang said, waving off the compliment. "I have *ein Dienstmädchen*, how do you say—a housekeeper—who comes to look after me. These are just some leftovers, so I apologize for the crudity. You must come over some night," Wolfgang looked directly at Susan, "and dine with me properly." It seemed the invitation might have been for her alone.

"Absolutely!" Jennifer inserted. "And you'll have to visit Samuel's wine restaurant in Phoenix, Fifty-Five Degrees." Jennifer produced one of the business cards from her purse and handed it to Wolfgang.

"*Ganz sicher*, (Of course) I would be honored."

As they ate, Jennifer said, "So, Wolfgang, do you think you'll be able to do anything with the wine downstairs?"

"Oh, *Ja*, nearly every barrel is full, and I have tested each one. I think it could easily be marketed and sold in its entirety."

"Wolfgang's going to make and sell wine," Jennifer said to Susan. "He has a special Austrian process he's going to implement. He's going to re-grow the vines and everything."

Wolfgang nodded and smiled in agreement. "*Das* current wine, which is Cabernet, is not the best, but it is well enough for my purposes."

"You should see the cellar," Samuel said to Susan.

Jennifer shot him a look of sudden horror.

Wolfgang's eye's darted from side to side as if looking for an escape. "*Nein*." Wolfgang said at the exact moment Jennifer said, "No." Together they seemed to harmonize an international tune. Wolfgang looked to Jennifer, "*Entschuldigung;* (Sorry) I did not mean to interrupt you."

"Oh no, that's quite alright." Jennifer smiled with nervous relief.

"It's just that I am arranging things down there, and I'm not sure if it is safe at this precise moment," Wolfgang said.

From the back corner of the dining room ceiling, Whitney could see a form underneath Wolfgang's thick turtleneck at the back of his trousers. She knew it was his gun. She wanted to warn Jennifer and the rest, but all she could do was watch the events unfold.

"Absolutely; we completely understand," Jennifer spoke for everyone before they could speak for themselves. "We'll see the cellar another time."

Jennifer felt the sweat on her forehead. She could see Susan walking immediately to the wine rack, led by some psychic notion directing her like a compass to the source of evil, and with the "beautiful" Whitney standing beside her pointing at the brick wall screaming, *It's behind there!* Then Wolfgang would be gone—after demanding his money back. The local newspaper would get it wrong and accuse *her* of child sacrifice. Her former cohorts at McWilliam's would all gather around one paper and read the story with their jaws open, and Samuel would say, "I—I just can't be involved with this." But Jennifer only smiled in their presence at the feast-of-sandwiches, the consummate salesperson—in every moment.

"*Gute Idee!* (Good idea) We must see the cellar at another time." Wolfgang quickly agreed.

"Yeah," Susan added, as if they were all waiting for her to make the final decision. Wolfgang watched her with the same glare she saw on the walkway. "If it's all the same, I'd rather not," she said.

"Sorry." Samuel said quietly as Jennifer glared at him. He took a large bite from his sandwich and tried to look away.

THIRTY-SEVEN

———— •—

hey took hours of back roads and trails through dry wash-
es requiring four-wheel drive. The only times they
stopped were once to eat and twice to urinate. At a quarter
past five the pickup finally came to a stop in a desolate
area thirty miles north of Nogales in a valley within the San
Cayetano Mountains.

"Why'd we stop?" Mike asked.

"This is where we meet them," Santiago grunted, struggling
with his English.

"And they're going to give us the girl?"

"*Por Seguro.*" (For sure)

Mike sipped from a bottle of water and marveled at how fast
the darkness fell, like a great malevolent shadow covering
them. He wished he had his wine with him, but Wolfgang was
keeping it to ensure his return.

Santiago got out of the truck and jumped up on the hood,
and using a pair of binoculars, he scanned the area south of
their position. "I see them!" he shouted.

Mike looked out through the windshield and then stuck his head out the passenger window, "How many are there?"

Santiago paused and counted. "Ten, maybe eleven."

"That's going to get pretty crowded in the back, isn't it?"

"No," Santiago said. He jumped off the hood of the truck as they approached.

"¡*Vamános!*" (Let's go!) Santiago said to Mike and motioned with a wave of his hand for him to get out of the truck. Santiago yelled to the approaching crowd. "*Vengan aquí. ¡Rapido!*" (Over here! Hurry!)

The crowd made its way to the pickup. When they were close, Mike saw three men, four women, and an old woman whose cracked and rugged face matched the surrounding terrain. There were three children, as well: two boys and one girl. The girl had large brown eyes and perfect mocha-smooth skin. She couldn't have been more than six, maybe seven. This would be the one Wolfgang wanted. Knowing her fate, Mike desperately avoided eye contact with her. It was easier that way.

Hola, ¿qué tal? (Hello, how are you?) Santiago said to the group.

The oldest of the men stepped forward: *Estamos bien. Gracias por encontrarnos aquí. Mi nombre es Sergio, y ella es mi esposa, Maria,* (We're all fine. Thank you for meeting us here. My name is Sergio, and this is my wife, Maria.) *Ella es mi madre,*" (And this is my mother) he said, pointing to the old woman. The old woman didn't smile, but only stared at Santiago with a hard non-committing face.

"*No se preocupe, Señora,*" (Don't worry, grandma) Santiago smiled as he spoke. "*Es casi terminado.*" (It's almost over.)

The woman stayed fixed in her cynical expression. Somewhere above them and off in the distance a hawk screeched in the desert air. The afternoon was waning fast, making it almost too dark to see.

"*Señor*," Sergio continued introducing the adults, "*son Hector, Jesús, Lucita, y Beth, y Josephina.*" (this is Hector, Jesus, Lucita, and Beth and Josephina)

"*¿Y quiénes son esta pequeña gente?*"(And who are these little people?) Santiago said as he knelt down in front of the children; they stood shy and reticent.

Sergio responded, "*Son Julio, Bernardo, y Cynthia.*"

Santiago looked at the little girl. "*Hola,* Cynthia," he said as he put his hand on her tiny shoulder. *¿Estás listo a ver lo qué esta América?*" (Are you ready to see what America is all about?) The little girl, not understanding, nodded her head obediently.

"Then let's get going," Santiago said in English to Mike who was standing at the back of the truck. Mike nodded. He was still unsure exactly how they were going to separate the girl from her family. They seemed very close, and not the type that would sell her.

Sergio smiled and motioned his family to follow after Santiago.

"Yeeehaaa!" Santiago suddenly yelled.

The family startled, apprehension struck across their faces. The one named, Maria, put her arms around the little girl.

The old woman remained stone-faced, as if she had lived too long to be startled by the actions of others. Mike noticed she looked nothing like someone starting a new life in the land of milk and honey. Rather, she looked like someone being herded into a cattle car—next stop, Auschwitz.

As Santiago walked on, the family shuffled behind him cautiously. Sergio tried to lift their spirits and even said, "yeehaa," albeit more quietly, as if it were very much a part of their new and hopeful beginning. He tried to reassure them, but their forced smiles remained.

Anticipating the entire family getting into the back, Mike raised the door of the topper and lowered the tailgate, but there were no cushions, no blankets, no water, or food. Instead there was only a zippered, soft-leather rifle case and a roll of gray duct tape.

Santiago whistled a simple tune as he approached and unzipped the case. When he removed the Colt AR-15, slapped in a thirty-round magazine and charged the receiver, the family began to scream.

Santiago shouldered the weapon and immediately shot Sergio in the chest. Mike covered his ears when the first two shots boomed in rapid succession. The second shot let out a large muzzle flash in the gathering darkness. Sergio dropped to his knees and fell forward, face first, into the desert gravel. Mike noticed a portion of thick white bone sticking out the back of his shirt. The entire family scrambled in panic, all of them screaming, except for the old woman who didn't move.

Santiago opened up on them with semi-automatic fire. Five shots hit Hector, Jesús, and Josephina. They all fell immediately to the dirt. Josephina wasn't killed outright, but her left femur was blown in half, and she fell to the ground when her thigh collapsed. She cried and drug herself in the dirt, but Santiago put another three rounds into her back. It rendered her lifeless, and the others rapidly exsanguinated.

Lucita tried to run with the two little boys, Julio and Bernardo, but she couldn't get them to move any faster than an adult would walk. They were stamping their feet as if in a temper tantrum, but their screams came from their reaction to their mother's fear, the noise of the gun, and not knowing what to do.

Santiago readjusted his aim. With a muzzle flash and deafening thunder, the top right quarter of Lucita's skull vaporized.

She dropped, and the two toddler boys ran around her in a frenzy. He put three rounds into Julio and four into Bernardo. Bernardo's right arm flew off with the third round before the fourth tore a hole through his tiny midsection.

Maria, squeezing Cynthia close to her chest, ran back the way they had come through the desert. Santiago took careful aim and shot five rounds at her legs. The first four missed and made small plumes of dust on the ground around her. The last one took out her left tibia. Bone visibly separating from her lower leg, she fell, and Cynthia cushioned her fall.

"Go get the girl," Santiago shouted at Mike.

Mike stood in abject terror, unable to move. Santiago spun and pointed the rifle at him. Mike saw the aggression in his eyes and the sweat on his face. He overcame himself and obeyed. He scrambled out to where they had fallen, like a perverse form of bird dog hot on a downed quail. He thought only two things as he ran: he wanted this horrible reality to go away, and he needed more wine.

The one called, Beth, was several yards off and running fast. Santiago swung the rifle around and opened up with five shots in rapid succession. Bursts of flame swelled around the muzzle of the gun on the third and fifth rounds. In the distance Beth fell hard. She didn't guard herself when she fell but rather hit the ground motionless and remained so. Santiago turned his attention from her to the grandmother, who had not moved from her spot.

She glared at him.

He pointed his rifle at her, and at the end of the elevated sights the woman's face judged him. "*¿Qué estas mirando, puta?*" (What are you looking at, whore?) he said.

"*Un hombre pequeño en el infierno,*" (A small man in hell) She replied.

Santiago rapid-fired twice at the old woman's head, and it opened up spraying red and cranial fragments. She crumpled to the ground as if someone pulled a supporting rod out of her spine. The bolt of the AR-15 held back on the empty magazine.

Santiago walked over to the truck and retrieved a full magazine from the rifle case. He ejected the empty clip, letting it fall to the dirt and slapped in the new one, then he pressed the bolt release and charged the weapon. He picked up the duct tape and headed off to where the last episodes of life were acting out ahead of the truck.

Mike was trying to wrench the screaming child from her mother's arms. Santiago laughed as he approached and saw that Mike was bawling as well. In his thick Spanish accent he asked, "Do you think we should fuck her first?"

"*Por favor no haga daño a mi niña!*" (Please don't hurt my little girl!) Maria cried to Mike. "*Por favor, es una nina.* (Please, she's just little.)

Mike couldn't understand the woman's Spanish, even though he could guess what her words meant. Never once did he think about what he had turned into. His need for the wine was becoming critical. All he could think about was the wine. The girl's sneaker came off in her mother's hand, and Mike was able to pull her free from Maria's grip that had fastened around her ankle. The child flailed in Mike's arms, instinctively, like a small animal trying to escape.

"I forgot; you don't fuck women." Santiago laughed again as the explosive blasts and muzzle flashes commenced. He let go ten rounds into Maria's upper back and head. Mike stumbled backward and fell into the dirt with the little girl screaming in his arms.

After kicking the woman to ensure her death, Santiago went over to Mike and knelt down. He laid the rifle beside him, and as

Mike held Cynthia around the waste, Santiago pulled off a piece of duct tape and affixed it across her mouth. Suddenly, the desert returned to its stunning dark silence. Santiago taped the girl's feet together around her ankles, and then taped her hands together at the wrists.

"What if she can't breathe?" Mike asked.

Santiago looked closely at the girl's face. Her eyes were filled with fear, and she struggled violently; slightly broken and muffled screams escaped through her nose.

"If she's dead when we get her back, she's worth nothing to Wolfgang," Santiago said. He watched her for a moment and put his hand on the front of her chest. "She's breathing. Throw her in the back, and let's get out of here. *Podría haber* patrulla fronteriza." (There could be Border Patrol.)

Mike carried the girl back under his arm and put her in the back of the pickup. "It's going to be a bumpy ride for her," Mike said. His mind screamed for black wine.

"Who gives a fuck," Santiago croaked, applying the safety on the AR-15. He threw the rifle in next to the wiggling child and guzzled from a bottle of water. Then he closed the tailgate and shut the topper.

THIRTY-EIGHT

———— • ————

The black pickup skidded to a stop on the gravel in front of Eternity Vineyards. They had risked returning on a main road and then the highway in order to be back by nine. It was 8:55.

Wolfgang, with a black wine bottle in his hand, walked out to the truck as Mike and Santiago climbed out and went to the back.

"Is she alive?" Wolfgang demanded.

"I think so," Mike answered. He pulled the duct-taped girl from the back of the pickup and positioned her supine on the tailgate. Her eyes were closed and her body limp.

"She was struggling when we put her in the truck," Mike said.

"*Sie ist keine guten toten*!" (She's no good dead!) Wolfgang bellowed. He quickly ripped the tape off her mouth and tilted her head back. In a practiced manner, he put his ear to the child's mouth, listening and feeling for any signs of breath. "*Scheisse* (Shit)! he said and quickly sealed his mouth over the girl's giving her two small breaths of his own. He felt for her pulse in the side of her neck. "*Sie hat einen Puls*, (She has a pulse) he said as if talking to himself. "Schnell, (quickly) Michael, bring her inside!"

Mike scooped up the girl.

Wolfgang turned to Santiago and spoke to him in Spanish: "*Venga mañana para sus botellas. Ellos estarán listos. Por el momento, tome a Michael's.* (Come tomorrow for your bottles. They will be ready. For now, take Michael's.)

Santiago nodded and took the wine before slamming the tailgate and the topper closed. Using his teeth, he quickly pulled the half-raised cork out of the neck of the bottle and spit it to the ground. He took a large swig of the wine and wiped his mouth on his shirt. "*Gracias, señor*," Santiago smiled and went back to the cab of the pickup. He hastily climbed in and closed the door.

Mike watched in horror as the small Mexican took his bottle with him. When the rear tires spun out on the gravel, Mike screamed, "No!"

Wolfgang turned and walked toward Mike, "*Sie idiot*, get her in the basement before her heart ceases, and she'll make three hundred gallons of your wine! *Wenn sich Herz anhält, bekommen Sie nichts.* (If her heart stops, you get nothing.) Schnell, Michael!"

Mike ran into the house, Cynthia's limbs flopping about as he ran with her in his arms. In the foyer, lit only by candlelight, Mike stopped and looked above him and all around. A high-pitched scream echoed throughout the house. He couldn't place its direction, but when he looked to the top of the staircase, Whitney, barely illuminated in candlelight, stood with empty black eyes and a jagged gaping mouth. She screamed so loud, Mike reflexively dropped the unconscious girl and covered his ears.

Accelerating exponentially with every inch, Whitney flew down to him. She covered the distance almost instantly, and as she flew into him, he threw up his hands to protect his face, but she only passed through. He felt nothing. Then she was gone. The dim house was empty again, the screaming barely audible in the distance.

Mike felt a hand slap down on the back of his shoulder. He screeched as he stumbled away from it, tripping over the girl and falling to the floor. When he looked, it was Wolfgang laughing at him.

"*Sie ist gerade ein Geist.* (She's just a ghost.) How can you be afraid of a little ghost? Pick up the girl now, and follow me. I have the room prepared." Wolfgang walked casually to the door behind the stairs, and descended into the basement.

Mike carefully retrieved the girl who lay unmoving on the floor. Her comatose eyes were open, but she looked at nothing. He carried her to the stairs and followed his leader into the basement.

Just as in the foyer, candles were burning in various locations providing the only light in the cellar. The wine rack was opened, and the small room was illuminated with the flickering light of a dozen candles blazing in the candelabrum.

When Mike carried the girl to the door, he saw that Wolfgang had changed into a black robe with its hood pulled over his head. He solemnly held the leather book from the bookshelf in his hands. He was the image of a monk-gone-bad, or worse, something that might walk circles around Stonehenge under a full moon.

There were chains with small shackles hanging from the table legs, and on either side of the table were silver basins lined up with the drain groves cut in the table's surface. He could still hear Whitney's screaming echoing from somewhere in the house, but it was subdued and distant. "Lay her on *der* table, Michael," Wolfgang instructed.

Mike did as he was told.

"Remove *der* tape from her hands *und* feet, *und* fasten them to *der* table legs with those chains, then leave."

Again, Mike did as he was told. When he ripped the tape from her wrists, Cynthia's arms fell flaccid over the sides of the table. He placed her wrists in the iron shackles. He did the same with her ankles. While he was twisting the fastening bolt on the left ankle shackle, Wolfgang put his finger on the side of the girl's neck, pressing into her soft flesh.

"*Sie wird bradycardic.* (She's becoming bradycardic.) *Schnell*, Michael, *schnell.*"

Mike finished and stood up. Wolfgang impatiently waved him out of the room. Mike left, but he stood just outside the door and watched the ceremony unfold.

Wolfgang put the book into a pocket of the robe and produced the ornate dagger from within the sleeve of it. Laying it carefully on the girl's chest—that had ceased all movement— he turned the dagger down to ensure it was pointing toward her feet. Then he backed away and turned to the pentagram. He breathed in deeply through his nose, and a painful grimace overtook his facial expression.

"*Mein Vater, Satan!*" (My Father, Satan!) A tear formed quickly in his left eye and ran down his cheek. "*Kommen Sie zu mir und füllen Sie mich. Lassen Sie uns unseren Wein machen—und futter die Welt.*" (Come to me and fill me. Let us make our wine—and feed the world.) Wolfgang's tears fell freely but he did not sob as he turned to the girl and picked the dagger up off her chest. Holding it high above his head, he aimed the tip at Cynthia's sternum. Then he recited quickly from memory:

"*Das Blut des Kindes* (The blood of the child)

"*Ist die Schuld der Welt* (Is the guilt of the world)

"*Der Tod der Wahrheit* (The death of truth)

"*Trank in der Kommunion von Dämonen*, (Drunk in the communion of demons)

"*Im Dienst des Grossen Herrn Satan.*" (In service to the Great Lord Satan)

Then he slammed the dagger into the heart of the child. When he felt it stick into the wood of the table beneath her, he moaned as if a great pain had been relieved. He pulled the knife and slammed it again and again. Mike counted ten stabbings in quick frenzied succession before Wolfgang regained his composure and laid the dagger on the table. He stepped back and turned to face the pentagram again. He raised his arms. "*Heil Satan!*" he shouted. Then quietly, with sincere solemnity, "*Danke, Vater.*" (Thank you, Father.)

Mike watched the blood running from under the girl and dripping into the silver basins. Wolfgang went to the wine rack and removed an empty, uncorked, black bottle. He knelt down, took the dagger and dipped it in the blood in one of the basins. He let the blood drip off the dagger into the bottle, two drops only. Then he walked out of the room into the cellar. He walked passed Mike as if he weren't there and over to one of the wine casks.

Using a wine thief, he withdrew enough to fill the bottle; then walked to the china cabinet, and from one of its drawers he took a cork and pressed it a third of the way in into the neck of the bottle. As he gently turned the bottle end over end mixing the wine and the blood, he looked at Mike and smiled like an indulging mother. "*Das Flasche* (The bottle) is for you, Michael, as soon as you bury *das Mädchen.*" (the girl)He tilted his head toward the room.

Nauseated, Mike peered in at the slaughtered girl on the table. "Where am I supposed to bury her?" His tone whined with impossibility.

"Bury her deep in the vineyard, where *der* dirt is soft. Go down at least one and a half meters, and make sure to remove her clothes. It will help her decompose. Then burn *die* clothes in *die* fireplace."

* * *

With little enthusiasm, Mike did as he was told, and when he arrived in the study for his reward, Wolfgang was sitting at the desk still in his black robe but with his hood pulled back. He rested his temple on two fingers and stared blankly into the fireplace, baldness and face glowing red with the firelight. "Did you bury her well?" Wolfgang asked.

"Yes," Mike said as he put the girls dress, stockings, shoes and coat onto the roaring logs. When the fire consumed them, it grew larger and brighter, illuminating the room in a chaotic brilliance.

The black bottle sat on the desk; Mike stared at it immodestly.

"Drink up," Wolfgang said.

Mike took it quickly, removed the cork and swallowed from it. "Oh God!" Mike said and fell into one of the chairs by the desk. His eyes became fixed on the ceiling, then rolled back slightly in his skull as if starting a seizure. "That is so good," He finally said, and took another sip.

"There's just one more to go," Wolfgang mentioned calmly. He stared intently at Mike, waiting for his reply.

"I know," Mike said.

* * *

Whitney sat in her chair and looked out of her bedroom window into the night. A three-quarter moon broke through holes in the clouds intermittently illuminating the vineyard. She had watched Mike bury the girl, just as she had seen her father do many times, even before he killed Kerrie—before she had traded Kerrie to him—and then many times after that. She longed to be buried in the vineyard, herself, but there was nothing she could do. She continued to moan, and her moaning became like the wind that blew through the lonely stone structures of the estate.

THIRTY-NINE

Jennifer wasn't sure what she was doing; unpaid labor wasn't something she aspired to, but she knew she liked it. The bar was busy at Fifty-Five Degrees, and she liked being busy. She got along well with the other staff, and she liked the friends she was making among them. She even liked the feel of the black combed-cotton slacks against her skin and the black blouse she wore while she worked. She was comfortable in her new clothes at the bar. It wasn't at all like McWilliam's Real Estate; she didn't feel in competition with anyone.

Samuel wanted to put her on the payroll, but she refused. If he needed her, she wanted to be there, but she could never be his employee. She was either much more than that or she'd walk away, nothing less could ever be tolerated.

The income from the Eternity Vineyards lease kept her in her small apartment, and if Wolfgang was successful, there could be more from the existing wine sales. Besides, she was able to eat and drink whatever she wanted at the restaurant or at the bar, and did so nearly every night with Samuel.

But she was forty-three, and couldn't' shake the feeling that she was merely killing time in a life going nowhere. *Where does a life go?* she thought. And when she thought it, Whitney came to mind. Suddenly she missed her, and didn't know why.

"Jennifer, you got to see this!" Samuel said walking quickly from the manager's office to the bar. He held an atlas of Arizona in his hand. Jennifer was drying glasses and lost in the thoughts about her life when he came up to her.

"What?" Jennifer asked, snapping out of it.

Samuel used the remote control and changed the channel on the flat screen TV behind the bar. The evening news was just running the story:

Again, the U.S. Border Patrol is reporting the gruesome discovery of ten bodies, some of them children, apparently illegal immigrants, shot to death in the desert north of Nogales.

There was an aerial image of the mass murder scene. The bodies were covered in yellow plastic sheets. Then came the footage of full body bags being loaded into a military helicopter.

"That's not that far from your place," Samuel said pointing to the location on his map. "This is where it happened. It's only about thirty miles southwest of you."

"Oh my God," Jennifer said.

These were probably illegals that came up on a drug deal gone bad," a uniformed authority was telling a reporter. *"Unfortunately, these people come up from Mexico looking for work and have no protection from the drug dealers and coyotes that typically make drug exchanges in the more remote areas of our state. These poor folks look like they've been dead about a week."*

"Five women, three men and two toddler-aged children were killed..." the news report continued.

Jennifer stopped watching when an armed Minuteman gave an obligatory press statement that even though they carried high-powered rifles with scopes, they only reported illegals to the Border Patrol and gave the desert-crossers water and food.

"I should call Wolfgang and let him know. I can't imagine what he must think of our country." Jennifer said. "I feel like I'm going to be sick. That's so close to us."

Samuel put his arms around her from behind and kissed her neck. "He's probably watching it," Samuel said.

"Who could kill children like that? Who could just wipe out a family, and for what? Drugs? Sometimes I swear I can't face this world alone."

"You don't have to," Samuel said.

Jennifer turned around from the sink and looked up directly into his eyes. His face was perfect to her, and the depth and warmth of his eyes felt like coming home. "What are you saying?" She asked.

FORTY

ennifer took the cardboard box into her kitchen. She told herself she was only bringing a few things over to Samuel's house, and only because they spent so much time there, absolutely not because they were moving in together. It was simply that Samuel's three-bedroom, twenty-eight hundred square foot contemporary adobe in Northern Phoenix was more comfortable than her apartment—for the both of them, and he had a pool that they didn't have to share with any neighbors. This was the only reason for the box, and as she looked into the living room at the two overstuffed suitcases, she allowed the same explanation for them. She made her own money; he made his own money. They were simply two independent people who spent a lot of time together.

Of course, her money depended on Wolfgang never finding out the truth about Eternity. Bringing the local tarot reader out there had almost blown it. That was her screw up, and she wouldn't make that same mistake again. Samuel was going to have to learn to be more careful, too. He wasn't a salesman, and she couldn't expect him to work off a partner, but thank God he caught on when he did. Thank God he stuck a sandwich in it before saying something that couldn't be retracted, something that would have to be explained. And thank God Wolfgang wasn't eager to show off the wine cellar.

As she put her good spatula in the box of temporary things to bring to Samuel's, a light went off somewhere in the darkest corner of her mind, just the slightest thought that wasn't in synch with the rest: *Wolfgang answered too fast.* He said *no* as quick as she did. It may have been in German, but it was *no* all the same, and he seemed almost as startled. She had a good reason; she was hiding something. She was hiding something evil. So what about Wolfgang? What were his reasons? That the place was a mess? When you quote a price to someone on a property, Jennifer thought, you know before they ever say a word, before they ever say yes or no whether or not they can afford it, whether they think the place isn't worth it, or whether there might be a slight chance they can get the financing. It's what their eyes do when you quote the price. You always have to watch the eyes when you quote, because that's where the truth is. Wolfgang wasn't worried about any mess; she'd seen his eyes.

Jennifer forced herself to stop thinking about it. She placed her thoughts elsewhere, a talent she'd developed throughout her life, a talent she used when her ex first said she wasn't spending enough time with Tammy, a talent she used when Joel at McWilliam's said she'd never make it alone, a talent she used after she promised Robert Maddock she'd never sell Eternity. Her technique was simple: You just stop thinking about what you think and concentrate only on what you know. What she *knew* was that Wolfgang Shlegel was a nice rich man who likes to make wine, that's all. It brought her four grand a month free and clear, and she would get a cut from the wine in the cellar. That was it. She put her cheese grater in the box.

Besides, there were serious things to consider: Call-It-Home Realty was dead. The bet was over. She'd taken a hit card and busted. It was inaccurate now to call herself *in real estate*. She only went to the strip mall office once a week, more to clear out the mail and check for break-ins than anything else. At the end of the month, she'd close it for good. There wasn't any reason to eat up money on office rent.

The professional loss felt like falling off a cliff. All she'd ever been was a Realtor. All she ever found success at was selling property. *But it cost you everything*. She tried to banish the thought. *Don't think about what you think; concentrate on what you know*. But she couldn't deny the truth: At the end of her career, all she had was a desolate, unsellable, horribly haunted mansion. Its only use was maybe making wine, and in Arizona at that!

She moved a box into the bedroom and reminded herself only to retrieve what was absolutely necessary for the times she visited him. She took an unopened four-pack of toilet paper from the cabinet under the bathroom sink and put it in the box.

If Wolfgang could make a go of the vineyards, then the commercial potential of the property could be realized, even if it couldn't be sold. Even if Wolfgang didn't stay long-term, if he was successful in proving good wine could be cultivated from the vineyards, others would want to lease it. And apparently, so long as she was keeping her deal with Robert Maddock not to sell the place, Whitney had no power to ruin her plans.

How strange to know for sure that the soul survived the body, but Whitney proved it. How few people knew what she now knew. They believed it, but they didn't know it, but what comfort was it? The idea of becoming a ghost after death only made the idea of dying more horrible. *How do you avoid becoming a ghost?* She thought. How did Whitney end up a ghost? Surely all little girls go to heaven; surely it was only the older ones like herself who had to worry.

Jennifer set the box down on the first step of the concrete stairs outside her apartment door. She reached up to unhook the small potted plant that hung from the roof, and carefully put it on top of the other things in the box. Without the hanging plant, her apartment didn't look like hers anymore. But a plant has to be tended to, she thought. She couldn't just leave it to itself in the Phoenix sun. Besides, it would be easier to water on the occasions she spent at Samuel's place.

She locked the door behind her and carried her box of things to her Durango. She came back for the suitcases. She wanted to drop them off before the evening shift at Fifty-Five Degrees.

FORTY-ONE

don't want to go out again. I don't ever want to leave the house again. What we did to that girl was horrible," Mike said.

"But *Sie sehen hier* (you see here), I've only been able to finish two of *diese* casks." Wolfgang motioned with his hand to the two barrels at the end of the row. He spoke offhand as if what he said naturally nullified everything Mike was requesting, or thinking. "With another child," he said, "one with greater health and hydration, we could finish at least another three."

Wolfgang lowered a hydrometer into one of the barrels and checked the specific gravity of the wine. Sun shone through the open loading doors, and in the directional rustic light, Wolfgang looked like a humble winemaker. He wore a leather bib apron and spectacles, the perfect ad in *Wine Spectator Magazine*. He sampled the untouched liquid from a glass as if all that mattered was the quality of the grapes he had grown with his own bare hands and hard work.

"Why can't Santiago do it himself? He doesn't need me; he didn't need me last time."

"I want you to be *mein Augen und Ohren*, Michael. I want you to be my eyes and ears out there."

Michael sat in a wooden chair by the wine rack that was now closed, concealing the room behind it. He raised a black bottle to his lips. He had come to learn that all he had to do was wet his lips to feel good. Drinking the wine in gulps was wasteful and pointless; it only required a taste. He looked at his bottle as if studying it. "Does the bottle matter," he asked.

"*Ja*," Wolfgang said. "But we don't need *Flaschen*. (bottles) We won't bottle and ship here. They come to us and we fill them. When we have enough, we will let them all know. There are thousands of bottles out there in countries you've never been to or heard of. What we do matters *sehr viel*. (very much)

Michael didn't understand Wolfgang's German. Most of the time he couldn't make out his English either, but he resigned himself to Wolfgang's will. He tried hard to imagine life before the wine, but found it increasingly difficult to do.

"Tomorrow, Santiago is coming to fill his *Flaschen*, and *Sie* will go with him again and bring to us another *Mädchen*. Then we can finish our work. Then the world is mine." Wolfgang paused, correcting himself and smiling at his less than innocent omission, "...ours."

* * *

Mike screamed as soon as he awoke. Whitney was sitting on the side of his bed staring out his window. She didn't turn to him when he screamed, she just stared, as if he was a silent stiff body and she was sitting with him grieving his loss.

Even before the orientation of time and place formed in his mind, he scrambled out the other side of the bed, pulling the blankets with him and falling to the hardwood floor with a thud. He felt nothing but fear when he hit.

"Leave me alone!" he yelled at the apparition.

Whitney didn't turn when she spoke, her gaze remained fixed on the pre-dawn light hitting the mountains in the distance—doing so preserved her energy. "He's going to kill you, too," she said. "When you're dead, you'll still want the wine, but you won't be able to drink it. The dead can't drink."

Though he could hear her, he was too scared for her words to register. He continued to scoot his naked body across the floor, making distance between himself and the ghost-girl. "You leave me alone! You can't hurt me!" Mike said. He grabbed a small vase for protection off a stand by the bedroom door.

"You're going to hell," Whitney said distantly, as if the fact were nothing more than a comment on the mild morning. "You're going to the hell you're making while you're alive— the same as I did." Then her apparition was gone.

Mike blinked looking at the spot where Whitney had been. He couldn't tell if he had been dreaming, but his day started with fear as all his days had since meeting Wolfgang. But leaving Wolfgang never entered his mind as a possibility. Even if Wolfgang had become nothing more than a symbol of unending addiction, pain, and all things bad, he didn't care. Only the wine mattered—making it, drinking it.

He stood and took his bottle from the night table. He couldn't help himself; he took a large swallow. When he heard the rumble of the pickup's exhaust and the crunching of gravel beneath rubber tires, he pulled his blanket around him and walked to the window and looked down; Santiago had arrived.

* * *

"Did you bring your rifle?" Mike asked as they drove. He didn't like Santiago. His Latin machismo disgusted him, so he wetted his lips with his bottle. Almost immediately after, Santiago didn't seem so bad. Santiago, as if on cue, did the same with his own black bottle. The pickup jerked and bounced over ruts in the dirt road, a road that no one seemed to know existed except for Santiago. Occasionally, he would stop the truck and consult the map he laid between himself and Mike.

"We don't need it this time." Santiago said and pulled a Smith and Wesson revolver out of a shoulder holster under his denim jacket. "This time you, little *jotto*, you're doing it." Santiago handed Mike the gun.

It was heavy, but he held it out in front of him as if studying it. He knew the nickel plating meant expensive. He looked through the sites at something out the front window.

"That's a .44 Magnum, *hombre*. You ever shoot a gun?" Santiago asked.

"Yes," Mike said. "I know what to do with it. I had a friend once who used to take me to an indoor range." Mike sat the gun on the seat beside him. "Isn't there some way we could just take the girl at...you know...gunpoint and leave the parents?"

Santiago scowled at Mike with paranoid fear. "You kill them, or I'll kill you; ¿*entienda*?" (understand?) Santiago took back the revolver and pushed its four-inch barrel against Mike's left temple while he steered the truck. "Shlegel promised you were good for this." He hissed through his teeth.

"I am." Mike recoiled from the gun and pressed himself against the passenger door. "I am."

Santiago put the gun back down on the seat between them. "*Bueno*. Now shut up," Santiago said, then mumbled to himself, "*No me gusta hablar con usted*." (I don't like talking with you.)

Mike stared out the passenger window as they drove, but had no idea where they were. It wasn't anywhere close to where they slaughtered the last group. It amazed him how whole groups made their way through Southern Arizona from Mexico. It was desolate in the winter—positively deadly in the summer—but illegals from south of the border were an endless stream throughout the year. There would be plenty of children wandering around at any time, and Wolfgang would have an endless supply, prime for the taking, and no one would ever know.

They hadn't made any turns on the dirt road since leaving the highway that led away from Eternity Vineyards. Mike supposed if he got out and just headed back, he'd find the highway, if he could walk that far in the desert that is. He figured they were at least twenty miles from the main road, and when Santiago finally stopped, Mike realized they had arrived in the middle of nowhere. They could have been on another planet or on earth before humans existed. And it seemed they were back in time before any morality had formed in the minds of men, in the middle of a desert with nothing else, just rocks and bushes, foothills—predators and prey.

Santiago took a bottle of water out of the holder on the dash and swallowed half the contents, then wet his lips with his black bottle. Mike noticed that Santiago wet his lips exactly as he had learned to do through trial and error. It must be a natural learning curve, he thought.

As they sat parked, Mike occasionally wetted his lips with his supply of wine, but his bottle was getting light. He was running out again, and he knew it. He had taken too many gulps and not enough sips, and the sips were a mistake, too, when all he needed was the taste on his lips.

Santiago was more disciplined. Mike noticed the bottle he turned up to his mouth chugged with fullness. The idea that

Santiago would share his wine was not something he wanted to inquire about. Santiago might shoot him for asking.

"Wait here; I have to take a piss," Santiago announced. He opened his door and the coolness of the winter day spilled in diluting the greenhouse heat generated by the windshield. Mike hardly noticed him leave. All he saw was Santiago's unattended black bottle sitting against the backrest of the driver's seat. He tried hard to look at it only with a sideways glance, the thought of stealing its contents already entering and possessing him. Santiago slammed the driver's door.

Mike wanted to ignore the full bottle sitting next to him. After all, soon they would have the child and be back home where Wolfgang could stab her heart, get her blood, and make more wine for him. Wolfgang, the provider of everything necessary, would refill his bottle. That's all he had to concentrate on, just that and nothing more.

Except this time he would have to do the killing. Santiago would kill him if he didn't kill the girl's parents, and Mike knew he meant it. He knew it as sure as he knew his wine was almost gone and Santiago's was almost full. He pretended Santiago's bottle wasn't there, and looked out at the vast emptiness of the Arizona landscape—Mars with plant life.

Then, not even looking, he reached over to it. His hand felt the cool smooth curve of the glass neck, and he gripped it. He'd gone too far; he couldn't stop. He pulled the bottle to his side, but when he turned to look at it, Santiago was at the driver's window watching everything with sociopathic eyes.

Mike screamed his surprise.

FORTY-TWO

———— • ————

Santiago jerked the truck door open: "Gim'me that fucking bottle!" He snarled.

"I swear I was just keeping it from falling." Mike tried to smile.

Santiago grabbed the bottle and tipped it back and forth carefully analyzing its weight for any hint of depreciation. His look was one of pitiful fear, the look of loss that comes just before revenge. Then Santiago raged, "I'm going to kill you, *jotto cabron*!" (faggot son of a bitch!) Santiago put a boot up on the running board to climb into the cab.

Just then Mike pointed out the windshield and shouted excitedly, "Santiago, look!"

In the distance, barely visible, two adults and a small child made their way towards them. The man waved his hand. Santiago glared at Mike and then returned a high and slow wave. "Pick up the gun," Santiago said, "and hide it in your pants." They watched the small group approach "Don't let them see you. We have to get them close."

Mike sighed in relief. Santiago was distracted from an appetizer of murder and on to his main course. He picked up the gun and felt its undiluted power in his hand, power to make anything the way he wanted it to be. He thought about what would soon take place. He saw himself pointing the pistol at the man. The man had to be taken out first. He'd see the father's expression of confusion just before the realization that the dark hole of the gun barrel would spit fire and end his life.

In his head, he could hear the woman screaming and the child crying. He reached for his bottle to wet his lips. The sight of the gun pressed against the woman's skull filled his mind. He could see her pathetic frown as she gripped her child, still believing she could save her, or maybe only comfort herself. Everything was planned; everything was ready to happen, but then he accepted what he had been trying not to know: he knew he wasn't going to kill a family; he knew that for certain. And because he knew that, he also knew that he was going to die very soon. If he wouldn't kill the man, his wife, and capture yet another child, he would not live another hour. In fact, given their proximity, he was in his last ten minutes of life.

Mike stepped out of the truck. A strange freedom melted over him, bonded to his impending death. Something he feared all his life was about to happen, and it wasn't that bad at all. The sun was shining brighter; the sky was somehow bluer. It was a good day. It was the only good day he'd had since he and Jennifer were still friends. The day was suddenly full of power, power like the weight of a large-framed .44 magnum held firmly in his grip. When he couldn't pull the trigger, Santiago would take the weapon and shoot the family, and then he would shoot him. Never had Mike felt so clear and sure of anything.

Mike walked around to the front of the truck where Santiago stood. His first shot, aimed at the black hair on Santiago's head, entered the small Mexican's arm instead and spun him around forcing him to face Mike. The bullet obviously dislocated Santiago's shoulder and tore off a bloody chunk of his bicep. The boom of it seemed to fill the entire world.

Mike stifled a hysterical laugh when he saw the look of confusion on Santiago's face, just as it would have been on the father's face—the father who now stood frozen, watching with his family from a hundred yards off. The next shot missed and exploded Santiago's black bottle. Wine sprayed in the desert air like blood. Mike screamed with rage and terror as he fired the gun. The next four shots entered Santiago's abdomen and chest. The blast and concussion of the shots were like artillery fire. The gun recoiled violently in Mike's hand, but he didn't feel the pounding of it.

Santiago stumbled and fell to the ground on his back. Mike approached and stood over him. He aimed the gun directly at Santiago's face. Santiago tried to swear, but only coughed up blood. Some of it splattered on Mike's jeans, and Mike instinctively pulled his leg back as if avoiding a dog's mess. Mike pulled the trigger again, but the hammer only clicked on a spent round.

He dropped the gun beside Santiago, stunned by his own actions, surprised that he had acted on his own at all. He turned to where the family had been and visored his eyes with his hand against the noon sun. He watched them running in the opposite direction, back into the desert from whence they'd come.

He was alive. The family was alive. Mike wondered if they'd survive in the desert long enough to find another pick-up or another pack of border-crossers. He wondered if they'd make it back to Mexico. Then he stopped caring, because he saw the fragments of the bottle he'd shot. He fell to his knees before the broken glass and grieved.

The freedom he felt at the idea of dying just seconds ago was fading, and the need for wine began pressing in on him. Returning to the pickup, he climbed in the driver's seat, and took a large swig from his own bottle, swallowing it without reserve. Immediately, he cursed himself for not conserving it.

There was no way to look into the bottle. The glass was entirely opaque. Even when he held it up to the sun, he couldn't determine how much was left, but it felt light. There couldn't be more than one or two swallows left. He had to get away. He had to get back to Wolfgang and explain and get his bottle refilled.

He started the pickup. He carefully turned it around and headed back on the dirt road that led to the highway. Surely if he just explained to Wolfgang that Santiago meant to kill him. But without a sacrifice, he was nothing to Wolfgang, and he knew it. There'd be no point in going back.

Rolling on Highway 83, he eventually sped past Eternity Vineyards' entrance road. Once again, he felt independent and free. He was defiant and self-affirming. He even flipped off the distant estate and let out a hoot of triumph, but there had been a little wine left at that point. By the time he was halfway to Phoenix, the gnawing sense of familiar panic was setting in.

He'd swallowed the last of his wine by exit 236, just north of Tucson, and while under its influence, he felt he might be able to get away from Wolfgang and Eternity Vineyards, return to Phoenix, his apartment, his job with Call-It-Home Realty, and Jennifer. But his wine was gone now, and that changed things.

By the time he reached the suburb of Chandler next to Mesa, he was trying to piece together a way to fix his situation. All he needed to do was explain things to Wolfgang; all he needed to do was arrange with him a chance to try again. Surely he would understand that. Surely he would be eager to regroup and try again. They were partners, after all.

In Mesa, he planned how to get a child. A child would fix everything. He couldn't go to Wolfgang empty-handed. Without the wine, he felt unclear. His rationale was turning to primal instinct. He needed Wolfgang to give him a refill; he needed to bring him a child, a young girl. That's all that mattered now. His eyes shifted back and forth, taking in the urban setting: the apartments, the bus stops, the people on bikes, and the kids in the cars that passed him.

Twenty minutes later, he wasn't headed for his apartment at all; he couldn't even remember who Jennifer was or what his previous life had been. He felt like a hawk circling above the desert floor, looking for the movement of a small creature below. It was Saturday afternoon; the schools would be empty. His need for wine was strengthening; his planning was breaking down in bits and desperation was taking over.

Then he saw it, just ahead and to the left was the winning ticket.

Mike turned onto 16th street, trying not to screech the tires as he did. He followed the signs for Eastlake Park. It was alive with cars, women with strollers, and kids skirting about like unsuspecting field mice. He had to hurry. It was a sunny day in the Arizona winter, but another hour and there wouldn't be enough sun to keep the serious chill away. Parents would look for their children and want to head home.

Mike swooped down and parked the truck near the restrooms.

FORTY-THREE

⬤

here were no customers in the store, otherwise she never would have turned the television on to watch the news, and Susan was thankful, because she felt sick after watching it.

A nervous nausea followed it, like the kind that followed her astrological study of Eternity Vineyards. Now, she wanted to vomit again.

The first time she'd vomited over Eternity Vineyards was on the way home with Jennifer and Samuel after lunch with Wolfgang Shlegel. Jennifer had to pull the Durango to the side of the road so she could hurl into the dirt. She played it off; she lied; she hadn't been feeling well all day, but in truth she had to get rid of everything that touched her from that place—inside and out.

Once home, she didn't lie on the sofa watching TV and drinking Sprite like Jennifer told her to. Instead, she scrubbed herself for forty-five minutes in the shower, crying even as the water went from hot, to lukewarm, to cold, but there was no washing Wolfgang's glare out of her head. Jeff even opened the bathroom door just to be sure she wasn't unconscious in the water. She lied to him, too, shouting out that everything was fine.

But her natal chart of the Vineyard, a horary astrological inquiry regarding the motivations of Wolfgang Shlegel, and finally a mundane astrological study of the murder of the ten illegal aliens in that same sector brought into focus a truth she knew instinctively since her first visit: Eternity Vineyards is, and has been from its inception, a black hole of evil, it sucked people into it.

She didn't have the specifics, but never had she encountered so much frank psychic energy before, so much power, and yet it was repulsive to her. The beautiful ghost, Shlegel, himself, and the history of a place desolated and lost in the past. It had become a noxious odor to her. Whatever innocence she entertained regarding the inherent good of the spiritual realm evaporated. Now she knew that everything, anything, could sometimes turn evil.

At first, she wasn't going to call. She was going to honor Samuel's wishes and let Jennifer handle the place on her own, but that was before channel nine repeated the alert.

"An Amber Alert has been issued for Tamara Patterson," said the blond anchor with inhumanly full lips. On screen beside her flashed the image of a tiny black girl in pigtails and a dress—an obvious school photo. *"Tamara Patterson is seven years old and went missing this afternoon at approximately four o'clock from Eastlake Park on sixteenth and East Jefferson in Phoenix. Anyone with information regarding her whereabouts is strongly encouraged to call 911 or the Phoenix Police Department and report what you know."*

The image switched to an on-scene interview capturing the up-close anguish of a heavyset mother wailing: *"My girl! My baby girl!"* and regularly dropping to the ground as her legs gave out under her even greater emotional weight. A man and a woman with her were doing their best to console her. They were successful only in keeping her from hitting the ground with full force whenever she dropped.

The video passed to a reporter on the scene standing near the public restrooms who listened intently to whatever was coming over his earpiece. Then he spoke into the camera: *"... That's right, Carol. According to friends of the girl's mother, Tamara Patterson was last seen entering these restrooms. It's my understanding that about fifteen minutes later, when the girl didn't return, her mother went looking for her and was unable to locate her. According to friends of the family, no one has seen little Tamara since that time. Right now, there are no witnesses, and no one knows exactly what might have happened to her, but the Phoenix Police have issued an Amber Alert at this time. Any missing child, of course, a great concern to the Phoenix PD and all of us here at channel nine..."*

When she first saw the report, Susan looked for the missing girl with a tarot reading. She did this any time she learned of a missing child. The girl still existed, her preliminary reading indicated that much. Her next step in tarot-location was a global hemisphere reading, then a quadrant, country, city, and finally she would pull out maps and concentrate on various areas of that city. This time, none of that was necessary. No matter how many times she shuffled her deck and laid out her cards, the pattern she flipped over was the existence pattern for Eternity Vineyards.

Susan picked up the phone while the report continued and called the business number at Fifty-Five Degrees. She had to call, even though Jennifer might get angry, even though she had no physical evidence the missing girl was linked to Eternity Vineyards. She might even be wrong, but how could she live if all her life was dedicated to the psychic arts, and now, when a little girl's life was on the line, she sat back and only vomited. She'd rather lose a friend and a good reputation than know for the rest of her life that even she believed she was a fraud.

"Fifty-Five Degrees, this is Jen." The noise of glasses clinking and dinner conversation filled the background.

"Jennifer, this is Susan. I'm sorry to bother you."

"Susan! How's it going? I hope you're feeling better."

"Actually, I'm not. I have something I need to talk to you about, and I don't think it can wait."

"What?" Jennifer switched to gravely concerned.

"I know Eternity Vineyards means a lot to you, but have you seen the news?"

"No, I haven't."

"On channel nine—" Susan began.

"Hold on, I'm turning it on." There was a pause. "It looks like there's another Amber Alert," Jennifer said with little concern.

"That's what I want to talk to you about. I think that girl's kidnapping and Eternity Vineyards are connected." There was another pause.

"What do you mean?" Jennifer sounded defensive.

"Jennifer, I have to tell you, I don't trust that Wolfgang Shlegel. There's something wrong with him, something evil, and that place, it's not just haunted, there's really something bad about it."

"It's just a house, Susan."

"I think it's more than that. I did a natal chart based on the origins of that place using a rough estimate of the time you said it was built, and I've never encountered such an ugly alignment of planets and stars. If a person had a chart like that, I'd never tell them about it; it's that bad. It's such an unusual and unlikely placement, it's so negative that I'm positive it was designed that way. It must have been deliberately built at the time and place it was in order to maximize the dark potential that its natal chart indicates."

"Whoa, Susan." Jennifer said, "I'm not following you. You know I'm not into all that stuff you're—"

"Jennifer, it's not just that. I did other readings, tarot readings as well. I firmly believe there's a connection between the murder of those Mexicans in the desert and Eternity Vineyards. I admit, I'm not sure what the connection means. I only know they are connected. And now this Amber Alert, I'm getting the same connection between it and Eternity Vineyards."

There was silence on the other end of the line. It seemed to last too long.

"Are you still there?" Susan asked.

"I'm still here," Jennifer said. "Susan, I'm not saying you're entirely wrong about the place. I mean, let's just say I could agree with you that it may not have always been a good place, but Wolfgang Shlegel pays a lot—"

"All I'm asking you to do," Susan interrupted, "is go out there and look around. I think this girl, this Tamara Patterson, might be out there. I don't understand any more than that, and I know you probably think I'm a fool, and it would take forever to explain all the techniques I use, and I don't think we have that kind of time."

"I never said I thought you were a fool," Jennifer replied.

"I'm just asking you to go look at your property closely. I honestly think this girl—"

"Why are you telling me this?" Jennifer asked quietly, incredulously. "Why don't you just call the police?"

"Because it's your place."

* * *

When Jennifer hung up the phone after admitting nothing, committing to nothing, she tried working the bar to ignore it, but an impending avalanche of responsibility was falling fast upon her shoulders. Distracted, she brought two glasses of the wrong wine to a couple sitting at the bar, but it was red, and when they drank it, they said "Thank you, that's great!" To them, the wine varieties were just words on a menu. Thankfully, they didn't know the difference.

She knew more than Susan about Eternity Vineyards. Even without astrology charts and tarot cards, she knew what Eternity Vineyards was all about. After all, it was her credit card that paid for the bricks.

How ironic, Jennifer thought: she didn't even believe in all the psychic stuff—or at least she didn't before Eternity Vineyards—and yet she held the undiluted proof that every impression Susan had was spot on. So how could she doubt her warning and do nothing? A month ago she would have done nothing, but that was another lifetime. Maybe it was Samuel, maybe it was the distance from the real estate business and their religious mottos, always be closing; fake it 'till you make it, and the little hymn they used to sing at sales conferences:

"Money is a friend of mine,
I can make it any time,
If I'm closing every day,
I can make it really pay!"

How could four grand a month matter so much?

She took off the black apron she wore behind the bar, and let the hostess know she was taking a break. Walking back to the manager's office and knocking quietly on the door, she let herself in, not waiting for an answer.

Samuel was sitting at the desk looking exasperated. "I'm not going to do this forever, you know? I'm constantly calculating invoices and filling out an order sheets. I could hire a fulltime manager who—"

"Samuel, I think we need to make a trip out to Eternity Vineyards tonight."

"What? Why?"

"I think Susan knows all about it."

"You told her?"

"I haven't told her a thing, but she knows everything; maybe not the exact specifics, but she knows there's something wrong. She just called me. Have you seen the news?" Jennifer's anxiety was growing.

"No," Samuel said as he sat back in his chair and put his hands behind his head.

"There's an Amber Alert. A little girl was taken from a bathroom at a park here in Phoenix. Susan called me and said she thinks—in fact, she seems almost certain—the little girl is at Eternity Vineyards."

"She thinks Wolfgang kidnapped a little girl?" Samuel looked as if he'd just heard the patently ridiculous.

"She didn't say that, exactly, she just thinks the two incidents are connected, and she asked me to go out and take a look around, and I don't want to go out there alone."

"It's a three-hour ride," Samuel said, "It'll be ten before we get there."

"I know. I just feel like if I go out there and everything is alright, then I can rest easy, and I won't have to keep worrying about what I've done—hiding that room and all. If everything's alright, then I'm free to just rent the place out and not worry about it anymore, and to hell with Susan's feelings."

"But if it's not *all* right..." Samuel began.

"If it's not alright; I can't ignore it. Susan even thinks the murder of those Mexicans in the desert is somehow connected to Eternity Vineyards. You know, Samuel, I think when things play out, when things are looked at as a whole, it's just like what you told me about that girl who let your wife and her friends take her car: not doing anything about a bad thing is even worse than doing something bad. It's like an infection that gets left alone to fester."

Samuel removed his glasses and set them on the stack of invoices. He rubbed his eyes, and then got up and grabbed his coat from a hook on the back of the office door. "Grab your coat," he said, "and let me tell Travis to take over. He can close tonight; He's working until close anyway."

"I'm sorry, Samuel, I know this is asking a lot."

"No, I agree with you," he said, but she thought he sounded a little perturbed. "We need to lay this thing to rest once and for all. We need to move forward."

FORTY-FOUR

She wouldn't shut up, but he didn't have the stomach to punch the girl hard enough to knock her out. He'd sealed her mouth with duct tape, but she screamed through her nose all the same. He wished he'd put her in the bed of the truck like they did the last time, but he didn't want to risk stopping now and have someone see him tossing a struggling, bound and gagged child into the back.

She lay on her side in the backseat of the extended cab kicking with both feet that were duct-taped together as one big foot. With each strike, Mike felt her shoes jack-hammering his lower spine.

"Stop it!" He yelled time and again, but she took no notice of his commands. She only kicked harder.

He took Highway 85 south out of Phoenix. It would take forever to get to Eternity Vineyards, but it was better to stay off the Interstate and main roads. The Amber Alert was all over the local radio stations. They didn't have a description of the pickup, but for all he knew he was in a stolen vehicle. It seemed unlikely Santiago would use his own truck for the tasks Wolfgang paid him to do.

The early evening settled into a black night. There was no moon, and the reach of the headlights was as far as Mike could see. All he thought of was his acute need for more wine. The acuity trumped every risk he'd taken in getting the girl. Yet it astonished him how easy it was to get her.

With the pickup just outside the bathrooms, it was a quick couple of steps with his hand over her mouth and nose to the privacy of the truck. She'd entered the stall where he was crouched down and perched on a toilet seat. The bathroom was otherwise empty, and when she opened the door, he sprang on her like a monster from a closet. Unfortunately, she wet herself when he jumped on her and slapped the duct tape across her mouth, and now he could smell her urine all the while they drove.

Mike tipped his empty bottle of wine up and tried to feel any drop at all on his dry lips. But there hadn't been anything the last time he tried, now it seemed almost dusty. He tried to focus on the warm welcome Wolfgang would give him, and the wine he would supply—just so long as the girl's heart was still beating when he got there, just like last time.

Wolfgang might even reward him extra for doing it on his own and finishing off Santiago in the process. It would prove to Wolfgang he was someone who could be more than just a gofer of sacrifices. It would prove he could be a legitimate partner, someone who could think and make decisions on his own for the good of them both. He couldn't help himself; he tipped the bottle onto his quivering outstretched lower lip, but again there was nothing.

FORTY-FIVE

They took Samuel's car, and once out of the city past the streetlights, Jennifer could feel the darkness as it closed in on her. She was thankful for the glowing dash lights; any light was better than none.

"Something's not right," Jennifer said. "I got the place too easy, and everything about me made me a prime mark. I got suckered in and now I'm being punished for my sins."

"What sins? You're a good person," Samuel said casually.

Jennifer turned on him as if he'd just slapped her. "No I'm not, Samuel! I'm not a good person. I've never been a good person. I traded my marriage for a career; I traded my daughter for a shot at success; I conned Robert Maddock for a cheap deal to make me rich. Because God knows if I was rich then, and only then, would I be good—and oh how I wanted to let everyone know how good I was. I'm not good; I'm selfish. I think Susan knows something," Jennifer said, her eyes shifting suspiciously from side to side. "I know she knows something, and I think this whole thing is going to blow up in my face." She started to cry and reached into her handbag for a travel pack of tissues.

As they drove through the darkness, Samuel said nothing until he finally asked: "If God was punishing you, why not just give you cancer or something, or give you some kind of drug addiction? Why go to all this trouble just to get you?"

But Jennifer wasn't receiving him. She had no answers for his questions, so she didn't answer him. She only dabbed at her eyes.

"When we get out there," Samuel said, "we're going to check out the basement. We'll just tell Wolfgang something—anything—tell him you have to check the boiler for God's sake. If he doesn't let you, then we'll force the issue. After all, you're the landlord. And Jennifer," Samuel became emphatic, "you've done nothing wrong—*nothing*."

"You're right;" Jennifer sounded far away. "I did nothing. But isn't it strange all the bad done by people who do nothing?" Jennifer turned to look out her window. She tried to drift away, but her anxiety stayed put.

"If something's happened out there," she said, "I can't be guilty for that. I just couldn't handle that." She wiped the corner of her eye with the tissue again.

"Even if something has happened," Samuel said, "that doesn't make it your fault."

Jennifer tried to smile at him, to thank him for his support, but her smile only patronized his lack of understanding. "I hope you're right," she said, and it was all she could manage.

* * *

When they arrived at the estate, Jennifer motioned to the maintenance shed at the bottom of the driveway near the entrance to the vineyard. "Park back there," she said. "I don't think we should go up to the house just yet. We need to get our story straight—figure out what we're going to say."

Samuel parked the Crown Vic on the gravel behind the shed and turned off the lights and ignition. They sat in the dark. "We should—" Jennifer began but stopped short. "Samuel, look." She pointed back toward the road.

Coming east on 82, a set of headlights drew closer to them. "It's ten o'clock," Jennifer said. "There's nothing out here for anyone at this time of night."

"Just this place," Samuel replied.

"Maybe it's Shlegel. Let's wait here for a minute."

"He'll think we're spying on him," Samuel said.

"If he goes straight up the driveway, I don't think he'll even see us."

The headlights approached and slowed at the entrance to make the turn.

"Whose pickup?" Samuel asked.

"I have no idea."

As the truck passed the shed, Jennifer saw through the driver's side window something impossible to her. "I think that's Mike!" She grabbed at Samuel's shoulder.

"What? Are you sure?"

"No, I'm not. I mean it can't be. He's in California. I got a letter—oh no, Samuel, something's not right. Something's not right at all."

The black pickup was coming to a stop at the front of the house. Just then a light came on in the dining room window as if the house were coming to life.

"Go, Samuel! Go now—get up there!" Jennifer was physically bouncing in her seat as if to make the car move faster.

Samuel started the engine and hit the lights. Gravel spit from the rear tires as he pulled onto the driveway road and sped toward the house. Jennifer held on to the passenger dash, glaring out the windshield, her lips grimacing tightly, her eyes wide and taking in the unbelievable.

Samuel skidded to an angled halt nearly hitting the pickup. Beams of dust glowed in his headlights and reflected off the rear taillights of Wolfgang's Mercedes parked at the side of the house.

Mike was already out, and Jennifer looked at him briefly through her closed window. Their startled eyes met, but he wasn't the same. He was thin, pale, and sickly, his hair a mess, and he'd grown a short ragged beard. He was unkempt and not at all how she remembered him.

Mike broke their mutual gaze and ran to the passenger side of the pickup. Jennifer tried to open her door to block his way, but he ran into it, slamming it closed.

"Fuck!" Jennifer shouted, and fumbled with the handle again.

Mike made it to the other side of the truck. He opened the passenger door, then reached in and opened the door of the extended cab. Just then Jennifer made it out of the car, and Samuel joined her from the driver's side.

"Mike! You asshole! You son-of-a-bitch! You fucking bas—" Jennifer froze in place. Mike wasn't acknowledging her as he viciously pulled the small black girl out of the truck and let her fall to the ground. She kicked in the dirt and gravel with her bound feet. Duct tape encircled her, pinning her arms to her sides, and a large piece of tape sealed her mouth.

"Good God!" Samuel said as he came around the back of the car.

"Mike, what are you doing?" Jennifer watched the bewildering horror of Mike dragging the girl toward the front door by the collar of her dress. He was grunting and panting, and his face strained with the stress of reaching his goal.

"Mike, stop it!" Jennifer moved toward him.

"Stay away!" Mike screamed. He managed to bring the girl up high enough to grip her under his arm and carry her like a bundle. He ran for the front door, and once there, he squeezed the latch and threw it open.

"Mike!" Jennifer shouted, "Put her down!"

Light spilled from the interior and through the open door. He stared into it like a long-awaited light at the end of a tunnel. But the hope and relief of his expression changed to terror, and he took a step back as Whitney walked from the house. She approached him with her arms stretched out as if begging for a hug.

Jennifer saw her, as did Samuel, but she looked worse than before. Her feet pointed downward as she began to float, making her taller than Mike, and from that vantage point, she looked down on him and reached out to grab his face in her hands.

Her own face was a wrinkled and pale mess, pruned, as if from decades in a damp grave. Her hair hung down in black strips of wet tangles, and blood covered most of her thin blue nightgown. The usual black voids replaced her eyes, and her mouth formed into the shape of a screaming black cavern. She looked the ghostly part of something murdered, buried, and dug up again for an unearthly encore.

Then she screamed, and Jennifer covered her ears, as did Samuel. Mike tried to cover his own but holding the girl gave him only one hand to put over one ear. Whitney screamed over and over.

Mike stumbled backwards and fell with the girl. Jennifer ran up, dropped to her knees and grabbed the girl's legs. For a moment she and Mike engaged in a tug-of-war. "Let go!" he shouted. "I have to have her!"

"Give her to me, Mike! Are you out of your fucking mind?"

That's when Jennifer felt the solid impact of Mike's hiking boot on the left side of her face and jaw. The impact stunned her, and her field of vision narrowed to black with lightning spikes flashing in the dark of her slipping consciousness. He kicked at her repeatedly, and with the force of each kick, she finally lost her grip on the girl's legs and fell back onto the gravel.

She was out for only seconds, but when she could see again, Samuel was already sitting on Mike's chest throwing punches at his face as Mike raised his hands in a futile defense. The girl was forgotten in the gravel, still kicking and screaming at low volume through her nose. Her eyes were terrified globes, instinctively looking for a way to survive. Whitney was gone. Jennifer tried to yell, but the dizziness from the boot strikes left her confused and searching. Finally, she found what she wanted to say and shouted it: "Samuel, no!"

She struggled to her feet and ran to the melee. She grabbed Samuel's arm just as he raised it for another strike, but the force of his swing broke free from her grip, and he hit Mike's face on the left. Blood streamed from Mike's nose and mouth, and Samuel's continued punches made dull wet slapping sounds. Mike's head lolled with each hit.

"Samuel, stop it. You'll kill him!" She grabbed Samuel by his shirt and with all her might pulled him back. He fell off of Mike and landed in the gravel on his backside. She'd never seen his face so angry, and his fury was frightening in its intensity. "Samuel, we have to get the girl and get out of here— Samuel!"

Just then, he seemed to snap out of his frenzy and looked at her. He was panting, his teeth bared, but he seemed to be getting what she was saying.

"Samuel," Jennifer repeated with slow emphasis, "we have to get that little girl out of here."

Mike was already struggling to his knees and crawling toward the front door. "Wolfgang," he shouted, "save me! Wolfgang, Wolfgang, help me! I got the girl, Wolfgang!"

Samuel looked at Jennifer, and finally got it. He forced himself up, and they ran together to the girl. He threw her over his shoulder and raced with her struggling body back to his car. Jennifer was slightly ahead of him and opened the driver's side back door. Samuel threw the girl in, as if completing his own smooth abduction, and Jennifer climbed in after her, then he slammed the door.

A second before Samuel climbed behind the wheel, Jennifer looked through the window at the front door of the house. Wolfgang Shlegel stood in the doorway. His bald head made his identity unmistakable. He wore a black monk's robe with the hood pulled back. He glared at Jennifer, and in that fraction of a moment she felt his extreme hatred for her. Mike pawed at Wolfgang's legs and reached up to him as if begging for water; blood ran off his lips and down his chin.

As Samuel reversed the car, backing away from the house, she saw Wolfgang raise his arm, and before her mind could record the reality of the object in his hand, she saw the muzzle flash and heard the deafening boom. The rear passenger window became nearly opaque in an instant with a million cracks in the shatterproof glass.

"Shit!" Samuel yelled, and dropped the gear lever into drive. He mashed the accelerator, and Jennifer grabbed hold of the girl. "Get down!" Samuel shouted, "Get on the floor!"

Jennifer rolled with the girl off the backseat and onto the floorboard landing on top of her. The rear end of the Crown Victoria spun around in the gravel, as more shots were fired.

The driver's side rear window was next to shatter, and in the back window, three small holes appeared one immediately after the other. One bullet passed through the passenger backrest and out the windshield as Samuel maneuvered the fishtailing vehicle down the driveway. The engine screamed in low gear, but the sound was dwarfed by the repetitive hits to the car's body as the bullets smacked into it, each one hitting like a hammer.

By the time they reached the bottom of the driveway, Samuel had the car up to seventy. He pressed hard on the brakes and skidded sideways onto the highway pointing west toward Elgin and Sonoita. He gunned the engine again, and accelerated to ninety.

"Jennifer, are you alright!"

"Yeah, I'm just stuck down here. Are they following us?"

Samuel checked the rearview mirror, but everything was dark—no headlights. "I don't think so. I don't see anything. I'm going to pull over up here."

Samuel went another two miles approaching one hundred miles an hour, then gradually slowed over a mile and pulled the car off to the side. He left the engine running and quickly exited.

Opening the back passenger door, he saw Jennifer struggling out of the space between the backrests and the backseat. Samuel helped her out of the car. "Get ready to go if we see lights," he said.

On the floorboard the small dark child laid face down, struggling against the duct tape. Jennifer reached in and pulled her up and out of the car. Together, she and Samuel removed the tape, and when the tape came off the girl's mouth, she began to bawl.

Jennifer reached out and took the girl in her arms. The girl was sweating and smelled of urine. "It's okay, now; we've got you honey; nothing's going to happen to you. We're going to get you back to your mommy."

The child was inconsolable.

"Are you Tamara? Is your name Tamara?" Jennifer asked. Jennifer held the girl away from her and the girl nodded her head with exaggeration. Jennifer hugged her again. "It's ok, we're going to take you back to your mommy, okay?"

Samuel looked at the damage to the car windows. Later he would count nine bullet holes in all. He reached back in the car and removed his cell phone from the center console and dialed 911. Jennifer was surprised by his calm on the phone.

"Yes, my name is Samuel Ansell. I'm with Jennifer Dickerman. I believe we have the child from the Amber Alert you issued this afternoon. I believe we have Tamara Patterson."

There was a pause.

"No, we didn't take her; I believe we rescued her from the ones who did. We're running from them now, they're at Eternity Vineyards off of Highway 83. We've been shot at and our vehicle is damaged, but we're headed toward Elgin.

Another pause as Samuel listened.

"No, none of us were shot, I don't think we need an ambulance, but I don't know about the girl. She looks okay, but she's really upset—Yes, I will stay on the line as long as I can."

Samuel looked down at Jennifer who was still kneeling on the ground hugging the little girl. "We have to go. They're going to meet us. Come on, get her in the car; we have to get out of here."

Jennifer put Tamara in the backseat and climbed in with her. She put her arm around the girl and held her close to her side. Tamara was still crying, but reached out and clung to Jennifer as if for her very life.

Samuel turned to face the pitch-black highway from where they'd come. There were still no headlights. All he could see was a small orange light glowing on a hill in the distance. He knew it was Eternity Vineyards shining in the desert night like a lone ship on a midnight ocean. Samuel closed the door behind Jennifer and quickly planted himself behind the wheel and peeled out from the gravel pullout back onto the highway. The tires squealed when they hit the pavement.

While they drove, Samuel talked to the 911 operator giving her the details and the exact address for Eternity Vineyards. Before they'd gone another ten miles, they saw headlights and the unmistakable red and blue strobe lights of authority coming toward them.

"I guess that's them, Jennifer said."

"I see the police," Samuel told the operator. "They're coming toward us; I'm going to hang up now—Yes, thank you very much; thank you." Samuel tapped off the phone.

FORTY-SIX

———— ●•● ————

I want my mommy," Tamara cried.

"Look," Jennifer pointed out the front windshield to the oncoming lights. "That's the police. They're going to get you back to your mommy. Everything's going to be alright now."

As the lights grew closer, Samuel pulled off the road into a pullout. The first Santa Cruz Sheriff's car sped past them, and behind it, an unmarked car followed closely at high speed.

"Where are they going? Didn't they see us?" Jennifer asked.

"They must be going out to the vineyard," Samuel said.

A third Sheriff's car stopped in front of Samuel's, nearly touching his front bumper. A bright white light from its light bar shone into the interior of the Ford. The last of the Sheriff's cars pulled in behind the Crown Vic effectively preventing any chance of escape, should there be such an inclination.

Two deputies, one from each car, exited their cruisers, and drew their weapons. The one in front commanded: "Keep your hands in plain view!" The second was aiming a shotgun at the broken back window. Samuel raised his hands above the steering wheel; Jennifer raised her hands, and Tamara followed suit by raising her hands.

"Let the girl out," The deputy at the back shouted. He came up and opened the back door.

"Go, see that man," Jennifer said

"No!" Tamara screamed and started crying again. She grabbed hold of Jennifer's blouse and held tighter as the officer reached in for her.

"It's okay, honey, he's here to help. He's going to get you to your mommy. You have to go with him so they can take you home."

Reluctantly Tamara moved toward the officer who took hold of her. "It's okay," the officer said. "Why don't you come see my police car and talk to your mommy? I've got her on the phone. She wants to talk to you." The deputy picked the girl up and carried her off to his car.

"Step out of the vehicle, one at a time," The front deputy ordered. "Driver, you first. Keep your hands in plain view at all times."

Samuel exited. The officer kept his weapon aimed at him. "Get down on your knees, and place your hands on top of your head."

Samuel complied.

The officer stepped forward and put his pistol in its holster. He placed Samuel's hands behind his back and handcuffed him. Then he stood him up and escorted him back to his cruiser. Pushing down on Samuel's head to protect it, he helped him into the backseat.

Jennifer went through the same ritual and joined Samuel in the back of the police car. When they were secured, the first deputy went to the patrol car at Samuel's back bumper and conversed with the other deputy. Jennifer strained to see and caught a glimpse of Tamara in the backseat of the other car talking on a cell phone.

"Oh my God, look at us," Samuel said. They looked at each other and burst into a short bit of laughter at the same time.

"Bonnie and Clyde," Jennifer said. "Do you think we're in trouble?"

"No. I don't think so. Hell, we haven't done anything. I don't see how anyone could think we have. They just don't know the whole story yet. They're just being careful; that's all." Samuel looked to see what the police were doing at the other car, but they were still only talking.

"What if they did know the whole story?" Jennifer asked.

"They won't," Samuel said. "Not from me, anyway. I don't know anything about any cellar, or room, or Satanism, and I only met Shlegel once, and I don't know him at all. So, whatever you say—that must be the way it is.

Jennifer rubbed her shoulder against Samuel's, "Thank you," she said. "And as for me, if there's something bad in the cellar, then Wolfgang Shlegel or Mike must have done it. I don't know squat about it either."

Samuel looked at her, "Then we're safe."

They watched as the first officer approached the car and opened Jennifer's door first. "I'm sorry," the deputy said, "we had to be sure. The girl says you two got her away from the man who took her. I think that family owes you a great deal of gratitude." "They owe us nothing at all, not a thing," Samuel said.

At that moment, a voice came over the deputy's radio: "1-Bravo-14."

The deputy turned away and keyed the radio mike clipped to his lapel: "1-Bravo 14."

"Are you Code 4, Sanders?"

"Code 4(situation under control)"

"Deputy Hanes will 10-14 (transport) the girl to Sonoita. Social Services will 45 (meet) with him there. I need you to detain and 10-14 S. Ansell and J. Dickerman and 45 with me at 113 Highway 83. That's Eternity Vineyards. We have a 903 (dead body) here. Are you 10-35 (able to receive confidential information)?

"Negative."

"10-4. Just 10-45 with me here.

"10-4. Show me 10-17 (en route)."

"Copy, 1-Bravo-14, 10-17."

Deputy Sanders turned back to Samuel and Jennifer, his face serious and hard. "I need to take you back to the house."

"What did we do?" Jennifer asked. "You said the girl told you we saved her."

Sanders climbed behind the wheel of the cruiser without responding.

"We haven't done anything," Samuel insisted.

"Ms. Dickerman," Deputy Sanders said, "There's a dead body on your property. Until we get this sorted out, we have to detain you and your friend. Do you understand what I'm telling you?" Sanders looked at Samuel, "You're not being arrested at this point, either of you, but I have to detain you for now. Just be patient, and we'll get this sorted out."

Deputy Hanes departed with Tamara Patterson back down the Highway toward Sonoita. As his car passed by Jennifer's window she took a last look at the girl. Tamara was looking back and waving. Jennifer wanted to wave back, but her hands were cuffed behind her, so she only nodded. Sanders pulled onto the highway and the three headed in the opposite direction en route to Eternity Vineyards.

"Did Wolfgang Shlegel shoot Mike?" Jennifer asked the deputy.

"Who's Wolfgang Shlegel? Who's Mike?"

"Wolfgang Shlegel lives there. I rent the vineyard to him."

"He's the one who shot at us. We told that to the 911 operator," Samuel said.

Sanders looked into his rearview mirror. "I'm going to let Detective Chamberlain fill you in."

* * *

1-Bravo-14 pulled off the Highway onto the driveway at Eternity Vineyards and drove slowly up the gravel road to the house. When they got there, Jennifer noticed the unmarked car they saw pass by them before was now parked behind Maddock's Range Rover, and the patrol car was parked at the front near the entrance. Most of the downstairs lights in the house were on, and the front door was opened, but there was no Mercedes.

Deputy Sanders exited, opened Jennifer's door first, and helped her out. He did the same for Samuel as Detective Chamberlain came out of the house and walked up to them. He was a fat man with a belly that hid his belt buckle, but on the left side of his belt was a plainly visible gold badge and on the right an automatic pistol in a padded nylon holster. "We don't need these," the detective said and selected a small silver key on his key ring. He unlocked Jennifer's handcuffs and Sanders followed suite with Samuel's.

As she massaged her wrists, Chamberlain reached out his hand to Jennifer first. "Ms. Dickerman, my name is Joe Chamberlain, I'm a detective for the Santa Cruz County Sheriff's Department, and I'd like to ask you some questions, if you don't mind." She shook his hand. He looked at Samuel and extended a hand to him as well. "You must be Samuel Ansell," Chamberlain said.

"Yes, I am," Samuel replied, and the two shook without enthusiasm.

"Mr. Ansell, I'd like you to remain out here with Deputy Sanders while I talk to Ms. Dickerman in private, would that be alright?" Chamberlain's polite manner stood in contrast to his obvious years of service catching the criminal element.

"Sure...of course," Samuel said.

Jennifer looked at Samuel with a hint of distress, but Samuel nodded indicating everything was fine. She found herself wishing they'd taken more time to piece together a story between them. Perhaps, she thought, as she walked with Chamberlain to the house, the time for formatting stories was over.

They entered the foyer, and Chamberlain stopped to ask, "Ms. Dickerman, what is your relationship to Michael Wilson?"

"He was my business partner. He owns part of this house. Well actually, he has a promissory note for the amount he invested and a portion of the proceeds when it sells."

"I don't think he'll be collecting on that," Chamberlain said and motioned for Jennifer to follow him into the study.

When they entered, Mike was sitting in the chair behind the desk. His head was lying on the desk and turned to one side so severely that it appeared as if his neck were broken. The cavernous wound on the top back of his skull stared at Jennifer even as she stared back at it. Blood was pooled over the top of the desk, and blood splattered on the window as if someone had taken a bloody paintbrush and whipped it at the glass. With his skullcap missing, Jennifer could see into the glistening meat that represented the remains of Mike's brain.

"Oh, Mike," Jennifer said and covered her mouth in horror. The scene was too grizzly. She wanted to vomit. She wanted to look away but couldn't stop staring at the human mess before her.

"Of course, he's dead," the detective mentioned rhetorically.

"Wolfgang shot him?" Jennifer asked.

"Who's Wolfgang?"

"Wolfgang Shlegel," Jennifer added with frustration. "He's my tenant. I was renting this winery to him. He shot at us."

"Ms. Dickerman, I don't think anyone shot Michael Wilson other than Michael Wilson. A crime scene investigator is on her way out here. We paged her as soon as we discovered the body. But if you look here…" Chamberlain motioned for Jennifer to follow him to the side of the desk, and she complied.

On the hardwood floor sat a shining nickel-plated revolver. "That's a Smith & Wesson .38 Special. It's a pretty old gun. I'll bet my salary it's the gun that killed him. Look at Mike's finger." Chamberlain pointed at Mike's right index finger with the antenna of his radio. It was bent in the opposite direction of the joint.

"Oh my God," Jennifer said. Seeing a finger set backwards at an almost ninety-degree angle was a foreign and bizarre image.

"When he shot himself, the gun must have flown out of his hand and broke his finger. The reason I show you all this is because of that open drawer there." Chamberlain pointed at the obvious. "I figure he got the gun out of that drawer. Is that your gun, Ms. Dickerman?"

Jennifer didn't know how to answer. She felt herself being led with questions the way she might lead a client into a positive buying decision. "I don't know; it could be. I mean I never really had a chance to go through everything in the house before I rented it. If it belonged to Robert Maddock, the former owner, I suppose it's mine now. I bought the house and all its contents."

"You said you had a promissory note with Mike."

"Yes, I did."

"Pretty convenient he's dead, financially speaking I mean," Chamberlain said casually.

Jennifer stepped back as if Chamberlain just spit at her. "What are you saying? I thought he was in California. I have a letter from him. This is the first time I've seen Mike in three months. None of this is convenient."

"I'm just trying to add up the numbers here, Ms. Dickerman, I don't want you to feel suspected of anything, but I certainly understand if you'd like to speak with an attorney first before talking about this."

Chamberlain was a master; he should have worked for McWilliam's, but she called his bluff. "I don't need a lawyer, Detective Chamberlain. We have holes all over our car. We rescued a little girl that was kidnapped. We're the good guys here. Remember?"

"Of course, Jennifer. May I call you Jennifer?"

"Call me, Jen."

"Jen," Chamberlain continued, "The girl backs up your story. Deputy Hanes, phoned me just before you got here and said she won't stop talking about it. She described Mike here to a tee. He definitely kidnapped her. You rescued her, and she says Mike, here, brought her out to this place. No doubt about it."

"Well then..." Jennifer said and shrugged her shoulders in conclusion.

"Who's Wolfgang Shlegel?"

"I told you; he's my tenant, or was anyway?"

"Where is he now?" Chamberlain drilled impatiently.

"I think that's what you're supposed to find out. How would I know? He tried to kill us. Samuel gave the 911 operator all this information."

"Oh, we have that. We put out your information to all agencies. We're looking for him and his Mercedes as we speak. It's just that we've searched the entire premises, and we can't find the slightest evidence that anyone named Wolfgang Shlegel ever lived here. There's no mail, no clothes in the closet, no dirty dishes, nothing."

"Did you check the cellar?" Jennifer had only one thing in mind when she asked, and it wasn't locating Wolfgang. She only wanted to see his reaction. She didn't even care what he said; his eyes would tell the truth. If he knew about the ritual room she was going to lawyer-up. She trusted Samuel would never mention it.

"Should we?" Chamberlain asked.

"Of course you should," Jennifer said with an Oscar-winning appearance of surprise. She turned quickly and began to walk out as if leading him to the cellar.

"Don't bother, Ms. Dickerman. We've searched the cellar completely. He's not there; there's nothing in the cellar, except wine barrels." Detective Chamberlain sounded as if he was giving her obvious information that she was too stupid to understand. He was patronizing her, but it comforted her. With her back turned to him, she allowed herself a slight smile before turning around with a straight face. She knew it was true: he hadn't found anything at all.

"I have Shlegel's signature on a rental agreement. I'll bet his prints are everywhere in this house. I'll bet his tire tracks are right out there on the other side of that Land Rover. That's where he used to park."

"Actually, Ms. Dickerman," Chamberlain interrupted, "I think Mike killed himself. I think there is a Wolfgang Shlegel. I know Mike kidnapped the girl. But one thing won't leave me alone." The detective put his fingers on his forehead as if trying to physically pull out the information he sought. "What I just can't figure is how you, and our man Samuel out there, happened to be here when Mike arrived. Why were you out here, Ms. Dickerman? How did you know Michael was bringing Tamara Patterson out here?" The detective stopped and looked directly at Jennifer as if to say, *Go on; try some bullshit on me.*

In a microsecond, Jennifer realized the fruition of everything she had learned as a salesperson. In a flash, she realized what Melissa once emphasized: *A salesperson has to keep their mouth shut until they know exactly what to say, and they always have to know exactly what to say, or make it up right then and there, and it better make sense. It's what you say about the wheel that just fell off the car you said was like new; it's what you say to the client who just turned on the hot water and got cold brown liquid at high pressure, and it's what you say to your partner when he asks you what the basement looks like in a multimillion-dollar winery that you failed to check. It's selling's finest millisecond.*

She answered him as soon as the unspoken period of his sentence sounded, "There's no moon tonight, Detective Chamberlain, and it's almost midnight. I brought Samuel out here to see the ghost."

"Ghost?" Chamberlain was incredulous. "What ghost?"

A call came over Chamberlain's radio: "Det-4, we have a problem out here!" Deputy Sanders sounded out of breath, obviously running and talking at the same time. In the background, with the mike keyed, Samuel was yelling, "Oh my God!" But Chamberlain never broke eye contact with Jennifer. He seemed to hear nothing from his radio as his concentration remained fixed, waiting on her response.

"That ghost," she finally said, and pointed to the picture window behind Chamberlain, behind the desk, framed in stained glass, and splattered with Mike's suicidal blood.

"Det-4, there's another minor on the property. Show me in pursuit behind the main house." The transmission ended abruptly.

Chamberlain turned; Whitney stood just beyond the glass. She reached out with her hands toward the window, her skin gothic white, her eyes black vacancies, her mouth its usual jagged cavern. Slowly, her thin blue nightgown moved, as if with the evening breeze. She was monstrous, and even more so when her moaning started up, deafening and mournful.

Chamberlain startled, dropped his radio and stumbled backwards. Jennifer smiled.

Behind Whitney, Deputy Sanders appeared in the window, running up as if he'd just caught up to her. Samuel was with him. Sanders lurched toward the window, reaching out to grab her arm, but Whitney vaporized into invisibility. Suddenly there was nothing. Chamberlain found himself staring open-mouthed at Sanders who was staring open-mouthed at him.

FORTY-SEVEN

When Sanders and Samuel came back around to the front entrance, Chamberlain met them with Jennifer close behind.

"I can't find her," Sanders said to Chamberlain, nearly muttering in confusion.

"Was there anything there?" Chamberlain asked.

"I don't know," Sanders replied.

Jennifer spoke to Samuel before Chamberlain could stop her, "I told you we'd see the ghost if we came out tonight."

It didn't take more than a blink for Samuel to back her up. "I can't believe I finally saw it!"

"Mike's dead," Jennifer announced.

"I take it Shlegel shot him?"

Jennifer turned to Chamberlain as if making sure she was accurate, "You think he killed himself, right?"

"Well, we still need the crime scene investigator and an autopsy," Chamberlain solemnly announced, "but it looks like it."

Two hours later, a crime scene investigator arrived. The coroner's office was called an hour after that. Suicide would later become the official cause of death determined by the Pima County Medical Examiner. Detective Chamberlain and Deputy Sanders would write in their reports that Jennifer and Samuel had come out on a scheduled inspection of the property. For their own professional survival, neither mentioned the pale girl in the blue nightdress.

Jennifer watched misty-eyed as Mike's body was put into a black vinyl body bag then seat-belted at the legs and chest to a gurney. She wept openly as they rolled him out. Samuel kept his arm around her, intermittently rubbing her shoulder.

Hating Mike for what he did, or what he had become, didn't make any sense to her. How could she hate what she didn't even understand? Whatever came over him the last time she saw him was a mystery to her—at least until the tow truck operator hooked up to the front end of Santiago's pickup an hour later.

The pickup was to be taken in as evidence, and when the operator opened the driver's door to shift the truck into neutral, a black bottle fell out onto the gravel driveway. The operator stopped and went over to tell the CSI deputy, who was interviewing Jennifer at the time.

Jennifer followed her over to the pickup and watched her retrieve the black, unlabeled bottle. With a gloved hand, she picked it up and looked at it. She shook it and listened for contents, smelled it, and tipped it over, but it was dry.

"Wine," she said, as if Jennifer had asked her. She placed the bottle in an evidence bag and labeled it.

"Mike must have been drinking it," Jennifer said despondently.

But the weight of Jennifer's understanding was lost on the CSI deputy who only shrugged. "In these cases, they've usually been drinking *something*," she said.

* * *

As the coroner's van made its way to the highway entrance, permanently removing Mike from Eternity Vineyards, Detective Chamberlain gave Jennifer a business card for a crime scene cleaning company located in Tucson. It had a twenty-four hour hotline, promised immediate response, but when she called the tired-sounding dispatcher admitted they couldn't be out until 10 a.m. The dispatcher recommended closing the door to the study for the time being.

Chamberlain was the last to leave. Jennifer and Samuel each shook his hand, and he thanked them for saving Tamara Patterson.

"These things so often turn out much worse," Chamberlain said. "It's too bad about your friend, but most of the time we never get the child back alive. It's a terrible tragedy."

Jennifer could still see traces of disbelief on Chamberlain's face, especially when he shook her hand. He was like a man who saw a magic trick he couldn't figure out, a mathematician unable to solve a formula that wouldn't add up.

"I hope you find Wolfgang Shlegel," Samuel added. "As long as he's out there—"

"He's always out there," Chamberlain interjected. "This time he just looked like a winemaker. Sometimes they look like skuzzy trash, sometimes like a parent, but it's always the same person: pedophiles are pedophiles. You catch one; another pops up in his place.

Samuel nodded somberly.

"Again, Ms. Dickerman, I'm sorry about your friend."

"Thank you," Jennifer said.

Chamberlain drove down the driveway in the cold temperature of the last vestiges of the Arizona winter. As the black of early morning morphed into light on the eastern horizon, Jennifer and Samuel watched him leave.

"So, do we burn the place to the ground?" Jennifer asked as they politely waved goodbye to the disappearing unmarked police car.

"They'll think we have something to hide," Samuel said.

"We do."

Jennifer walked out to the middle of the graveled front lot. She closed her jacket around her and stared out toward the east mountain ranges waiting for the sun to show. Samuel followed her and put his arm around her. She moved in as close to him as she could.

He looked out at the vineyards, then he turned to look at the house. "This place, if you didn't know anything about it, is absolutely beautiful."

"Just like an angel of light," Jennifer said. "You know, I think Susan was right that time we met her in her store. She said even if we destroyed the place, Whitney would probably still haunt it. Maybe the same goes for the evil that revolves around it."

"What do you mean?"

"I mean even if we tore it down, someone would come along on some astrologically perfect day, or some shit, and build another winery, or something else that could be used for the evil that surrounds this area. I think that's why Robert Maddock thought the place had to have a caretaker."

Samuel considered what she said and replied, "Maybe what Susan said when we brought her out here is true: the place has power; it isn't good or bad—just power."

"I don't know how I'll even pay the property taxes, but I think I have to live here. If I boarded it up and tried to forget about it, how would I ever know if Wolfgang Shlegel returned? But I'll tell you this right now, I damn sure won't be insuring it." They both chuckled at her declaration.

"Make wine," Samuel said casually.

"I don't know wine from mustard," Jennifer said with simple resignation. "You know that."

"But I do," Samuel replied.

She looked to him; his brown eyes were full of sincerity. He meant more; she knew it, but she asked the obvious: "Are you suggesting a partnership?"

"I'll be in charge of making it;" he ventured, "you sell it; what could be better?"

"Is that the extent of it?" She queried, feeling vulnerable to his answer.

"No, there's something else I want."

"And that is?"

"Will you marry me?" Samuel never broke his eye contact with her.

"Yes," Jennifer said without hesitation, without having to think, without calling the shot, without calculating the impact of her response, without concern for the future.

He kissed her deeply, and she fell into him. Whitney watched from her bedroom window, silently witnessing their fledgling happiness and feeling it for herself.

* * *

The cleaners wore biohazard suits, masks, gloves and goggles. Once Jennifer showed them the room, they took over like they'd cleaned a million pounds of gray matter from a million suicide scenes. Their indifferent efficiency had its own kind of ghastliness.

"We have a room to clean, too." Samuel said to Jennifer, and she knew the room he meant. Together they walked to the cellar entrance behind the staircase and descended the wooden steps. Jennifer recalled the first time she walked down the steps in response to Michael's find. Back then the heels of her dress shoes clunked loudly on the wooden surfaces. This time her trainers made no sound whatsoever. She liked the sound of her new shoes.

"God knows how old these steps are," Samuel observed. "You'd think they were built yesterday."

When they got to the cellar, the wine rack was still closed. The place was clean. "No one's been making wine down here, that's for sure," Samuel said.

"Not good wine, anyway," Jennifer added. She went to the wine rack, and hesitated. "What do you think is behind here?"

"My guess is it's not a brick wall."

Jennifer looked through an empty wine bottle slot. "You would be right," she said.

"Wait!" Samuel took hold of her arm. "Before we open that, we could just weld it closed, build a wall over this whole damn rack and never look behind it again. If we look, we become responsible."

Jennifer considered, and then responded unemotionally: "If we don't, we're worse. I don't care what I find. I'm not afraid of this place anymore." With smooth effort, she pulled open the heavy wine rack.

They looked into the dark chamber. Jennifer tried the light switch, but Mike had never rewired the electric after pulling it. Jennifer walked into the darkness and unceremoniously plucked one of the black candles off the candelabra. She stepped back out. "Do you have a match?" She asked.

Samuel patted himself down and produced the Bic lighter he used at Fifty-Five Degrees and lit her candle.

Cupping the flame against the draft of her movement, she walked back in.

The chamber was the same as she remembered it, but she noticed there was no dust. The room had been thoroughly cleaned. The leather book was on the shelf, the pentagram still on the wall, the shackles and chains in their place.

Samuel stepped in behind her. "Good God," he said as he marveled at the room. The candle cast dim orange light and dark shadows around the objects therein.

"More like godforsaken," Jennifer said.

"It's like a chamber of horrors."

"Except it's real."

Jennifer touched the table surface and felt a slight dampness. She jerked her hand back. "Jesus," she gasped.

"What?" Samuel asked.

"The table—it's still wet."

Samuel ran his fingers over its surface. He took the candle from Jennifer and held it closer to the table. "I think it's just water."

"I know it is. That means it's been washed off. You don't have to wash a dusty table."

Samuel stepped back. "Oh God, you're right. What do we do with all this stuff?"

"I can't risk getting rid of it. If it fell into the wrong hands... I don't know what kind of power it has."

"I know what you mean," Samuel said. "This is incredible."

"Are you tempted by this?" Jennifer asked without the slightest hesitation or hint of judgment, only curiosity.

"I feel like I'm in pure evil," Samuel replied.

"Me, too."

"I'm not tempted by this at all. I'm sickened by it. I just don't understand how one person could torture another to gain—what? Power? I've got everything I want in this life, especially now, with you. Let's get out of here. Let's brick this fucking place back up."

Jennifer looked relieved at his response. "There's no point in that," she said. "Besides, I want to always verify that it's gathering dust. That's my responsibility now. Let's just close the door. No one's getting in here while I'm alive." Jennifer blew out the candle and tossed it on the table.

Together they walked out, but just as Samuel was moving the rack back into place, Jennifer stopped him: "Samuel, look!"

Samuel looked in. Glowing dimly in the darkness, just barely bright enough to make out, Whitney stood at the table. She looked down at it, her long black hair falling in front of her pale face. She rested her hand lightly on its surface.

"Do you hear that," Samuel whispered.

"She's crying," Jennifer said. "Come on, let's leave her alone." Jennifer helped Samuel ease the wine rack closed as if quietly shutting the door on a crypt. They tried not to disturb its ghost.

FORTY-EIGHT

T hanks, Susan," Jennifer said as she took a box of dishes from her that she'd carried in from Jennifer's Durango. They stood together in the kitchen, and Susan took another drink from her glass of iced tea. Jennifer stared out the kitchen windows at the green leaves forming on the vines in the northern vineyard.

April arrived, and the temperature was in the bottom seventies. The clean cool air, brilliant sky, and only scattered clouds made the task of moving easy, but the annual wildflowers growing everywhere on the estate, transforming it into an impressionist's pallet of color, made any task other than sitting in the chairs on the walkway hard to do.

"I appreciate you letting me research this place," Susan said.

"Psychic phenomena, the verifiable stuff anyway, can't be easy to come by," Jennifer remarked as she began hanging coffee cups on the pegboard near the sink.

"Not really. Come to think of it, I'm not sure of one case where you can go to the place, or meet the person, or anything like that and actually experience the phenomena—not ESP, not precognition, not apparitions—nothing. And I don't know how much different this is going to be. I mean I can see her; I hear her, but I can't take a picture of her. She doesn't come out on film or digital, or for that matter, audiotape or video. There are no electromagnetic fluctuations and no temperature changes. A person would have to just experience her. And what good would that do? I see pictures of ghosts all the time, but I don't believe they're authentic. I've heard supposed audio, and I think it's silly, and I'm in the business. If we had daily tours, even then people wouldn't believe it. They'd think it was a hoax. The Haunted Mansion at Disneyland, to be honest, is more realistic than the real thing."

"True," Jennifer said, "but we can bring out other experts in your field, the one's you trust. They can see her, and—"

Jennifer paused and suddenly looked perturbed: "Whitney," she said, "if you can't walk and show your eyes and mouth at the same time, then just sit still. We've already talked about that. Practice in your room by the mirror if you have to, but when you come in here, you have to be in full form; remember?"

Whitney passed by Jennifer and Susan on her way toward the wooden table and chairs. She sat and put her hands on the table. She turned and looked slowly at the two women; her blue eyes appeared first, then the pink of her lips, and then the structure of her mouth came into full view.

"God, she's beautiful," Susan remarked, "and I'm not just saying that because she's a ghost."

"She is pretty, isn't she?" Jennifer said like a proud parent. She took a moment to look at Whitney. Lately her mouth had started forming little smiles. Now Whitney tried her best to make one as Susan stared at her.

"Show off," Jennifer teased and went back to placing the cups.

"I think your idea is better. Have those special wine tastings at night, play it up like a séance and let her make her appearance. You know more about it than me, but that would be a serious marketing tool, or at least I think it would," Susan said. "What do you think, Whitney?"

Whitney managed one of her best smiles.

"Oh, she'd love it!" Jennifer laughed. "She's nothing if not the biggest ham in the world. Samuel thinks if we play our cards right, we can make good wine here, a decent Cabernet Sauvignon anyway. I guess you can grow those grapes just about anywhere."

"So what did you do with the wine casks in the cellar?" Susan asked.

Jennifer stopped placing dishes. "We didn't want to take any chances. We drained them and poured the wine out in the desert, and then we broke the barrels down. We had a big bonfire with the wood. We're going to start over with new casks— new casks for new wine."

Jennifer put her hand on Susan's shoulder as she walked past her to get to another box. "I'm sorry I didn't tell you the whole thing up front."

"It wasn't any of my business," Susan said, trying not to sound hurt.

"Actually, I think it was your business, strictly speaking. It sure wasn't the real estate business. We should have consulted you."

"But you had to work it out," Susan said. "It was your thing. If I can advise you along the way, I'm glad to do it." Susan walked into the kitchen and placed some plates in a cupboard.

"Just get a big advance on your book; I want my fifteen per-cent," Jennifer said making them both laugh.

"What if he comes back?" Susan asked.

"You mean Wolfgang?"

Susan nodded.

"I doubt it. I think if he wanted this place bad enough to take it, or if he could, he would have gotten it from Robert Maddock. Besides, we're going to be a legitimate business. This place isn't going to stay hidden anymore. That's where Maddock screwed up, if you ask me. He came here and spent his life burying his family secrets." Jennifer paused and con-templated: "He should have just dragged this whole place into the light."

"You sound so New Age," Susan said. "You're going to have to start wearing long dresses and beads if you're going to talk like that. You gotta let your hair grow, too."

"Oh my God," Jennifer said, as if suddenly realizing she had nothing to wear to an event, "You've got to show me where you shop!"

"I will!" Susan perked. "In fact, there's this great place I know, and you can do your grocery shopping there, too." They both laughed again.

Whitney watched from the table as the women chatted. She liked to be with them when they talked, so she worked on her smile as they put away the kitchen utensils.

FORTY-NINE

i, this is Tammy. I'm not in right now, but leave a message, and I'll call you back!" The electronic voice was cheery.

"Hello, Tammy, this is your mom. Since I can't get you to pick up, I'm just going to talk to your voicemail. You might not want to call me back, but I wish you would.

"I'm sorry, Tammy. I was wrong. I hurt you, and I left you when you needed your mom to help you. You don't need that now, and I know it. I never needed a daughter either, but now I want one. Maybe it's the same for you. Maybe you want a mother.

"Things are a lot different. Samuel and I are married, you know, and you should see our house. I wish you would see our house, but I'm not going to beg you, Tammy. I love you, but I won't call you again after this. I can love you, even if I can't have you in my future.

"But on a brighter note, I have a new friend; she's a fortuneteller—imagine that! She says we do have a future, and I believe her. I wish you could meet her. You can't help but like her, and Samuel's just fantastic.

"Would you believe I've given up real estate? We have a wine restaurant, and this house sits on a vineyard. We're going to make and sell wine. Can you imagine your mother working the land? Crazy notion, huh? Look, call me if you get a chance. Call me if there's anything left. I love you, Tammy."

Jennifer reluctantly pressed END and continued cleaning the study. There were decades of dust still everywhere in the house. Whitney sat behind the desk watching from the high back leather chair as Jennifer worked. She seemed to be playing a game she remembered from her life more than a half-century before.

They both looked at the cell phone when it vibrated on the desktop.

THE END

ABOUT THE AUTHOR

Caretakers of Eternity is Edward Gordon's debut novel. Throughout most of his life, he travelled extensively abroad, including the Cotswold area of England where he lived for nearly a decade. It was there, while hiking around the endless ruined castles and ancient graveyards of Great Britain, that he formed many of the ideas for his stories and poems. Currently, he lives and writes in the New Orleans area and is married to Michelle, his wife of twenty-two years.